What th

"An electrifying tale about a Vampire and a Fae, who are thrown into an vortex of danger, lust and love. The plot is very exciting and keeps you guessing what will happen next." ~ *Cupid Library's Review*

"This was a great story and very well written...a phenomenal book." ~ *Fallen Angel Reviews*

"This whole series is just one of the best I've read and vampire lovers can't go wrong with any of the *Embraced* stories. Well done *Ms. Bast!!*" ~ *eCataromance*

Anya Bast

Blood of an Angel

ELLORA'S CAVE
ROMANTICA PUBLISHING

An Ellora's Cave Romantica Publication

www.ellorascave.com

Blood of an Angel

ISBN # 1419952455
ALL RIGHTS RESERVED.
Blood of an Angel Copyright © 2005 Anya Bast
Edited by: Briana St. James
Cover art by: Syneca

Electronic book Publication: March, 2005
Trade paperback Publication: September, 2005

Excerpt from *Blood of the Rose* Copyright © Anya Bast, 2004

Warning:

The following material contains graphic sexual content meant for mature readers. *Blood of an Angel* has been rated *E-rotic* by a minimum of three independent reviewers.

Ellora's Cave Publishing offers three levels of Romantica™ reading entertainment: S (S-ensuous), E (E-rotic), and X (X-treme).

S-*ensuous* love scenes are explicit and leave nothing to the imagination.

E-*rotic* love scenes are explicit, leave nothing to the imagination, and are high in volume per the overall word count. In addition, some E-rated titles might contain fantasy material that some readers find objectionable, such as bondage, submission, same sex encounters, forced seductions, etc. E-rated titles are the most graphic titles we carry; it is common, for instance, for an author to use words such as "fucking", "cock", "pussy", etc., within their work of literature.

X-*treme* titles differ from E-rated titles only in plot premise and storyline execution. Unlike E-rated titles, stories designated with the letter X tend to contain controversial subject matter not for the faint of heart.

Also by Anya Bast:

Autumn Pleasures: The Union
Ellora's Cavemen: Tales from the Temple III
Ordinary Charm
The Embraced: Blood of the Raven
The Embraced: Blood of the Rose
Spring Pleasures: The Transformation
Summer Pleasures: The Capture
Winter Pleasures: The Training
Water Crystal

Blood of an Angel
The Embraced

Dedication

This book is dedicated to super-editor Briana St. James, the one who makes all my books better and provides me with much needed encouragement. Thanks for all your hard work. It's very appreciated.

Chapter One

If only he could've fallen for a woman like that one.

Charlie leaned against the wall of the café of the upscale bookstore he'd been dragged into by his friend Vincent. A small distance away a diminutive blonde wearing glasses, a burgundy sweater and pair of baggy cargo pants perused the books in the philosophy section. Petite, delicate, brainy-looking, those were all terms he would use to describe her.

Angelic. That one seemed all encompassing.

He wondered what she'd be like with her clothes off.

He looked away from her, berating himself for even contemplating the seduction of an unmarked human female. An entire household of Demi females willing to fuck him whenever, wherever and however he wanted awaited him this evening...awaited him every evening. He shouldn't even be thinking about how this woman in front of him would look with her clothes off, or how she'd feel under his hands, or how she'd taste against his tongue...both her sex and her blood. Charlie gave his head a sharp shake. Like many Vampir, sometimes he craved the blood of a human. When something was forbidden, it made it more attractive.

Not that he was looking for anything beyond a one-night stand and a little blood at this point. He'd had enough heartbreak to last him a century. Literally.

Still, he was bored and the woman was compelling. He watched as she selected a thick tome from the shelf, cracked it and scanned the first page. Maybe she was a university student. The University of Minnesota wasn't that far away. A wave of violet scent wafted toward him and he inhaled it like a drug. The scent seemed almost intoxicating. Her long blonde hair was pulled back in a French braid, revealing a long swanlike neck that featured the fair skin of the naturally light-haired. If he looked closely enough, he could see the fine blue veins in her throat.

The *sacyr*, the blood-hunger of the Embraced, flickered to life in his stomach. Uneasily, he shifted against the wall. He hadn't fed yet today, though the *sacyr* seemed unusually strong despite that.

The woman replaced the tome and tilted her head to the side as she examined the book spines, showcasing that wonderful expanse of neck that he wanted to taste. Charlie cleared his throat and looked away. It wasn't like he was a new Vampir. He should be able to control the *sacyr* better than this.

Where the hell was Vincent anyway?

They'd come to the bookstore so Vincent could pick up a novel for Evelyn, the mate of this territory's keeper, Anlon. Vincent was continually trying to curry Anlon's favor and offering to do errands for Evelyn was one way to do it. Earlier, Evelyn had mentioned she wanted a new mystery novel that had just released, so here was Vincent, shopping for it.

Vincent was a fairly young Vampir. It had been about twenty-five years since he'd been Embraced. Despite his youth, Vincent had a lot of power. That power had not gone unnoticed by Anlon. Still, Anlon didn't treat him any differently than the rest of the territory's Vampir. Anlon wanted Vincent to earn a place in the top ranks of his Vampir, not automatically get it because he was exceptionally strong. Anlon thought Vincent needed to mature into the responsibility of taking a high position with the territory, and Charlie agreed.

Charlie watched the situation in this vampiric territory with interest, but he had no ambitions here himself. Here, Charlie was only a guest and he was content to leave it so. His place was in a territory south of here, with a keeper named Gabriel Letourneau. Charlie used to be Gabriel's right hand. Now he wasn't so sure what he was, and Charlie wasn't sure he cared. Something bad had happened down there and Charlie had left without word to anyone.

He'd just needed to get away. Away from Gabriel and his new love, Fate Harding. Away from Raven House, where the memories of the one he'd lost still remained, where the scent of her had clung to the furniture. He'd needed to get away from his own apartment, where her scent and the psychic impression of her had lingered, especially in his bedroom…especially in his bed. He'd spent so many years loving her, wanting her to love him back, allowing her to fill up so much space within him that when she'd died, she'd left a gaping hole.

The term *immortal* was such a misnomer. The immortal could live forever, yes, but they could also die if the right weapon was used. Charlie shuddered against the unwelcome memories of that night.

"Charlie, come on, man."

Charlie felt a tug on his elbow, turned his head and saw Vincent's scowling face. Black eyes stared at him from the visage of a twenty-five-year-old man, though Vincent was actually closer to fifty. His glossy hair, as coal black as his eyes, brushed the collar of his black leather jacket.

Vincent shrugged. "I said your name five times. I don't know where you went, but it wasn't anywhere around here. Let's go."

Charlie pushed away from the wall and shot one last glance at the alluring little bookworm in the philosophy section. He bet her blood would be so sweet. He bet the woman's body would feel even sweeter. The *sacyr* kicked up a notch and Charlie forced it back down. He turned away. Yes, leaving the store and this unnaturally tempting woman was the best option.

Charlie turned up the collar of his black leather duster and walked down the street with Vincent. Griffin House was about five blocks down Grand Avenue and one block over on Summit. Summit Avenue was an older, elegant part of St. Paul. Huge, historical well-taken care of homes lined the wide street along with towering one hundred-year-old oaks. The lawns were well-kept, manicured by fussy owners who employed professionals to keep things *just so.*

Vincent turned to him and showed him the bag. He grinned. "I got it."

"Great," answered Charlie, unenthused. Vincent reminded him of an eager puppy at times. Though Charlie knew he, too, had been the same way at one time. Years and experience had matured Charlie into a shadow of his former self. Charlie didn't much resemble the man he'd been at the time he'd been Embraced. The same would happen to Vincent in time. "Evelyn will be surprised and pleased, I'm sure."

"I hope so."

Their boots crunched on the autumn leaves. Charlie watched the shopkeepers closing up for the night as they progressed down the street in companionable silence.

"How long did it take for you to make it in Gabriel's territory?" Vincent asked finally. "How long until Gabriel let you into his inner circle and gave you power?"

Charlie shrugged. "I was pretty weak after I was first Embraced. It took me a long time to grow into my powers, but once I did I was very strong. Still, it took many years and a lot of proving myself before Gabriel learned to trust me."

Charlie's thoughts strayed to Adam, another Vampir in Gabriel's territory. Adam had been giving Gabriel some problems when Charlie left. Adam was an undisciplined Vampir, always getting into trouble. He was true to the time he'd been Embraced, the Wild West. Adam was a perfect product of his time—wild, always out for the thrill. Always looking for the next new thing around the corner. Charlie knew that Niccolo, Gabriel's other hand, had left at the same time. That would have left Gabriel with few truly trusted Vampir around him.

Charlie cringed inwardly, and then stopped himself. *No.* He was not going to concern himself with what was going on down there. Charlie had his own issues to deal with right now, and Gabriel was strong enough to take care of his own shit.

They turned down a residential alley that linked Grand Avenue to Summit. Griffin House wasn't far. About halfway down the alley, the clang of metal trash cans sounded behind them. At the same time Charlie caught a scent in the air that didn't belong there.

The scent of violet.

"What was that?" Vincent muttered as he turned. "And what's that sm—"

A blur of blonde and burgundy rushed into their vision. The scent of violet filled the night air right before Vincent went down. The blur disappeared.

What the…?

"Vincent?" Charlie shouted as he raced to where Vincent lay and knelt. Blood welled from a deep gash in Vincent's stomach. "You okay?"

Vincent groaned.

Charlie's mind whirled as he tried to get a fix on what happened and where the attacker had gone. He stood up and turned in a hard circle, ready to fight whoever it was, but all he saw were garages, chain link fences and trash cans. Somewhere in the distance, a dog barked.

Out of nowhere came the blur. Something hard hit Charlie's solar plexus, knocking him back and spilling him on his ass on the ground of the alley. What the hell was faster than a Vampir?

His stomach clenched in agony. Not much could harm the Embraced, but whatever the blur had done to him, it had *harmed*. He rolled to the side for a moment, one palm on the pavement. Pebbles bit into his palm. He held his stomach with his other hand and groaned. His whole body screamed in pain. Something hot and wet touched his forearm and he pulled it away to see his white shirt stained dark with his own blood. Piercing physical anguish consumed him. It bowed his spine and made him squeeze his eyes shut.

Had she hit him with a hawthorn stake?

No. Hell, he'd be completely incapacitated right now and on his way to death if the blur had done that.

Movement in front of him caught his attention. He looked up and saw the bookstore blonde staring down at him. Her eyes were cold now, the cold gray of a winter storm or of gunmetal. "Let me finish this business I have with the other and I'll let you go. I have no quarrel with you." She had a slight accent he couldn't place. English, maybe?

She backed into the darkness and Charlie's gaze fell to Vincent, who lay unmoving on the ground.

The woman moved over Vincent, a hawthorn stake loose in her hand. She knelt. They spoke in low tones for a few moments. Charlie was too injured to pitch his hearing and listen in. Every part of his body felt like it was slowly dying and he felt so unbelievably bad that he almost wished for it. His head pounded with the rush of blood. His legs and arms were growing cold. Pain lanced through his stomach as though someone continually stabbed him. He was prey for any animal that came along right now. Charlie tried to push up, but collapsed back down.

The woman's voice grew strident, as though enraged. She raised the stake.

Charlie's mind struggled to comprehend the world beyond his pain. He squinted at her.

She was going to kill Vincent.

That fact gave Charlie enough motivation to push past the ravaging pain in his body. His muscles and mind protesting the movement, Charlie pushed off from the ground and launched himself at the woman with an anguished roar. She cried out in surprise, as he slammed full-force into her midsection, driving them both back into the door of a garage behind them. A hot slickness coated his stomach and chest and it took him a moment to realize it was his own blood. She struggled against him, waving that hawthorn stake dangerously close to his back.

Hawthorn wood was highly toxic to the Embraced. The wound made by a hawthorn stake not only poisoned their blood, it wouldn't close up. Ironically, most Embraced died of blood loss if someone staked them. So the fact that the hawthorn was now scraping his shoulder didn't make Charlie feel exactly warm and fuzzy.

He shifted to the side and grabbed the wrist of the hand wielding the stake. His whole body screamed from whatever it was she'd done to him. The wound made him weak and she was exceptionally strong. *Way* too strong for a human female. The result made them almost evenly matched in a fight. *Almost.* He suspected he was still the stronger one.

There was something off here. What was it?

With single-minded intensity, he pushed her down the garage door to the pavement. She shrieked in rage, but she couldn't stop him from pressing that wrist down to the ground. The woman might be faster than him, but it turned out that, even injured, he was still stronger. He wrested the stake from her grasp and threw it to the side. It ended up behind a row of trash cans that stood nearby.

She kicked, coming dangerously close to his balls with her knee, and slammed her fist into his jaw. His head snapped to the side under the force of the punch. Pain blossomed through his skull.

Damn, she was strong. She *couldn't* be human, but she didn't feel like an Embraced.

What the hell was she?

He needed to further control the woman, and he needed to do it fast. Using his inner thighs, he pressed in, pinning her legs together. He also grabbed her other flailing arm at the wrist and pressed it down to the ground.

She shrieked again and Charlie wondered when someone in one of these nearby houses would call the cops. They didn't need that. The police would call in the local SPAVA unit—Squad for Paranormal and Vampiric Activity—and they'd give both

Charlie and Anlon absolute hell. Any conflict between a human and an Embraced — if *human* really was what this woman was — got extra-special attention from the local law enforcement, always at the expense of the Embraced, no matter which party was truly at fault. Prejudice against the Embraced was alive and well in the United States.

But more important than avoiding SPAVA was finding out if Vincent was all right. He hadn't moved or made a sound since the woman had knelt over him with the stake in her hand. The fact that Charlie had wrested the hawthorn away from her before she'd had a chance to strike Vincent gave him hope that he was probably okay.

The woman went limp beneath him. Charlie was thankful, since the blood he'd lost was making him feel weak and the *sacyr* was rising hard and fast as a result. Plus, the closeness of his peculiar woman and her violet scent, combined with his own rage, was fueling his blood hunger.

She stared up with him with complete and utter animosity in her eyes.

Gone were the glasses. Gone was the illusion of bookishness and fragility. Completely gone was the impression that this woman was *angelic*. She felt delicate beneath him, but the way she'd kicked his ass contradicted that image.

"You should have let me kill him. He deserves to die," she spat.

Charlie's brow furrowed. Vincent was harmless. He was one of the most harmless Embraced he'd ever met. Vincent was almost *naïve*. What could Vincent have done to gain this woman's wrath? The question posed on his lips was *why* in the moment the woman suddenly pushed up hard. Caught off-guard by the jolt of inhuman strength, Charlie toppled to the side.

The woman sprang to her feet, eyeing the dark corner behind the row of trash cans where Charlie had thrown the stake. She lunged in that direction, but he stretched out quick as a striking snake and caught her by the ankle. He toppled her to the ground face-first and pushed to his feet.

The *sacyr* roared within him, overwhelming his weakness. It screamed in his head. He needed to feed. He needed to feed *now*.

Too bad for the woman in front him. She was about to become a meal.

With an intense gaze, he watched her flip to her back and spot him. He was the predator now. He might be injured. He might be weak. The rising *sacyr* didn't care about any of that. It just wanted the blood of this woman. Her gray eyes widened as she realized the tables had suddenly turned. Charlie watched her crabwalk back a few paces, then lurch to her feet.

Charlie lunged.

The woman spun to the side, kicking her booted foot up and around in a roundhouse kick. Her heel caught him hard in the solar plexus, right where she'd wounded him. He grunted, but the *sacyr* held him upright, made him push through the intense pain. The *sacyr* was unstoppable now. He had no say in his actions and was a slave to its whims. She threw a punch, but he blocked it. He took a step forward, she took a step back. It was like a dance, but one wholly without romance.

She turned to run, but he grabbed her by her upper arms and dragged her back flush up against his chest.

He lowered his head to her ear, scenting the violet in her hair and the blood that ran through those delicate veins under her pale, soft skin. He inhaled and closed his eyes, letting her aroma infuse him. His breath left him in a groan of ecstasy. "All the gentleman's been beaten right out of me," he murmured into her ear. "You're in trouble now, angel."

She stilled. Her breathing sounded harsh in the suddenly quiet air. It was as if the whole world had fallen away and only this alley, only he and this mysterious woman, remained.

Charlie dipped his head to the place where her shoulder met her throat and rubbed his lips against her skin. The woman shivered. From fear? He didn't know. He didn't smell any fear on her, but by rights she *should've* been afraid. Charlie only knew that her shudder increased the pull and strength of the *sacyr*.

He had to have her…*now.*

He flicked his tongue out and tasted her skin, tasted the hard pulse under her earlobe. So sweet. So soft. So perfect. He stifled a groan. His fangs extended and he brushed them across her vulnerable throat. At the same, he readied his glamour. Charlie was exceptionally good with glamour. The woman would feel nothing but pleasure when he bit her.

It was far more than she deserved.

The sudden scent of arousal filled the air, delicately musky. The woman whimpered in her throat. She relaxed against him and the tang of her sex, plumped with excitement, teased him.

That sound, along with the fragrance of her, gripped him and wouldn't let him free. Feeling drugged, he grazed his fangs along her shoulder. He felt the skin slice open in a thin, neat line and tasted just a drop of her blood on his tongue.

Somewhere in the *sacyr*-controlled, pain-fogged back of his mind, Charlie noted that she didn't taste like a human. Her blood was smoother, silkier on his tongue. It reminded him of milk flavored with a bit of sugar.

So, delicious… He lowered his mouth to take another taste.

Suddenly, the woman thrust her elbows up hard and twisted to the side. Charlie tried to maintain his grip on her, but she was gone in a blur of speed.

An angelic tinkle of laughter was all he heard from the mouth of the alley. Then, nothing.

The *sacyr* wailed within him at being denied sustenance. His wound overwhelmed him. Charlie groaned, dropped to his knees and knew nothing more.

Chapter Two

Tiya's boots pounded on the pavement as hard as her heart pounded in her chest. She slowed her speed to a rate more in keeping with a human's, though she was tempted to simply take off like a shot and get as far away from the alley and that damn Vampir as she could get. As she ran, she used just enough magick to disguise the blood on her clothing. Her emotional state was too unsteady right now to risk using the kind of magick it would take to conceal how fast she could move.

Even now the sound of the sirens reached her ears. Someone had likely heard the struggles and her screams, and called the police.

Tears pricked her eyes as she rounded the corner that led to her apartment building. She was covered in the blood of the Embraced. All she wanted was for it to be cleansed from her skin. She wanted the scent of that Vampir's calming breath out of her nose. His glamour, along with the chemical in his breath that comforted a Vampir's prey, had almost been her undoing back in the alley. She'd almost allowed the vamp to sink his fangs into her. As it was, he'd gotten a small taste of her blood.

The slight slice in her shoulder hardly pained her. It was the knowledge she'd allowed him to do it that really stung. Hell, her body had reacted as though he was readying her for sex. She'd almost begged him to bite her before her senses snapped back into action and she'd freed herself. God, she'd nearly begged him to fuck her.

She ran to the tall brown building on Grand Avenue where she'd rented an apartment and pulled open the double doors. She'd just moved to St. Paul and had selected a place to live that wasn't far from Griffin House and her quarry.

She raced past the row of metal mailboxes and pounded up the three flights of stairs that led to her apartment, fumbling for her keys as she went. Finally, she stood in front of her apartment door, the wooden railing of the stairway behind her.

A light bulb hanging above her swung under the force of her agitation. She slid the key in the lock, threw the door open and slammed it shut behind her angrily. As soon as she was in, she pulled at her blood-smeared clothes, ripping them from her body by the seams and ruining them. Tears flowed down her face as she made her way into the bathroom and started the water.

She'd almost had him. She'd almost had her revenge on one of the Embraced responsible for the slaughter of her family. She'd been *so* close.

Tiya tore the elastic band from the end of her braid and shook out her hair, then climbed into the bathtub and stuck her head under the hot water. The blood ran from her body in rivulets and swirled down the drain at her feet. The water pressure stung the cut on her shoulder where she'd allowed the Vampir to taste her. Her blood flowed in with the rest. Sidhe and Embraced blood mixed.

Blood. More of it. Would she ever be free of the sight?

She leaned her head against the tile wall and sobbed. Her sobs turned to wails of grief and she slid down the tiled shower wall to sit in the bathtub with the pounding of the water punishing her head and body. The soul-deep grief she seemed unable to cure herself of racked her in sob after sob until it hurt to draw a breath.

Unwanted memories, the same ones that haunted her dreams, slammed into her.

She remembered entering her family's home in the hills of Wales. They'd lived there for centuries, away from the cities and most humans in an enclave of OtherKin Tuatha Dé Danaan. There weren't many OtherKin Sidhe. The ones that still remained tended to stick together. That way, they didn't have to move every ten years to disguise the fact they didn't age like humans. Humans didn't even know the OtherKin existed. Neither did the Embraced, for that matter.

That day she'd been visiting from the U.S. where she'd moved about thirty years prior. She'd arrived just in time to see the carnage wrought by a group of renegade Embraced. One of them had been draining her mother of her blood when Tiya had entered. Tiya had dropped her suitcase at the same time the Vamp had dropped her mother. Her mother had made a sick thudding sound on the floor when she'd fallen. Her wrists and ankles had been bound with cold iron cuffs.

Blood. Blood had been everywhere. On the floor, the walls. The smell of it had caught in her nostrils and made her stomach roil.

Tiya was an excellent fighter. Her father had made sure she knew self-defense. That day, she'd fought for her life. In rage, disbelief and grief, she'd battled the three vamps in her parent's house who'd killed her mother, father and sister before she'd arrived. The Vampir had been strong, really strong, but she'd fought as though possessed. As though she'd been Cúchulainn in the throes of a berserker state. Her adrenaline had been pumping hard enough to take out an army, or so she imagined.

The murderers had all gotten away, save one.

Those Vampir must've known what she and her family were, because they'd been ready to fight the OtherKin, who, whether they were shifters or the Sidhe, were faster and stronger than humans. Every member of her family had been bound with cold iron manacles, which was the only substance that could negate the OtherKin's abilities.

She had stunned the vamps. They'd been awed by her strength and speed. Their surprise had given her an advantage. They hadn't been expecting a fourth OtherKin Sidhe to fight that day. They hadn't brought that many sets of handcuffs, which let her known they'd planned the attack. She'd used her muscles and her magick and had vanquished all of them, save one.

The one who'd killed her mother had not escaped. Tiya had managed to incapacitate that one by crushing one of his knees. Vamps healed fast, but not that fast. While he writhed on the floor of the kitchen, she'd stalked out into the front yard and broken a branch off the hawthorn tree. Luckily the plant grew all over Wales. Right before she'd staked the bastard, she'd gotten two bits of information about the people responsible.

Vincent.

St. Paul, Minnesota.

When she'd asked why they'd done this to her family, he'd just laughed at her. That laugh had been the last sound the vamp had ever made. It still haunted her sleep in the dead of night.

His life had been the first life she'd ever taken in her two hundred years.

But she'd take more before she was through. She hungered for it. The desire to see their spilled blood made her cold inside. It made her feel partially dead and mostly numb. None of that mattered. She'd be little more than a shell when this was through, traumatized by the acts she was about to commit. None of that mattered either.

Now she was driven by one goal and one goal only—to find those responsible for what had happened and stop it from occurring to any more of her people. The OtherKin had largely concealed themselves for thousands of years from both humankind and the Embraced. It appeared someone, somewhere now knew.

And apparently, whoever it was, they wanted them dead.

Tiya had grieved over her family and then buried them with the aid of the OtherKin in that area. The very afternoon they were in the ground, Tiya purchased plane tickets back to the U.S. She hadn't been bound for her home in Seattle, but to Minneapolis, Minnesota.

Tiya sat in the bathtub and sobbed out her grief and frustration until the water grew cold. Her people, the Tuatha Dé Danaan, prayed to the goddess Danu. Tiya had never been particularly religious, but she prayed now that Danu would see her vengeance through.

Next time she'd get Vincent.

* * * * *

"Charlie."

Charlie roused at the feminine voice purring his name in his ear. It was the angel's voice. The beguiling, bloodthirsty angel. He reached out, searching for her small, curved body, her sweet blood…those cold, cold gunmetal eyes.

"Charlie," came the voice again. He felt the touch of a cool hand on his shoulder. It wasn't hot like the angel's skin. He opened his eyes.

Dark brown eyes met his, shining from a face with full lips, high cheekbones and a small, perfect nose.

Evelyn. Not his blood-splattered angel.

Evelyn's face wore a concerned expression. "Charlie, are you all right?" she asked in her charming, lilting English accent.

He blinked, and then squeezed his eyes shut. The *sacyr* twisted through his body, tightening every muscle as if in a vise. He gasped and clenched his fists, forcing himself to get a handle on it, struggling to gain mastery over it. How long had it been since he'd fed? He drew a shuddering breath and felt it recede. He opened his eyes.

"Charlie," came a deep voice beside him.

He turned his head and blinked again. "Adam?"

"Hey, pard," Adam Ridge smiled. His brown eyes glinted with pleasure. "Long time, no see."

Adam was here? How was that possible? Adam was Gabriel's Vampir. Adam belonged south of here.

Charlie tried to push up into a sitting position, but Evelyn pressed him back down onto the bed. "No. Stay still," she said. "You've been badly hurt. You've been out for days now."

Days? SPAVA or someone must've found him in the alley and taken him to Griffin House. Human medicine didn't do anything for a Vampir, so the Embraced tended to take care of their own. Hellish flashes of that night assaulted his mind's eye and made his stomach roll.

"Vincent?" Charlie rasped. Had he survived?

Evelyn ran long, cool fingers down the side of his face. "He's awake, but not well. His wound was worse than yours, deeper. Your attacker used a strange weapon on you both. If it's what Anlon thinks it is, it's a rare kind of blade that Vampir hunters sometimes use. It almost killed both of you."

Charlie cleared his dry throat and spoke in a rasping voice. "Did you catch her?"

Evelyn shared a glance with Adam. "Her?" she asked.

Charlie pushed up, noticing for the first time they'd dressed him a white T-shirt and a pair of blue boxers. Pain speared through his midsection. He touched his stomach and felt a bandage wrapping him. This time he wouldn't allow Evelyn to press him back down when she tried. "It was a woman who attacked **us**. She wasn't Embraced." He shook his head. "But she couldn't **have** been human, either."

Evelyn pursed her lips and nodded. "What was she, then?"

Charlie shook his head. "I don't know."

Adam nodded his closely shorn blond head. "Okay, Charlie, **you** need to feed, man. We'll talk more about what happened after you satisfy the *sacyr*. I can feel it raging within you from ten feet away."

Charlie nodded slightly. The *sacyr* was bad. He could barely keep it in check. "What are you doing here, Adam?" he asked in a gravelly voice.

"When you were out, you contacted Gabriel in your mind. Your subconscious did it, man. He sent me up here to check if you were all right." He paused. "Gabriel didn't come himself because he could sense he wasn't on your list of favorite people right now. He thought you needed some distance from him. Gabriel says, 'Come home when you're ready.'"

Home. It sounded good.

Evelyn turned and walked to the door. Adam followed in his slow, rambling gait, hands tucked into the pockets of his jeans. "We will send Jaela to you," said Evelyn. She turned, her long ebony hair swirling around her with the motion. "She is a favorite of yours, isn't she?" She winked and closed the door behind herself and Adam.

Charlie tipped his head back against the headboard, letting out a slow breath, and examined his surroundings. They'd put him in a guest room here at Griffin House. Liking his privacy, he had his own place across town. This room was decorated with heavy wood furniture and dark green fabrics. It had an old-fashioned feel to it, as did the entire house. Most the Houses of the Embraced did. Charlie guessed it was just more comfortable for most of them to surround themselves with things from the past.

It wasn't long before the door opened again and a tall, dark-skinned Demi padded across the plush cream-colored carpet toward him. She was dressed in a short, silky plum-colored negligee. Her hips swayed seductively with every step and her eyes were heavy-lidded. The full pout of her mouth curved in a smile. "Evelyn said you were hungry." Her dark eyes glinted in a predatory way.

The Demi were always hungry.

Charlie's gaze zeroed in on the pulse at her throat. The *sacyr* roared within him like some caged beast in his skin that fought tooth and nail to free itself. "Come here," he managed to growl.

Jaela's slight smile widened. She knew she'd be fed as well. Being Demi meant that she'd been unmarked when she'd been Embraced and hadn't been strong enough to push through the Demi stage of the process to make it to a full-blown Vampir. The Demi fed from sex and lust, instead of life force. The Council of the Embraced had decreed that the Vampir were to feed from the Demi and not humans. Though the Vampir broke that rule pretty often. Most humans enjoyed being bitten by a vamp. Some of them even actively sought it out. Some were even addicted.

Jaela slid in beside him in on the king-sized four-poster bed. Charlie made a growling sound in his throat and rolled her over and then under him, pinning her to the bed beneath him. The blankets were tangled between them and their clothes separated them. The clothing and blankets would have to go soon. Charlie wanted to feel her skin on his. He pushed her negligee up, feeling her smooth thighs. He closed his eyes and inhaled the scent of her perfume. It was musky, seductive. So unlike fresh, naïve violet.

At the thought of the violet scent of the angel, her face filled his mind. He saw her in the bookstore, where he'd thought her innocent. On its heels followed an image of her rising over Vincent with the stake in her hand.

He opened his eyes and banished the disturbing illusion by growling and dragging Jaela's negligee up to her waist. Jaela cooed, pleased at his rough treatment. The scent of her arousal painted the air, increasing his hunger.

Charlie wanted nothing more than to drive the vision of the angel out of his mind, so he planned to drive himself into Jaela. He would slake his thirst on Jaela while feeding her hunger. He would fuck her senseless, fuck Jaela until she couldn't think, until he couldn't think. Until he couldn't remember what had happened in the alley.

He'd burn the angel straight out of his mind.

He moved down Jaela's body, taking in every smooth, cocoa curve of her stomach and hips. When he reached her thighs, he spread them and lowered his mouth to her sex. He lapped her up, enjoying the musky taste of her, reveling in the feel of her swollen labia in between his lips and how he could make her clit plump full with arousal. Beneath him, Jaela moaned and writhed with pleasure.

In his mind, it was the angel's soft sound of pleasure he heard. The scent of violet filled his nostrils. Her face filled his mind. She was like a drug, a horrible temptation. No. Goddamn it.

No!

He licked the spot where Jaela's inner thigh and sex met. As his fangs descended, he ramped up his glamour. Without any warning to Jaela, he sank through her tender flesh and into her femoral artery. In the same instant, he covered her with his glamour to lessen the pain and make it pleasurable. He found the entrance to her slick pussy and pushed two fingers inside her to find the sweet spot that he knew she most wanted him to touch.

Jaela cried out and arched her back.

Her sweet blood rushed into Charlie's mouth and the *sacyr* cried its approval. His vision darkened at the sensation of his hunger being satisfied. It was akin to being famished and consuming a four-course meal. At the same time her blood started to flow, Jaela came hard. The muscles of her pussy rippled and pulsed around his fingers as she writhed under him and cried out.

With the glamour, he extended her orgasm so he could drink his fill of her. The blood flowed into him, making him strong. He could feel the wound on his stomach healing as he took in badly needed sustenance. The exhaustion he'd felt earlier now transformed into invigoration, as if he hadn't just been unconscious for a few days, he'd only been resting.

Charlie released Jaela's upper thigh, tipped his back and panted out his satisfaction. The *sacyr* was well-fed.

Jaela released her grip on the blankets, her chest heaving. Already the wound he'd made on her upper thigh was almost closed. The Demi also healed fast.

She twisted on the bed like a cat stretching and smiled. "Come on, baby. Time to return the favor."

Lust poured through his body like liquefied steel and pooled in his cock. He shed his clothes and came down between Jaela's thighs. The heat from her pussy rose up and caressed the tender flesh of his rock-hard shaft. She ran his fingers over his chest and arms, compelling his head down for a kiss.

As soon as his lips touched hers, he saw her…*the angel*. She smiled at him in the bookstore, full of purity and friendliness. Next he saw her pinned beneath him in the alley, smeared with his and Vincent's blood.

Charlie pulled away from the kiss and roared. At the same time, he thrust inside Jaela in one hard, forward motion and seated himself inside to the base of his shaft. He pulled out and rammed back into her creamy sex, quickly setting up a vicious, hard rhythm. Beneath him, Jaela tossed her head back and forth, grasping his shoulders. "Yes, baby, harder. That's it. Oh, yes," she chanted.

Charlie gave Jaela what she wanted and needed and did his best to rid himself of the unwanted images of the angel in his mind. When he came, it was hard enough to darken his vision. When he came, it was with Jaela's pussy muscles pulsing around his shaft from her climax.

When he came, within his mind, it was the angel's body he poured himself into.

Charlie collapsed on Jaela's perspiration-sheened body and rolled to the side. She curled up next to him, cooing and kissing him, telling him how good he'd been to her. He stared at the ceiling, wondering why that woman's face was so burned into his mind, why a vicious, deceptive angel was haunting him.

After Jaela had gathered her shredded nightgown and left him alone, Charlie rose from the bed and pulled the bandage from around his waist. He dropped it on a nearby table and ran a finger over the thin red line that bisected his stomach. The wound had healed while he'd fed from Jaela's blood. Even that mark would disappear within a day's time since he'd fed the *sacyr* so well today. It would leave a thin white scar for a while, and then even that would disappear.

He ran his index finger over the mark. The sight of the scar brought back memories of his life before, when he'd been a child.

Charlie been born in 1862 in Boston to a family with a lot of money and a high place in society. The Scythchildes had ruled everything they'd touched. Not only had Charlie been born with a silver spoon in his mouth, he'd been born marked with a caul, meaning he was destined to one day be Embraced.

He'd also been born with a horrible disfigurement to his face.

The disfigurement had appalled his father. Especially since Charlie had been eldest and his heir. So strong had his father's revulsion been, that his parents told the world the baby had died. Then they'd placed Charlie with another family. When he was older, his mother had located him, taken him back into the family mansion and hidden him, but when his father had discovered his presence, he'd kicked him out. Charlie could still remember the look of disgust and contempt on his father's face.

For years, Charlie had survived on the streets of Boston on his own. Eventually, he'd traveled south, to New York City, simply to get away from the pain of having to hear his family name, or glimpse it printed on a newspaper as he passed a street corner. Knowing that he'd be labeled insane for claiming it, Charlie had kept quiet about his parentage. He'd simply endured. He'd been too disfigured to gain employment, so surviving had been tricky, especially in the harsh wintertime.

Charlie walked to a mirror hanging on the wall next to the bed and stared at his reflection. He rubbed a hand over the three day's growth of beard on his face.

Then, one day, he'd been Embraced.

The Embrace had transformed his visage. The change had taken away the deformity, leaving behind the face of the man he would've been without it. It was a good-looking face. Handsome. One with features that society considered ideal. It was a face that made women susceptible to his charms.

All the women, that was, except the two in his lifetime he'd truly loved.

Charlie stared into his dark brown eyes.

He was still disfigured, though it didn't show on his face or his body. The rejection he'd endured by his father had marked his soul. Not that he dwelt on it. He'd long since dealt with the issue, although its mark was in some ways indelible. The things that happened to a person when they were young sculpted them into their adult form. You could accept and deal with the trauma and reshape parts of the sculpture, but never the whole thing.

Turning away, he clenched his fist. No more of this. He had things to see to. Charlie pulled on a pair of jeans and left his chest shirtless. On bare feet, he walked out of the room to find Vincent and ensure he was all right.

Charlie found Vincent in a large room on the third floor of the mansion. This one was decorated in silky, calming blues and greens. It was Vincent's room and, as such, was crammed to bursting with bookshelves filled with obscure texts. A large computer desk sat in one corner, upon which rested state-of-the-art equipment. Vincent was a bookworm and always had been. Overstuffed furniture in striped patterns scattered the room. Anlon sat in a straight-backed chair by the bed. Adam leaned against a wall in the corner of the room, wearing a pair of black jeans and a plain white T-shirt. He nodded when Charlie entered the room.

Vincent sat up in the bed, leaning against the carved wooden headboard. His breathing came harsh in the quiet air. His eyelids flickered open and his pupils fought to focus on Charlie's face. His lips were a sickly white and his normally shiny black eyes seemed dull.

Charlie tried to hide his reaction to Vincent's pallor and the gauntness of his face with a smile. "Hey, Vincent, you're awake."

Vincent tried to smile back, but it looked more like a grimace.

Anlon stood. He wore a silky red shirt that contrasted with the fall of his long, dark hair. "Charlie, I'm so glad you pulled through. I've never known anyone to come through hawthorn poisoning the way you two did." His voice held the slightest hint of an Irish accent.

It didn't look to Charlie that Vincent had "pulled through" yet, but he'd keep that opinion to himself. He pushed a hand through his unruly hair. "It was hawthorn she used, then?"

"Yes. It appears the attacker had some kind of weapon that was blended with a very small amount of hawthorn. She didn't mean to kill you, at least not at first. Her goal was incapacitation. She went for Vincent a lot harder than you. She struck deeper with her weapon and slashed him twice."

Images from the alley fight flicked through Charlie's mind. He heard her voice. "She told me she didn't have a quarrel with me. That if I let her conclude her *business* with Vincent she'd let me live."

Anlon pushed a hand through his hair and sighed. "It doesn't make sense. What could have Vincent have done to her?"

Charlie glanced at Vincent. His eyes were closed once more. Obviously, he wasn't in a condition to speak yet. "Has Vincent fed yet?" Charlie asked.

Adam pushed away from the wall and ambled toward them. "A Demi came in, gave him her blood. He could barely break the skin of her wrist and couldn't use any glamour on the poor woman. He'll need another feeding soon. He's real weak and it's going to take a lot of blood to get him up and running again."

Charlie nodded. He hated talking about Vincent as if he wasn't in the room, but Vincent didn't look up for discussion at the moment.

"Charlie, you told Evelyn your attacker was a woman and that you didn't think she was human," said Anlon. He paused. "What do you think she was?"

Charlie shook his head. "I don't know. She was fast, faster than a vamp and stronger than a human, but not as strong as me. I don't know, Anlon, but you better believe I'm going to find out."

"You need any help, I'm here, Charlie," said Adam. "Just like old times."

Just like old times. Guilt speared through Charlie for leaving Gabriel's territory. He needed to have a long talk with Adam and soon, but now was not the time.

He only had one thing on his mind right now.

Charlie gritted his teeth as Vincent fell into a coughing fit and expelled blood onto the white sheets. He'd find the angel and make her pay for what she'd done. He had her blood in him now. Her life force coursed through his veins, even if it was only a minute amount. She didn't realize, as most didn't, just how strong a Vampir he truly was. He'd grown in strength steadily over the years, but concealed most of his abilities from others.

Right now he could feel the angel within him and also her physical location in the city. It pulsed like a homing beacon. He'd be able to find her and, next time, he'd be ready for her.

She wouldn't fight free of him when their paths crossed next and he planned to arrange a meeting soon.

Chapter Three

What was she, invisible?

Tiya crossed her arms and leaned up against the wall behind her. She settled in for a baleful staring session at the redheaded clerk at the DMV while the older lady chatted on the phone to Karen.

Karen, Tiya learned, had recently bought a brand-new sedan with a sunroof two weeks ago and *already* it was in the shop. *Can you imagine?* Tiya rolled her eyes and made a show of checking her watch.

Redheaded DMV lady finally figured out Tiya was growing perturbed and ceased the ongoing automobile drama with Karen. She hung up the phone. "Can I help you?"

Tiya pushed off from the wall and walked to the counter. "I've had a change of address and need a new license." She pushed her old license across the counter and let redhead do what she needed to do.

"Stand against that wall on the X so I can take your picture," the redhead instructed.

Tiya walked over and stood there. She knew she was slouching. She wasn't wearing a bit of makeup. The picture would suck.

"Come on, smile!" the DMV lady said brightly. "Don't you want to look happy?"

Tiya scowled at her until the woman's smile faded.

The DMV lady shrugged. "Have it your way."

"Thank you."

The flashbulb flashed and minutes later the lady handed her a new license. Tiya had decided to move after her failed attempt to take Vincent in the alley. Why was she bothering with a new license right in the middle of a blood vendetta? First, she didn't need any extra hassle with local law enforcement. Second, it helped make her feel that she was still connected in some way to mundane day-to-day life and society. A trip to the DMV definitely cemented one in reality.

Tiya was doing all she could to prevent that tenuous thread of sanity from snapping and leaving her on the edge as some crazed woman on a mission of revenge.

She'd moved because she'd needed to get away from Griffin House to reduce the risk of the vamp she'd fought ever spotting her walking down the street or something. Things hadn't gone as planned in the alley. Moving was a part of her damage control.

That vamp had been one of the stronger ones she'd ever encountered. He had a lot of tightly leashed, violent power coiled within him. The fact he'd managed to get a taste of her blood was a testament to that fact. She never wanted to be the recipient of that power completely freed. She shivered.

"Here you go, Tee-ya," DMV lady said with a broad, cheery smile.

This woman was getting on Tiya's nerves. Weren't government workers supposed to be surly? Tiya wanted surly and quiet now. The last thing she was in the mood for was fucking little Miss Mary Sunshine.

"You have a gorgeous accent and that's a beautiful name," DMV lady said as Tiya took the license. "What's the origin?"

Tiya pocketed the new license in her black leather coat and turned. "It's Tie-ya, and you wouldn't understand the origin."

Tiya stalked out of the DMV and went toward her dark blue four-door sedan. She'd moved out to Woodbury, which was clear on the other side of St. Paul. Pretty much, it was yuppie grand central. The neighborhood hardly fit her current state of mind with its fancy, overpriced grocery stores and top-end restaurants, but it had been far from Griffin House and that made it attractive. The location was far from the powerful vamp who had stolen a taste of her blood, foiled her attempt at getting more information out of Vincent before she killed him and, surprisingly enough, had frightened her.

She thought she'd had no fear before she ran into him. How quickly he'd taught her otherwise.

She climbed into her car and started the engine.

There had been something about that vamp that had bothered her even before she'd stalked them through the streets and launched her attack. In the bookstore, she'd noticed him right away and it had had little to do with the fact that she could feel he was Embraced. She'd tried to read his mind, but no dice. The man could shield hard.

The OtherKin Sidhe, indeed all the varieties of OtherKin from the shifters to the witches and mages, could feel the Embraced when they were near. It was as if the very molecules of the Embraced vibrated at a different rate than humans — faster, harder, more alive. Perhaps it was the result of feeding from life force or sex.

The vamp had been resting his lean, powerful body against the wall of the store café when she'd first seen him. He'd been like a predator at rest, yet watchful. His gaze had taken in every part of the store, and especially her.

He'd been *very* focused on her for some reason.

And, for some reason, she'd felt that intent, watchful gaze like it had been his hand on her skin. She's felt it all the way through to her pussy. Even in the bookstore, she'd felt the vamp's sexual appeal. Why he affected her that way remained a mystery. Some kind of strange OtherKin chemistry? Who knew?

His hair was dark and glossy. Hanks of it had continually fallen across his eye on the left side and he'd been repeatedly flipping it back. His face was nicely formed — handsome. She wouldn't be inclined to call him a pretty boy, but he was damn close. He would've looked at home dressed in an expensive suit and posed on the cover of a trendy men's magazine. His lips were full and he'd had a bit of five o'clock shadow on his jaw. Just enough to make him look sexy.

But it was his eyes that had captured her attention most.

There had been a thinly masked expression of pain and torment in those dark eyes. There had been an *oldness* in his gaze. The same look of jaded exhaustion she found reflected in her own eyes when she looked in a mirror. What she saw in his gaze had aligned with her own, and that had bothered her. She'd done her best to act the part of the bookish store patron, yet she'd felt drawn to him in some indefinable way.

Her hands clenched the steering wheel of her car.

The bastard had been with Vincent. For all she knew, he was a part of the group targeting OtherKin Fae.

"Goddamn it," she said aloud to her quiet car.

She should've given him her hawthorn stake in the alley. Why had she spared him? Had it been the tormented look in those chocolate brown eyes? If so, her silly empathy had cost her dearly.

Right now she could afford no tenderhearted feelings, no misplaced mercy. She couldn't afford to let herself fall victim to a gorgeous Vampir with eyes as wounded as hers. Next time she came across the vamp, she'd use her hawthorn stake right away.

No hesitation. No compassion.

In the alley she'd used a weapon she'd made that had just a little bit of hawthorn blended into a sharp steel blade. It was called a malchete. It was a short sword, essentially. She'd seen Vampir hunters use them in Europe and had recreated one from memory.

The small bit of hawthorn poisoned the Vampir and incapacitated the victim, but since the hawthorn was not full-strength, did not kill on penetration. It was a good weapon to use when you wanted to wound a vamp and put him near death, but keep him in the world of the living. She'd used the malchete on Vincent, with the intent of threatening him with the pure hawthorn stake and drawing information out of him.

A part of her hoped Vincent had died from the deep wound she'd inflicted on him with the malchete. Another part of her hoped he hadn't because she still needed information.

She closed her eyes. With every wound she inflicted on another living being, with every thought of bloodlust she had, she felt another part of her soul slip away. This thirst for vengeance was a foreign thing to her. She'd always been a peaceful, loving person.

Heart heavy, Tiya started her car and headed home. By the time she'd fought rush-hour traffic over the bridge from South St. Paul into Woodbury, the sun was descending. She drove through a neighborhood of large homes and finally reached her own sparsely furnished house. These days, she traveled light since she had to be ready to pick up and move at moment's notice in order to conceal herself.

Her house was a small, white, two bedroom with a yard dotted through by mature trees at the end of a dead end street. She'd bought the house for two reasons. The first was that it had already been vacant, so she could pay cash for it and be moved in soon as she wanted. The other was the privacy it afforded her. Trees and high hedges lined the yard on all sides.

On the way into Woodbury, she'd stopped and picked up a little takeout from Wok This Way, a Chinese eatery she'd discovered. She grabbed her purse and her paper bag filled with chicken chow mein and eggrolls and got out of the car.

She balanced the bag and her purse and shut the driver's side door. Before she turned away from the car, something slammed her hard from behind. The bag with the Chinese food crushed between her body and car door and fell the ground. Strong hands jerked her purse from her arm. She watched it fly into the bushes.

Tiya punched her elbow back in an effort to connect with her attacker's face and hit pay dirt. The man oofed at the punch and fell back a little, enough for her to push away from the car and whirl around to face him.

It was the Vampir. The one she'd taken mercy on. The stake was in her purse, but she had a small malchete dagger sheathed in a holster at the small of her back. She groped for it, but he lunged at her with Vampir speed and knocked her backward.

Her breath whooshed out of her as her back made contact with the pavement. The Vampir's hard body pressed down on her from above. She kicked and struggled, having *déjà vu*. This was the second time the bastard had been on top in a fight.

She fucking wanted to be on top for once.

He grabbed her wrists and forced them down to either side of her. She cried out in anguish and pain. The Vampir was strong, way too strong for her. He pinned her wrists and pressed her thighs between his legs.

More goddamn *déjà vu*.

She tried to read his mind and encountered a thick protective wall. Maybe that was for the best. She didn't really want to see what he wanted to do to her. In effort to free herself, she gathered the magick she had within her, coiling it into a hard fastball of energy. With a hard mental push, she sent it out as a punch to the solar plexus, but her magick withered and died as soon as it touched the Vampir. She yelled out incoherently in frustration. What was wrong? Why wouldn't it work?

She tried again and again. Nothing. Every time her magick hit him, it died.

Despair washed over her. Maybe her family wouldn't be avenged after all.

Tiya closed her eyes against the beating of her heart, waiting for him to roll his glamour over her and bite her. She waited for him to drain her blood the way her family's blood had been drained.

"Look at me," said the Vampir in a voice that sound more like a low growl than anything else.

She squeezed her eyes shut tighter, feeling her heart slam against her rib cage.

"Woman, look at me," came his voice again, controlled, calm, as though he had all the time in the world.

A warm sensation washed over her. *Glamour.* It felt comforting, like a hug or the scent of her grandmother's cookies baking in the oven. God, his glamour was so strong. Maybe that's why her magick wouldn't work on him, she wondered sluggishly.

Look at me. This time he said the words in her mind.

She turned her head and opened her eyes, her gaze finding and fixing on his dark brown orbs. Despite the glamour he'd unfurled, there was nothing comforting or kind in those eyes. They should've seemed warm because of their color, but they were frosty and murderous.

Her gaze locked on his and it seemed she couldn't look away. She felt a trickle of power, not unlike her own magick, flow through her body. His eyes seemed to glow with a strange light. That light penetrated her mind, making her eyes roll back in her head. A small noise slipped from her throat and her eyelids drooped.

What the hell?

Her body felt heavy, as though she was very, very tired. Her mind screamed for her to move, to roll away and fight when he released her wrists and stood, but her muscles wouldn't obey her. It was like he'd drugged her.

The Vampir stood over her, looking down. Tiya felt like a wounded fawn ready for slaughter and there wasn't a damn thing she could do about it. The Vampir knelt and scooped her into his arms like she weighed nothing. She was limp as a rag doll, though her mind screamed and railed against what was happening. A soft whimper escaped her throat as he walked up to her front door and simply kicked it in.

Great.

None of the magickal shields she'd placed around her house had even slowed him down. A human would have been too discouraged by them to even approach the lawn, but they didn't even faze this vamp. It was like he couldn't even feel them.

The Vampir headed into her sparsely furnished living room and down the hall to her bedroom. Her heart rate sped up so fast she thought she'd have a heart attack. Not that the OtherKin Sidhe could have heart attacks. Did he mean to rape her before he drained her?

He dropped her onto the bed and searched her body for weapons. It was fast and efficient, his hands moving with purpose over her limbs and torso. He didn't so much as try to cop a feel. Maybe rape wasn't on the agenda.

Maybe her death was the only thing he wanted from her.

The damned vamp found the dagger in the sheath at the small of her back and threw it across the room. She tried to watch where it landed, but it was so hard to move her head. She felt so tired.

He left the room and when he came back, he held two sturdy lengths of rope in his hand. It took him no time at all to position her limp body spread-eagle on the bed and tie her wrists to the headboard rails.

Well, wasn't this nice and kinky.

"You should be able to do no harm now, huh, angel?" he murmured.

Angel? If only he knew. She'd like to show him just how little *angel* there was in her, but all she could do was glare at him with murder in her eyes.

He passed a hand in front of her face and it was like a wave of ice-cold water hit her. The lethargy left her in a rush and she took a gulp of air as though she'd been swimming in the ocean and had come up after being pulled down by the undertow.

"Asshole," she shrieked and kicked out at the same time.

He calmly grabbed her ankles and pressed them back onto the mattress. "Don't make me tie those, too."

She pulled on her bonds, but of course he'd tied them tight. Tiya was strong, but not strong enough to snap the thick rope.

"Don't fight or scream," he said, "or I'll have to get more serious. Right now, you're in no danger."

Right now. Those words were not lost on her. She quieted and stared at him. "If I screamed loud enough and long enough, the police would come."

He cocked his head to the side and smiled. A hank of glossy hair fell across his eye. "If the police came, so would SPAVA. I can't think you'd want that too much. You're not exactly human—" he paused and flipped his hair back "—are you?"

She gritted her teeth until her jaw ached. "Look, I'd say I'm sorry about jumping you and your friend in the alley, but I'm not. Your friend deserves to die."

"Oh, really? Vincent deserves to die? What did Vincent do to you that was so bad? 'Cause, see, I know Vincent, and he's not exactly what you'd call a lethal vamp."

She looked away. "I have information that says otherwise."

"So, what? You're playing judge, jury and executioner? You know, if a vamp has done something truly bad, The Council of the Embraced has its own Executioners. I even know one, a truly lethal one, personally."

She looked at him. "Bully for you."

He paused and stared down at her. "What's your name?"

She only laughed.

He sat down on the bed beside her. She stared up at him. He was really stunning. Tiya bet he made every little girl's heart go pitter-patter.

But not hers.

"I'm Charles Alexander Scythchilde, but everyone calls me Charlie."

She tipped her head back and smirked. "Gee, Charlie—" she moved her wrists, pulling on her bonds, "—I'm so happy to meet you. Maybe we can do lunch sometime."

"You're not going to be cooperative, are you? Too bad, angel, that's really too bad. Because you're lucky it was me who tracked you down. After what you did, I know a whole lotta vamps who'd just kill you on sight. I thought long and hard about doing just that. I almost did out there in your driveway."

"Funny, because that's what I was planning to do if I ever had the misfortune to see you again."

Charlie stood and left the room without a word. When he returned, he was holding her purse.

She rolled her eyes. "It doesn't go with your shoes," she quipped.

He ignored her. Using his sleeve pulled over his hand, he carefully pulled out the hawthorn stake and raised his eyebrows.

"Be careful. Don't get a sliver," she said sweetly.

He took the stake and the dagger from the room, came back and continued to rifle through her bag. Finally, he pulled out her billfold and let the purse drop to the floor. She'd moved her new license from her coat pocket to her wallet when she'd stopped for her food.

"Tiya Mitchell."

He even said her name right.

He raised an eyebrow. "So you stop at the DMV to update your license in between attempted murders, huh? That's interesting."

"Yeah, well, I want to be sure dickheads like you can find me so I kick their asses."

"I think I did most the ass-kicking in this round."

She gritted her teeth and looked down, unable to deny it.

Charlie walked over and sat down on the bed beside her once more. She felt the heat of his body roll off and warm hers and resisted the urge to wriggle to the side, away from him. "So, tell me, Tiya. What the hell are you, because it sure as hell isn't human."

She tipped her head toward him and narrowed her eyes. "How'd you track me down, anyway?"

He shook his head. "Tell me what you are and maybe I'll tell you how I found you."

There was no way she could reveal what she was. The OtherKin had kept the secret of their existence since 1699 B.C. when the Milesians had given them their ultimatum. Sure, there were likely pockets of Embraced or humans who knew of them. The OtherKin hadn't mingled together with other species on this planet for so long without that happening. But, generally, the OtherKin had done a much better job of keeping their secrets than the Embraced. The OtherKin didn't need the same problems the Embraced had with humankind.

She narrowed her eyes at him. "I'm fucking human, jackass," she lied.

He laughed. "Sure. Incredible strength and speed are skills lots of normal people have. Come on. You're not going to fool me, so you might as well give it up."

She glanced away and gave her head a sharp shake. "Not happening."

Charlie fixed her with a stare that was part predator and part pity.

Tiya tightened her grip on the ropes that bound her hands and swallowed hard. That look he gave her now and the thoughts he seemed to be having that fueled the look, caused something obscene, something completely out of place and ridiculous to happen in her body.

The man aroused her.

Impossible, but true.

Charlie allowed his gaze rove over her mouth and then let it descend to take in her throat and collarbones. It roved over her breasts, making her nipples harden. It descended over her stomach, down over her pelvis and thighs.

Tiya's breath quickened under his slow perusal and the sense of possession he seemed to have while he did it. She should have been screaming and kicking and struggling under that look. Instead, her breasts felt heavy, the nipples suddenly sensitive. Her sex slickened with moisture. Her pussy plumped, her clit growing full and responsive. It was as if his gaze alone was foreplay.

The Vampir could probably scent her excitement. The Embraced had senses like an OtherKin Shifter during a change. Like a wolf or a cougar. That slow, dark gaze returned to her face. He smiled.

The bastard.

Her lips parted in horror as the realization swept over her. "You're using glamour on me again, you pig," she said softly.

That had to be it.

His gaze found hers. A dark brow rose speculatively. "I'm not using any glamour on you and you know it. Your reactions are your own."

Chapter Four

The *sacyr* rode Charlie hard as he took in the woman spread like a gourmet meal before him. He should hate her for what she'd done. This woman had nearly killed Vincent, not to mention him. She deserved to pay for what she'd done. She shouldn't be turning him on. She shouldn't be making his cock so damned hard.

All he wanted to do was fuck her and drink her sweet blood. Not necessarily in that order, although doing both things at once sounded pretty good. He wanted to roll like a dog in that maddening scent of arousal and violet combined. It made the *sacyr* play havoc with him. Charlie wanted to taste this woman's blood more than he'd wanted to drink anyone's in a long time.

Charlie could tamp down the *sacyr*, but he wondered what was causing it to hunger so badly in this particular woman's presence. Hell, he'd just fed that morning.

He let his gaze drift back down over her body. Her black skirt had started to ride up her shapely thighs. Her feet were encased in thigh-high black leather boots and she wasn't wearing nylons. Charlie wondered if she'd omitted any other part of her outfit that morning. He wondered if he should push that little black skirt up a bit more and find out. Hell, she'd probably welcome it. She was creaming hard for him. The scent of it painted the air.

It was intoxicating, near irresistible. Charlie clenched his hands into fists against the *sacyr* and the sexual temptation she represented.

She shook her head and her long hair spilled around her shoulders like spun gold. The fall of it came nearly to her waist and the ends curled under prettily in tendrils he wanted to rub between his fingers. He wondered would that hair would feel like brushing his bare skin, his upper thighs while that luscious mouth closed over his cock, worked him until he came...

The *sacyr* rose within him and with it came his glamour. He sent a thread of his glamour out to flick over her and savored the power she had stored within her. It was so sweet, so tempting. So strong. With supreme effort and willpower, he reined in his glamour and the *sacyr*. He'd told her he wasn't using his power and he didn't want to make that a lie.

Although the soft flesh of her throat beckoned him to dip his head forward, toward her. Her skin looked so smooth and perfect. He did it before he'd realized he had. The violet mixed with the scent of her ever-deepening arousal intoxicated him and made common sense slip away.

"No," she said softly as his mouth came down toward her throat. Then she yelled, "No!"

Charlie shook his head as though waking from a dream. He stood up and backed away. "Calm down." He didn't know if he was talking to himself or her.

Her eyes were bright and her chest heaved as if in hyperventilation. Did she think he was going to harm her? Rape her? Perhaps. She had reason to think it, though he'd never do it. At least, he didn't think he would. The woman's scent made things so confusing.

She closed her eyes and inhaled and exhaled slowly. After a few moments, she opened her eyes and seemed to have regained control. "You're telling me to relax?" she asked. "You just tried to kill me."

"Whoa, hold on. I didn't just try to kill you." He held up a hand, palm out. "I don't know what happened there, but it won't happen again. Relax."

"So, what were you going to do?" she yelled. "Just take a little taste?"

Yes. *Just a little taste*. What was the harm in that?

He gave his head a sharp shake once more to clear it. "There is something about you," he muttered. "Something strange. It affects me." He raised his gaze to hers and projected his voice. "You need to tell me everything, Tiya. You don't understand how badly you pissed off Anlon and the vamps closest to him. You're lucky I found you first."

"Why aren't you with Anlon now? Isn't he your keeper?"

He shook his head, but he wasn't about to reveal any more information than he had to her. "No."

"So, what's the deal? You tracked me down first to, what, protect me?"

He laughed. To his own ears, it sounded cold and brutal. "No. I'm not interested in *protecting* you. I tracked you down first because I *could*. And also because I want to know why you attacked Vincent and me before Anlon and his boys drain you for dinner. They won't ask many questions and by the time they're through with you, you won't be able to tell anyone anything."

She shuddered and looked away. Her face, already fair, seemed to go pasty white.

In reality, he'd tracked her down because she'd called to him. The small bit of blood that had spread across his tongue in the alley had become a part of him that seemed ever fixed on her. Like a homing signal. If he concentrated hard enough, he could feel that drop of blood flowing through his veins even now.

His mind was filled with *why*. Only she had the answers to those questions. That's why he'd tracked her down before Anlon could. He needed to get answers before Anlon decided what kind of revenge to take on her for what she'd done to Vincent, who even now still lay on the edge of death in a bed at Griffin House.

"Anlon, Evelyn, Colin, and the rest of Anlon's inner circle, they won't go easy on you once they find you." He sat back down on the bed. "You want to know what they'll do to you once they track you down?" What he was about to say was a lie, through and through, but maybe it would help persuade her to talk. Fear could be an effective tool.

She shot a look of scorn at him. Her eyes flared momentarily with anger. "Gee, I can't guess."

"If Vincent dies and they track you down with the intention of taking an eye for an eye, you won't get a fast death." Charlie shook his head. "They'll tie you down and snack on you for a while. They'll each take a taste, then let you sweat for a while before they come back to take another taste. They'll let you die slow…so slow."

Her face became deathly white and she looked away. "S-shut up."

"What? I thought you couldn't guess. I'm just helping you out, telling you what you can expect. They'll drain your sweet, luscious body dry, Tiya, drop by drop, nibble by nibble."

Tiya took in an audible gulp of air and swayed against her bonds. All the bravado had suddenly seemed to leave her. She muttered something unintelligible. Her eyelids drooped, then closed. Her head lolled to the side and her body sagged, held up only by the ropes around her wrists.

"Shit," Charlie muttered in surprise. He hadn't meant to make her faint. He ran his hand over his jaw, feeling the scrape of stubble against his palm. He'd been trying to scare her into telling him what he wanted to know, that's all.

Yeah, Anlon would track her down, but he doubted he'd take the law into his own hands. Most likely, even if Vincent died as a result of the wounds she'd inflicted, Anlon would let SPAVA deal with her.

Well, hell. Now what? She looked damned uncomfortable like that. She'd probably wake up with a painful crick in her neck.

What the hell was he thinking? He shouldn't care about that.

Charlie watched the gentle rise and fall of her chest and the way her sooty lashes swept over her pale cheeks. Her silken hair spilled over the pillow and her shoulders. She was beautiful, but he couldn't allow himself to be swayed by her pretty face. He couldn't start thinking she was innocent or delicate just because she looked that way, or because she'd fainted on him. He still recalled the strength she'd had in the alley. Underestimating this woman meant death.

What could be so bad that it would motivate her to take on an entire territory of Embraced? What was her deal? Was she just screwed in the head, or had she suffered some trauma she believed Vincent had been responsible for? The woman was a mess of mysteries.

His gaze traveled over her. The skin of her wrists looked red and mottled from the ropes. Goddamn it, he couldn't leave her like that.

He let out a string of curses as he untied her bonds and settled her more comfortably on the bed. Quickly, he wound the rope around both her wrists and positioned them on the pillow above her head and tied the ends to the headboard.

When he'd finished re-securing her, he stood in the darkness, staring down at her for a long time before he left the room.

* * * * *

Blood dripped from her mother's throat onto the white linoleum of the kitchen floor. The Vampir holding her in a macabre embrace looked up from her throat when Tiya entered the house and watched her with eyes heavy with satiation.

In horror and surprise, Tiya dropped her suitcase. The vamp dropped her mother at the same time and stepped forward, a laugh bubbling up out of a blood-choked throat. The thick thud of her mother's body and the clank of the cold iron handcuffs around her wrists as they hit the floor echoed through the house.

"No!" *Tiya cried out. She kicked and twisted and fought, but the Vampir suddenly had her wrists. She couldn't move her arms, couldn't fight…*

"Tiya. Tiya, wake up!"

Wake up? Why was he yelling that? The Vampir, whose mouth was smeared with her mother's blood, shook her hard. She kicked out and connected, hearing him grunt. Then her legs were pinned. A hard body covered hers.

Conscious swelled once, twice. Awareness overwhelmed the nightmare. Panting hard, she opened her eyes.

Charlie's face was an inch from her own. The heavy weight of his body covered her. His hands were on her wrists, which were bound above her head. No longer was she propped in a sitting position on the bed, now she lay flat on her back.

Perspiration, despite the cool temperature of the room, plastered her hair to her forehead. Her heart beat like she'd run a marathon.

And she was very aware of the male body against her.

Very aware.

She froze like a deer in headlights. Every muscle in her body went taut.

Charlie's breath tickled her nostrils and she felt a wave of relaxation pass over her. Deliberately, he breathed against her face. A Vampir's body took the blood they drank and converted it into life force. Their breath was like a sedative, and always sweet-smelling. Some said their breath was a weapon, lulling their victim enough for them to take blood.

By rights, as an OtherKin Sidhe, his breath should not have been sedating her, but it was. It was only supposed to work on a human's biological makeup, not hers.

Why was it she was so damned vulnerable to this vamp? The more troublesome question was why wasn't he vulnerable to her? *That* was a really inconvenient bitch.

His chest was muscled, his thighs strong. She could see the strain of his biceps as he reached over her head, apparently in an effort to keep her from moving her arms and hurting herself.

A rush of arousal pooled in her pussy and breasts. He moved a bit, rubbing against her chest and she noticed it. Her nipples turned into hard, sensitive little peaks.

Charlie must have noticed it, too, because he went very still.

She lay there, staring into his eyes for a long moment. In that instant all she wanted was for him to pull up her skirt and slide his cock into her. She wanted him to remind her she was still alive, that she could still feel something other than this cold thirst for vengeance that she held so tight within her.

The realization that she wanted to fuck this vamp who lay on top of her right now was almost more than she could bear. Tears pricked her eyes and her rage rose. "Get off me," she snarled hoarsely. "Get off!"

Charlie rolled to the side and off the bed. "You were screaming your head off in here, thrashing around on the bed." He motioned at her wrists. "You hurt yourself."

As soon as he pointed it out, she felt a rush of pain around her wrists and the slow, hot trickle of blood down her skin. "Great," she muttered.

"You were screaming about marauding Vampir."

She stared up at him with murder in her eyes. "My dreams aren't open for discussion."

"Look, I could thrall you with my glamour and make you tell me everything. You know that, don't you?"

She swallowed hard. "Yeah."

"I haven't done it because I want you to tell me on your own." He pushed a hand through his hair. "I didn't come here to hurt you, okay? I just want to know what's going on."

She bit her lip. This one was definitely not involved with what had been done to her family. If he'd been a part of it, Tiya had no doubt that she'd be dead right now. "Let me free and I'll tell you some of it."

He stared down at her, unmoving.

She tipped her chin up at him and smiled. "What's the matter? Are you afraid I'd hurt you, big guy?"

His face went steely.

She hadn't lived two hundred years and not learned how to manipulate a man's ego to get what she wanted.

"No." That's all he said.

"So what's the problem?"

"I'm afraid you'll get away and Anlon will find you. I'm afraid I'll lose you before I get my answers."

She felt the blood drain from her face as the memories of Charlie's description of what Anlon would do to her rose back up and smacked her in the face.

"Hey, I'm sorry I mentioned it. Don't faint again," he said.

She looked up sharply. "I didn't *faint*," she snapped.

He raised a brow. "Really? You do a damned good impression of fainting, then."

She just looked away and ground her teeth.

"Here's what I don't understand, Tiya. Why would a person who passes out when she hears a description of a Vampir draining her be willing to bait an entire territory of them?"

"Let me free and maybe I'll tell you."

He went still. "Only if you allow me to use a bit of glamour on you."

She gave her head an empathic shake. "No way."

He shrugged. "All right then." Charlie turned to leave the room.

"Wait."

He turned back.

She licked her lips. "What ...*exactly*...would you need to do to me?"

"Just a light glamour to keep you from bolting on me. Something to make you feel nice and relaxed, like a sedative."

"Ah, so bonds for my mind instead of my wrists."

He shrugged again. "If you choose to think of them that way. You're especially susceptible to my glamour, I've found. I won't have to use much."

Yeah, she'd noticed the same thing. His breath, his glamour, everything thralled her so damn hard. As OtherKin Sidhe, it shouldn't be so. The only reason that made sense was that this vamp's glamour was especially strong, so strong that it negated her powers.

She bit her lip until she tasted blood. His gaze zeroed in on her mouth and his pupils contracted. The muscles of his body went hard and tight. Slowly, she released her lip, sucking the blood to make it disappear.

Bad move, Tiya, she chided herself. *Bad move.* There was already blood trickling from her wrist. That little bit extra had been more than this vamp's will appeared able to resist.

His body relaxed and his eyes returned to normal. "So, what's it going to be?" he asked. "Bondage or freedom?"

"Freedom," she muttered.

"Didn't quite hear that. Want to repeat?"

"Do it. Trot out your damn glamour, thrall me and free me, already."

He moved to take a place beside her on the bed. "You're sure?"

She nodded slightly.

"Look into my eyes," he commanded.

Reluctantly, she turned her head toward him and found his gaze.

His eyes were a nice chocolate color. The color of comfort. She let her consciousness slide into that warm hue and float. A breeze seemed to blow over her skin. It stroked her hair like a lover's hand, smoothed over her skin with fingers made of silk.

Tiya sighed.

The next thing she knew her wrists were free. She felt so relaxed, like she'd taken a tranquilizer. She was still aware. Her mind was still sharp but she felt so infinitely peaceful. As though nothing at all in the world was wrong.

"You all right?" Charlie asked. He rubbed her wrists above her wounds with long, strong fingers. His touch sent little fissures of pleasure throughout her body. She wondered what those fingers would feel like exploring her sex, thrusting into her.

Instantly, as if sensing her arousal, he stopped and put her hands down on the bed. "We'll need to disinfect and wrap those."

"It's okay," she murmured. "I'm a fast healer."

"Fast healer?" he repeated with a note of interest.

Damn. This soft cotton-wrapped relaxation was making her forget herself. Maybe that had been his plan all along. She didn't feel at all compelled to tell him anything she didn't want to, however, so the glamour he'd cast over her wasn't that strong.

She rubbed her wrist absently and shrugged. "Ever since I was young I've been a fast healer." She wouldn't reveal that "when she was young" had been a couple centuries ago. "I need some water, all right?"

He nodded and stood.

She got to her feet shakily and headed out to the kitchen, making her way around the few still unpacked boxes that held her meager belongings. She had a home in Seattle, a *real* home. It was decorated just to her liking, very comfortable and warm with soft, overstuffed couches and chairs. The artwork of her favorite artists, collected over the years, hung the walls. Her wooden wraparound deck had a lovely view of the Seattle skyline. In the winter, she burned wood in her creek stone hearth. It was beautiful. It was home. She didn't know if she'd ever see it again, though.

She flipped on the overhead light in the kitchen. It was clean and nearly completely bare. She didn't even have a kitchen table. Tiya sought one of the two glasses she currently owned and filled it with tap water. She turned and leaned against the counter to drink. The cool water slid down her throat and she closed her eyes in ecstasy. After she'd drained it, she set the glass aside and allowed her gaze to meet Charlie's evenly.

"So?" he asked.

"So."

He crossed his arms over his chest. The action defined his nice biceps and broad shoulders. He sighed.

Just watching him made her body go alert with feminine interest. What the hell was wrong with her that she would react to him this way? God, he was a Vampir! She looked away.

"Do I have to tie you up again?" he asked in a low voice.

Now came the part where she either lied, or told a half-truth. She thought the half-truth the better option. Vamps had a whole host of otherworldly senses, like the OtherKin Sidhe. He might be able to tell if she was lying outright. He might be able to smell it on her.

"Why were you targeting Vincent?" he asked.

She whirled and headed into the living room. Just the sound of his name angered her. Charlie followed. A couch lined one wall. That was the extent of the furniture. Stacked boxes sat in the corner of the neutrally decorated room.

She turned toward him and stood with her arms clasped over her chest. "Vincent is part of a group of Vampir that did harm to my family."

Charlie went still. "Vincent? How do you know this?"

She tipped her chin up. "It's reliable information. I...researched it."

He pushed a hand through his hair. "Uh. What exactly do you think he did?"

Memories rushed up to greet her. She swallowed hard and felt the blood drain from her face again. Her knees buckled.

Charlie was there in a flash. His arms were the only reason she didn't crumple like a cardboard box in the rain. He half-carried her to the couch and sat her down. "Okay?" he asked.

She drew a shaky breath and nodded. What a lie. She was not okay. Not at all.

"For now, let's not go down that road, all right? Whatever it was, I know it was bad," he said.

Tiya couldn't speak for a moment. Sorrow and rage warred within her. "He deserves to die," she managed to grind out.

Charlie leaned back against the coach. She could feel him, his body heat and his life force. She could smell the man of him, spicy and strong. It troubled her and excited her at the same time.

"You're wrong about Vincent, Tiya," he said. "I don't know the whole story. I don't know what happened that was so bad. But I *know* Vincent, and he's not capable of doing something horrible enough to make you want to faint at the mention of it."

"I did *not* almost faint."

A small smile twisted his lips. "Have it your way."

He turned toward her, putting his arm on the coach behind her. The action put her square in his powerful aura. The woody spicy scent of his cologne assaulted her nose. She could almost name the brand he used. Before, she'd paid attention to things like men's cologne. Now the names of well-known brands seemed beyond her mental reach. She wanted to move to the side, out of his immediate area. But if she did that, it would be admitting that he really did affect her.

Charlie sighed and his breath teased her long strands of hair. She fought a shiver of arousal. "Look, maybe I can help you."

She gave him a sharp look. "Help me? I tried to kill you, remember? What are you, crazy?"

He shrugged. "Yeah, well, it's not the first time in my life I had the piss walloped out of me. Anyway, I'm a sucker for a damsel in distress."

It was a good excuse to shoot up from the couch and get away from him. She folded her arms across her chest and turned. "I'm not a damsel, and I'm not in distress," she snapped in a steely voice.

"Man, you never give you up, do you?" He shook his head. "What do you think, Tiya? You want my help, or not?"

"Why would I want the help of someone I can't trust? What good does that do me?"

He shrugged. "I have an ulterior motive. If I can prove to you that Vincent wasn't involved in whatever you think he was, maybe you'll go away and leave him the fuck alone. Maybe that way I won't have to watch Anlon—" He paused. "Never mind."

She bit her lip. Why would he want to do anything but kill her? Why would he offer her anything but a pair of cold iron cuffs and a bloodletting?

Charlie stood. "What's the matter? Do you have some kind of prejudice against the Embraced or something?"

"No." She shook her head. "I'm smart enough not to take the actions of a few and hate the many." Fact of the matter was, she'd known her share of Embraced. There were good ones and there were bad ones, same as in the OtherKin community, or in the human race.

"Good. So what's the problem? You don't trust me?"

"Have you given me a reason to trust you?"

"Tiya, I'm the one who should have the bigger trust issue in this situation, don't you think?"

Tiya didn't answer.

He took a step forward. "I'll drop that little bit of glamour I have over you now, okay? I'll trust you if you trust me. Deal?"

She hesitated.

"Look, Tiya. I think we sized each other up pretty good in the alley. I'm stronger than you are, but you're a hell of a lot faster. That makes us more or less evenly matched. Come on."

She nodded. "Okay."

He walked toward her and the closer he got, the harder her heart seemed to pound. It wasn't a reaction that came from fear. Oh, no, it wasn't *fear* at all. It was far closer to lust than she liked. She couldn't keep her eyes off his chest, his shoulders, or his face with the silky hank of hair that kept falling into it. She wanted to brush it to the side every time it did that.

Damn. Damn. Double damn. What the hell was going on?

He touched her shoulder and she flinched. "It's okay," he said. "Look into my eyes."

Reluctantly, she raised her gaze to his. She felt the light blanket that had seemed to cover her awareness lift away. She blinked. The feeling of deep relaxation dissipated and tension settled into her shoulders. She grimaced.

"Feel like running?"

"A little, but I won't. Anyway, you know where I live now, and I don't feel like moving again. I wouldn't be able to take another trip to the DMV."

He drew a breath. "Tell me what you are, Tiya, Tell me what happened to you and what you're doing."

She closed her eyes against the temptation to just unload on him, tell him everything down to the year she was born and what she did for a living. Instead, she turned away.

Strong hands grasped her shoulders and turned her back toward him. He shook her once, gently. "I want to help you."

Desire steamrolled over her at the scent of him and the feel of his hands on her. Compared to what she'd felt before, this was like he'd primed her body for an hour with foreplay. Her pussy was ready for him, ready for his cock. All she wanted was to pull her skirt up, rip his pants off and sink herself down onto his rigid shaft.

"Oh, God," she breathed. She knew the hot perfume of her lust scented the air. Charlie knew what she wanted. There was no way in hell he didn't.

He crushed her to him, dragging her up against his chest. She grabbed onto his waist, inhaling the scent of him, feeling him so hard and warm against her, hearing the beat of his heart.

He ran his hands up her back and into her hair. When he tipped her head back and lowered his mouth to hers, she gasped against his lips. His breath caressed her mouth for a moment, infusing her senses with calm, then descended to gently taste.

She fisted her hands in his shirt at his upper arms. *Gentle* was the last thing she wanted from him right now.

Maybe it was the fucked-up state of her emotions. Maybe it was just the circumstances. Maybe it was that Charlie represented a temporary escape from all of the above. Maybe it was that she wanted to feel something other than angry and afraid and grieved. Whatever it was, she felt like she could melt into this man's body and never want to return.

She was one large mass of desire. Her panties were soaked and her nipples were erect. Her body was crying out for release.

Charlie tipped his head back. His Adam's apple bobbed as he groaned. "I smell your excitement, Tiya. It's making me insane."

He stared down at her, his gaze hot and promising even hotter things to come. The muscles of his body were visibly tense. Sensually, he trailed a hand up her body and palmed her breast through her shirt. She fought the urge to arch into his hand and bit her lower lip. Her nipple stabbed up, demanding attention, and he gave it, rubbing over it with the pad of his thumb. Swallowing hard, she fought the rising moan in her throat.

She fisted her hands and squeezed her eyes shut. All she wanted was to back away and leave him, but no amount of money could make her do it.

He slipped a hand down and fingered the waistband of her skirt. "You're burning up against me. I can feel how worked up you are, but I can sense your unease. Let me take the edge off." His voice was a silken rasp moving over her skin. "Give me permission to touch you, Tiya."

Chapter Five

She closed her eyes against the magic of his voice and arched her back, giving in to him. Unable to speak, she nodded. She couldn't fight her body any longer. It was almost like she was in heat.

He pulled the hem of her skirt up and ran his fingers over the lacy front of her panties. She shuddered in pleasure at his touch. He pressed his hips forward and she felt the wide ridge of his cock pressing into her hip. She'd made him hard and that knowledge only made her hotter.

He slipped his hand down her panties and ran his fingers over her clit. She couldn't help the thrust of her hips against him, or the small sound that escaped her throat.

Charlie leaned down and brushed his lips over her earlobe. "Part your legs for me, angel. Let me in," he murmured.

She spread her thighs as wide as they'd go, constricted by her skirt the way they were. He slicked his finger through her cream and used it as lubricant around her clit. Around and around he circled it until Tiya made a keening sound of pleasure.

"Do you like that?" he asked softly.

She closed her eyes and nodded slowly, losing herself in sensation. She felt like such a wanton slut, but hell if she cared right now.

"I like it, too," he murmured. He dipped his mouth to her ear and brushed his lips across it. "It feels like you have a very pretty little pussy, angel. Exquisite. Wish I could see it. Wish I could taste all that luscious cream I feel."

Tiya tightened her hold on his shoulders at his words and let a small moan escape her. She couldn't help but imagine him between her thighs, laving over her sex, teasing her clit with his tongue.

Charlie pressed his free hand to the base of her spine and drew his lips up over her jaw to her mouth. At the same time, he traced his fingers a little lower, caressing her labia, then pressed one thick digit into her cunt. Tiya gasped at the invasion. It had been a while since she'd had sex and she was tight. He thrust in and out, widening her and drawing her cream out to lubricate his finger. Tiya thought she'd go insane at how slow he allowed himself to slide in and out. He added a second finger, and Tiya groaned deep and animalistic in the back of her throat.

"Ah, angel, you feel so good," Charlie whispered against her mouth. "So sweet."

He thrust those two fingers in and out of her pussy. Tiya moaned long and low, reveling in the magical friction he exerted over her body. It was nearly making her come undone. He picked up the pace of his thrusting and her body tensed to climax.

"Come for me, Tiya," he murmured. "Come all over my hand." He flicked his thumb over her clit and she climaxed hard and fast.

Pleasure washed over her body. She felt the muscles of her pussy convulse around Charlie's pistoning fingers. He slanted his mouth hard over hers, eating up every moan and sigh.

Tremors racked her body and she clung to him as they eased. When it was over, when she no longer trembled from the force of her orgasm, she pushed away from him and backed up. His hand pulled free of her sex and panties in one movement.

Panting, she backed up against the wall, looking at him warily. "Did you just use glamour on me?"

He shook his head. "No. I swear I didn't."

She put a hand to her feverish forehead. She tried to read his mind, but he was shielding hard. Still, Tiya knew he hadn't thralled her. She was simply looking for an explanation other than that she was an uncontrollable slut. "What the hell was that?" she breathed, more to herself than to him.

"I don't know."

"Will you please leave?" she snapped.

Charlie didn't say anything, didn't move a muscle.

She looked up at him. "*Please leave*. I need time. Time to get my head together. Look, I won't bolt on you, all right? Come by tomorrow night. I'll think about telling you...everything, then."

Still Charlie didn't move. "I don't think—"

"Trust, remember? Trust that I'll still be here. Trust that I'll be ready to talk about things a little more than I am right now."

"I don't have a reason to trust you."

"Yeah, that's true. You don't have a reason to help me, either, right? But you seem to want to do it anyway. Let me process everything. Come back tomorrow night. I'll be here."

* * * * *

Charlie watched Tiya from across the room. The sweet scent of her that still lingered on his fingers was intoxicating.

Had he ever wanted Penelope this much...or Laila? He had loved both those women. He'd slept with Laila repeatedly over the years, since she'd been Demi, but what he felt for Tiya was more purely sexual than anything he'd felt before. It was almost an animalistic response to the sight and scent of her.

And he wanted her blood.

The *sacyr* seemed insatiable in her presence. It rolled and kicked in his stomach. It clenched his muscles and prodded him. It whispered in his ear about how sweet her blood would taste, how much it would satisfy him. It drew his gaze to her long, pale throat. It made him utterly fascinated with the pulse that beat there.

It was a constant battle for Charlie to tamp down and control the *sacyr* in her presence. What would Anlon do if he reacted this way to her? What would Evelyn or Vincent, if he recovered, do? Charlie had the strength to resist the call because there was one crucial difference between him and the others when it came to the woman who now stood before him.

Charlie cared about her.

For some reason, there was a part of him that cared about her. A part that didn't want to see her hurt. Inwardly, he berated himself. What was he, a fucking masochist? A man would have to be a masochist to care about this woman.

He looked at Tiya, who stared at him with accusation in her gray eyes. Then he glanced at the door. Charlie didn't feel right about leaving her, but he couldn't figure out why he had this compulsion to see her protected. Was it the old-world part of him? Was it that part of him that was raised to be a gentleman, taught to guard a lady from harm no matter what? Even if it was, it was clear this particular lady didn't need guarding.

He steeled his emotions. Anyway, she'd tried to kill him. There was no reason for him to be agonizing over her protection.

"I didn't try to kill you." She put her hand to her mouth as soon as the words shot out.

He arched a brow. "Excuse me?"

She lowered her hand and a cool mask slid over her features. "I could see that look on your face and assumed you must be thinking I'd tried to kill you. I didn't."

Anger bubbled up within him. She was lying to him. She'd just read his mind. She'd made a big old oopsie in her indignation over his thoughts and let him know she'd done it. Now she was trying to cover it up. The little, nonhuman, lying minx. He pulled walls up in his mind, blocking anyone who tried to enter his thoughts. Usually, he only had to do that with the Embraced. Hell, he'd only let his shields down for a moment. He thought he'd been safe to do it. After all, he hadn't figured Tiya for a mind reader.

He stalked toward her. "What are you?" he demanded to know.

She backed up, straight up against the wall behind her.

"What are you?" he repeated, louder.

Her eyes widened at the tone of his voice. She started to move to the side, but he caught her by the upper arms and held her in place. "You're not going anywhere. Tell me what you are."

She winced and he eased his grip a little. "You wouldn't believe me if I told you."

"Try me."

She bit her lip and looked away. "Really, you wouldn't."

Charlie fought the urge to shake her. "Do you think that one hundred and fifty years ago, if I'd told someone I was a vampire they would've believed me? The world is filled with all kinds of strange surprises." He let her go and stepped back. "I'll leave you alone for today, if you tell me what you are. One answer. I'm asking for just one."

She raised her gaze to his and sighed from the depths of her soul. "I'm tired of fighting you, you know that? You're worse than a starving dog with a juicy bone. You just won't fucking leave it alone. Fine. I'll tell you. Fat lot the information will do for you." She fell silent.

He raised an eyebrow. "Any day."

She pushed past him and turned. "I'm OtherKin Sidhe. Satisfied?"

He blinked. "She? You're an OtherKin, er, female? What's the OtherKin?"

Tiya sighed. "S-i-d-h-e. Shee."

He blinked again. "Oh, the *Sidhe*."

She threw up her hands. "See. I knew you wouldn't believe me."

"The Sidhe…as in the beings in the stories parents tell their children? Faeries? The Tuatha Dé Danaan?"

"I don't know another kind of Sidhe, do you? You want to drag me down to the hospital psych ward now?"

His mind stuttered, trying to understand the notion of the Tuatha Dé Danaan being real. If he hadn't experienced her strength, speed and telepathic ability, he would've told her to seek psychiatric help. "Sidhe," he repeated.

She turned around and walked away from him. "Did I fucking stutter or something?"

"It's just hard to believe faeries are real. Give me a minute."

She turned toward him and rolled her eyes. "Yeah, well, we're not really too much like Titania or Tinkerbell, okay? Get that stereotype out of your head. We're not small. We don't have wings, and we can't fly. We're human-sized. We don't live in the woods or under faery mounds, waiting for unwary travelers or whatever else the legends say. We're a race, like any other. We have our own customs and religion and traditions, but we live among humankind in secret." She shrugged. "We're the fae."

"Wow."

"Want to know something else, Vampir?" She pointed a finger at him. "The Embraced are related to us. Even the Dominion are related to the OtherKin. You guys just don't know it. The Embraced were severed from the OtherKin Sidhe a millennia ago and you have forgotten your history."

"Uh…huh?"

She sighed like he was an idiot. "You have *glamour*, which is a form of magick, and you have familiars sometimes, don't you? Why would you think you weren't related to us? You're *evolved* from us, Charlie. The OtherKin Sidhe and their cousins, the witches, are primarily the magick users. We belong to the bright and shiny Seelie Court, according to the legends. The shifters and the blood consumers, the creatures of nightmares…in other words, the Embraced and the Dominion…you're the Unseelie. Like it or not, we're all one big happy family. There's a light side and a dark side, according the legends the humans have concocted. In reality there are a lot of shades of gray."

His mind was on overload. It felt like it was about to pop. For the moment, he needed to leave that information alone. It was too much. "All I know is that you sure can wallop the piss of a vampire." He winced, suddenly realizing that he'd had the shit kicked out of him by a faery.

She smiled sweetly. "It was my pleasure."

He believed her. God, did he have a death wish? Why was he always attracted to women who seemed to have no other goal than injure him? Here he was, having some kind of lust/hate relationship with this woman in front of him. She seemed to share his feelings, too, judging by the way she'd let him get her off a couple minutes ago.

Letting his gaze slide over her from her head to her toes, Charlie knew he'd do it again if given the chance. He wanted nothing more than to feel her sweet, silken muscles tense around his fingers again, the scent of her perfuming the air. Damn, he wanted to get his cock in her.

He'd never figured himself for this kind of primal reaction to a woman. Gabriel, Adam and Niccolo pretty much had the market cornered on that. He went for the long, unrequited love in which he got his shredded heart handed to him at the end.

Abruptly, he turned away and pushed a hand through his hair. "So, you're telling me that the Sidhe, the Tuatha Dé Danaan, are a race, like humans or the Embraced?" He turned back to look at her. "You're also saying the Embraced are actually a form of OtherKin that was split off from the rest of their people a million or so years ago."

She leaned up against the side of the couch. "Basically. We ruled what are now known as the British Isles, before the Milesians came to call around 1699 B.C. There was a big battle. In the end, the Milesians defeated us. When they did, they gave us a choice, either rule alongside them or go underground. The Sidhe were a proud, magickal race and there was no way they were going to lower themselves to sharing power with mere mortals, so they went underground."

"I know the legend, but I thought...well, I thought it was only a legend."

She gave him a bitter little smile. "You thought wrong."

"So underground didn't mean literally *underground*, it meant—"

"Conceal your true nature. That's what it meant." Tiya turned and paced away from him. "The Embraced evolved to protect the OtherKin and humankind from their natural predators, the Dominion. Even though the Embraced were born protectors, the rest of the bright and shiny OtherKin couldn't accept those among them who had to drink blood or tap lust to survive, so they drummed the Embraced out of their society. Okay, I told you. Now, leave."

Charlie stared at her for a long moment in stunned silence, then turned toward the door. He had a lot of questions, but a deal was a deal. Stunned, he walked out of the house.

"Hey, Vampir."

He turned in the doorway to see Tiya looking at him with her head cocked to one side. Her fall of blonde hair cascaded down her shoulder. "What's it taste like?"

He frowned. "What?"

"Blood."

"Human blood tastes the same to me as it would to you. It's coppery, metallic."

"How can you stand it?"

He smiled. "It's not so bad. It's great cut with a little vodka and lemon juice. Makes for a delicious cocktail."

A smile flickered over her lips. "See you tomorrow night."

Charlie turned and walked out the door, wondering if he'd get a chance to taste a faery's blood again.

* * * * *

It had been a year since Charlie had seen Adam. Staring at him across the table now made Charlie almost feel like he'd never left Newville.

Adam raised his beer and took a swig. "So, you like it up here?"

Charlie sat back in his chair and surveyed Grand Avenue from the outdoor bar they were in. It was dusk on a Saturday night and everyone was coming out to play. Conversation, laughter and the general swell of Minneapolis' humanity surrounded him. "It's not a bad place to be."

"It's not home, though."

Charlie regarded Adam. "Where's home? Boston. New York. Chicago. Newville. I've lived in a lot places."

"Newville the longest."

Score one for Adam. He'd gone straight for blood. Charlie looked out at the street.

Adam leaned forward. The blue button-down shirt he wore was almost the same color as his eyes. "I'm not trying to make you come back, Charlie. You gotta do what you feel like you gotta do. I'm just trying to understand."

"Understand what?"

Adam paused, took another swig. "Why you're blaming Gabriel so hard about Laila's death. It's not like Gabe was holding that hawthorn stake in his hand when it happened. He was trying to stop it."

Unwelcome memories flickered through his mind's eye. A year ago, Xavier, a lover from Laila's past had returned still holding a grudge against Gabriel. Xavier had blamed Gabriel for Laila being Demi and had punished Gabriel by trying to turn Fate Harding, Gabriel's love, into a Demi. He'd failed. Fate had passed through the Demi phase of her forced Embrace and was now a Vampir. This had enraged Xavier and eventually he'd killed Laila.

It was the reason Charlie had left Gabriel's territory.

Charlie felt his jaw lock. Anger flickered. It went through his eyes, so he knew Adam saw it. Adam needed to back off. Right now.

Adam raised a hand palm out. "I'm sorry, man. I shouldn't have mentioned it."

"Yeah, you're right about that."

Adam ran a hand over his jaw. "Look, I'll shut up about it now, okay?"

"Gabriel was the reason she was killed," Charlie answered abruptly. "Xavier did it all for him. To get back at him."

"Yeah, but Charlie, that wasn't his fault. Gabe mourned Laila, too."

"Shit, I know that. I just couldn't stay there, looking at him every day after it happened. Every time I looked at him, I was looking at the reason Laila was killed. Do you understand?"

"So, that's why you left."

"Yeah."

"Well, now." Adam tipped the neck of his beer bottle toward him and winked. "That makes sense." He smiled and took a swig.

If only everyone was as easy to please as Adam.

Charlie picked up his bourbon and drained it. "So, anyone heard from Niccolo?"

Adam shook his head. "It's like he fucking disappeared off the face of the Earth."

"If Niccolo doesn't want to be found, he won't be found. He's old enough and powerful enough to mask himself from everyone, even the Council of the Embraced."

"That's the truth. The man's moves like a goddamned shadow half the time and a ghost the rest." Adam laughed. "It's kind of creepy."

"He's gone to ground, trying to avoid SPAVA. Either that, or he left the country. He'll contact us when he's ready."

"Yeah, I hope so."

A little over a year ago, he, Gabriel, Adam, and Niccolo had battled the Dominion back in Newville. The Dominion were a race of psychic vampires that existed beyond the physical constraints of reality and were the reason the Embraced existed. The Embraced acted as a natural predator to the Dominion, keeping them in check. Not in check, the Dominion would feed like locusts from the positive thoughts and emotions of humans through their dreams. Left uncontrolled, the Dominion had the potential to actually destroy the world.

In that battle a year ago, the Dominion had killed a prominent businessman in Newville named Dorian Cross. They'd got his assistant, Cynthia Hamilton, as well. Unfortunately, the circumstances of the crimes made it appear that Niccolo had done it. Now Niccolo was a wanted man, running from murders he hadn't committed.

That was truly ironic considering that Niccolo was 1,951 years old and had been taking life constantly for about 1,936 of those years. As an Executioner Niccolo was a man of many, *many* killings, most of them council-commanded. Now he was wanted for two he hadn't even committed.

Charlie tapped a nail on the side of his empty glass. "And how are Fate and Gabriel?"

"Uh, they fuck a lot. Can't go into Gabe's house without interrupting something. But Fate's been good for Gabe. He's a lot more relaxed than he used to be."

Charlie nodded. He wanted Gabriel to be happy and he liked Fate. Still, he was damned glad he'd left and not had to watch them be in love. Watching other people in love bothered him these days. That's why he didn't hang out at Griffin House very often with Anlon and Evelyn.

Adam indicated his clothing. "So where the hell are you going all fancied up like that?"

Charlie glanced down. He'd worn a pair of tailored black pants and a white half-collar chambray shirt tonight. Maybe he had taken a little extra care with his appearance because he was meeting Tiya. It was the masochist in him. "Nowhere special."

Adam laughed. "You never did lie well, Charlie. Don't worry, I'm not going to push it."

"Where are you going?"

Adam leaned back in his chair. "There is this fine little woman who works in a gift store on this street. She's got pretty strawberry-blonde hair and big brown eyes. I thought she might like to take in a movie, or something."

"Or something."

"Yeah, or something." He grinned.

Adam always broke the rules. One of the ones he was especially fond of busting through was the one about no Vampir taking blood from a human. The Council of the Embraced knew that sometimes the Vampir did anyway, so there was a failsafe rule. No taking blood from a human without erasing the memory from them. Adam broke both, continually. He liked to know they remembered it.

Charlie raised an eyebrow at Adam, but he wasn't going to say anything. He wasn't Adam's keeper, nor was he serving Gabriel right now. Adam could do what he wanted. Instead, Charlie stood, pulled a bill from his pocket and threw it on the table. "Have a good time." He turned to walk out of the café.

"Hey, Charlie."

He turned at the arched doorway leading out of the bar and onto the street.

"You remember what I said, now, all right? If you ever need my help, you just call. I figure you and I, we're both brothers in a strange territory."

"Thanks, Adam. Good luck hunting tonight."

"You too."

Yeah, he needed all the luck he could get dealing with Tiya.

Chapter Six

Tiya's body knew Charlie was at the door before her mind did. Every hair on the back of her neck stood up and her nipples did too. Her pussy was also ultra-aware of the man standing outside her front door. Her whole body seemed to be a fucking Charlie barometer.

Wasn't that nice?

As Tiya crossed the floor toward the door, she cursed herself out.

She'd contemplated running. After all, Charlie had trusted her enough to leave her alone. That wasn't exactly smart on his part. She could've just taken off. Except that Vincent was here and she wanted him. If she left her residence again, it would still have to be for a location close to Griffin House. There was a big chance that Charlie would just find her again. That's probably why he'd agreed to leave her alone for a day and a half, anyway. Next time he tracked her down, he might not be so understanding.

It was a risk Tiya wasn't willing to take at this point. Her agenda didn't need any more complications than it already had. It was better to deal with "The Charlie Factor" head-on than try to run from it. Anyway, what if Charlie wasn't lying about helping her out? She really could use his aid, if he was truly offering it.

Tiya only hoped the price she'd have to pay for it wouldn't be too high.

Her heart did a little stupid kerthump when she opened the door and saw Charlie standing there, backlit by the light of the full moon.

"You going to let me in?" he asked.

Tiya moved to the side, realizing she'd been standing there, staring at him like an idiot. "Sorry."

Charlie walked over the threshold. The sleeve of the long black leather duster he wore just brushed her as he passed. The scent of his cologne suffused the air around her for a moment.

She closed the door and followed him in, folding her arms over her chest as though she could protect herself from him.

"Feeling better?" he asked. "Got your head on a little straighter now?"

She walked past him, into the kitchen. She needed something to distract herself. Charlie followed her. "Want some coffee?" she asked as she reached for a cup in the cabinet. She'd unpacked the small amount of dishes she owned that afternoon.

"Sure, why not."

She got down another cup and filled them both. Tiya handed him one. "There's milk in the fridge if you want it. I don't have any sugar."

"You didn't answer my question."

"Yeah, sure, I feel better." She took a sip of the hot black coffee.

A lie. This man still disturbed the hell out of her. Before, she'd wanted him to leave just to get away from him for a while, just to relax. It had worked, but now that he was back that same tension hung in the air between them. Partly, it was dark and just plain stressful, but mostly it was sexual. It was as if he'd taken all that frozen wasteland within her and heated it into simmering lava. Like he'd awoken a part of her that had gone asleep.

"Good. So you're ready to tell me more, then?"

"How's Vincent?" she asked abruptly.

"There you go, changing the subject again."

"Just answer the question."

Charlie took a sip of coffee, staring at her for a moment over the rim. "He's still in a rough shape. He's not able to speak yet."

"Does he show any signs of getting better?"

Charlie paused before responding. "Why? So you can try and kill him again? Why do you care?"

Guilt speared through her. It wasn't like she wanted to maim and kill. "Goddamn it... I don't know." Suddenly not wanting it anymore, she set her cup down on the counter and moved into the living room.

"Tiya, tell me what happened." His voice followed her.

She sank down on the couch and stared up at him. "Honestly, I-I'm not sure I can."

His face softened. He sank down next to her and put his coffee cup on the floor. "Do you want me to use glamour on you? I could make the retelling a little less traumatic. Or, I could just enter your memories and see what happened for myself."

She looked up sharply. "You can do that?"

He nodded. "But only if you really want me to know. Otherwise, your subconscious will block me."

She bit her lower lip. A part of her wanted to share the burden she was carrying. She needed for someone else to have a record of what had befallen her family. What if she died? All knowledge of the violent event would die with her. There would be no one investigate it, no one to stop it from happening to another fae family. "Okay."

Charlie stood, took off the duster and laid it over the back of the couch. "Come into the bedroom with me."

Shock rippled through her at his request. "What? Why the bedroom?"

"We need a larger area than the couch for this and the floor will be uncomfortable. The bed's the best place."

"Uh."

"I'm not going to try and seduce you, Tiya. Okay?"

Yeah, but would she try and seduce him? That was the real question. Hell, she'd practically jumped him the day before. She let her gaze trail from his expensive, polished black shoes to the top of head. God, she was pathetic. It was like the mere sight of him made her libido kick into overdrive.

"Come on, Tiya. I think we can resist each other."

She wasn't so sure, but she stood anyway. "Fine."

They ended up facing each other in the center of the scarlet comforter that covered her bed. Charlie put his hands to her shoulders and she felt the heat of him bleed through her black shirt and into her skin.

"You need to be calm for this," he murmured. 'That means you need my breath. Will you let me lean in?"

Already mesmerized by the feel of his hands on her and his voice, she nodded.

He leaned forward, dipping his head toward hers, and caressed her lips in the softest of kisses. At the same time, he bathed her nose with his peace-inducing breath. A ripple of excitement eased up her spine, but the tension leaked out of her shoulders. Calmness spread through her body.

"Ready?" he murmured against her lips.

No. She nodded yes.

"Look at me, angel."

She opened her eyes and stared into his warm, brown gaze. She felt a thin blanket of glamour slip over her. Tiya took in a sharp breath and resisted the urge to close her eyes. The stress left her body bit by bit. A girl could become addicted to this, she thought sluggishly.

Something brushed against her mind, as though exploring. The brush became a tickle. The tickle became a knock. She didn't resist when she felt the door open and a foreign consciousness slip within.

"Okay?" Charlie breathed.

"Uh-huh."

"Close your eyes."

Her eyes slipped closed and she felt his glamour deepen. Soon felt herself pulled completely under his thrall. She floated in a comforting, velvet-swathed darkness. Here, there was no thought, no emotion. There was almost nothing at all.

It was beautiful. Tranquil.

Then something knocked against her awareness. Once. Twice. It ripped her from that place and back to the world. Charlie's glamour didn't roll back slowly this time, it snapped back like an old-fashioned shade over a window. The bright light it let in jarred her to the center of her bones. Her eyes opened and she gasped for a breath.

Charlie sat on the edge of the bed with his head in his hands and his back to her. His breathing sounded harsh in the quiet air.

"Charlie?"

He just shook his head.

It was then she knew he'd accessed her memories of that day. He'd done it while shielding her from having to relive them. She hadn't even known he'd done it, his glamour was that strong.

"God, Tiya. I've seen the Embraced take human lives, but that—that was beyond brutal. They played with them before they did it."

Sorrow choked her throat. She couldn't speak. The blood ran from her face, making her cheeks go clammy. "I know," she finally squeaked out.

Charlie went into the bathroom. She heard the sound of running water and when he returned, his shirt collar was wet. He'd splashed his face. He looked at her with troubled eyes. "You're pale. Are you okay?"

She nodded. A tear rolled down her cheek. She was not going to cry, goddamn it. The last thing she needed to do was show Charlie her weakness. She still wasn't sure of him enough to trust him with her vulnerabilities.

Charlie walked to the side of the bed she was closest to and sat down on the mattress. "I'd say I was sorry, but that would be totally inadequate."

She felt another tear fall and angrily wiped it away. She licked her dry lips. "I don't want your *sorry*, I just want you to help me find out who did this."

He ran a hand over his jaw. "The Council of the Embraced should know about this. There are rogue Vampir out there. They could hunt down others and do the same thing they did to your family."

She shook her head vigorously. "They'd take the matter into their own hands, send in Executioners. I want to kill the bastards myself. It's my right."

"Tiya," he said gently, like he was talking to a recalcitrant child. "I can understand your rage, but—"

She slid from the bed and turned. "Oh, can you? Can you understand the pain of having to watch the people you love killed right in front of you? Could you live with the knowledge that you were too late to stop it from happening by only *minutes*?" Anger boiled high and hot within her.

Charlie stood. "Yes, I can. I can imagine that, Tiya, because it's happened to me."

Speechless, she just stood looking at him.

"It's the reason I'm here, in a territory where I don't fit in. There was no one for me to slake my need for revenge on, so I got the hell away from the memory of it."

"Then you should understand my need to see this through on my own."

He pushed a hand through his hair. "Yeah, okay, I do. That doesn't mean I think it's the best course of action."

She set a hand to her hip. "Even though I want your help, I don't need your permission." Her voice sounded icy to her ears. She felt icy, too. A chill had seemed to settle into her body.

"I understand that." He took a step toward her. "Tiya."

Her eyes widened at his proximity and the scent of him. Her breath caught in her throat. Like a flash fire, desire started low in her belly. God, she was so schizophrenic when it came to this man. One minute she wanted to fight him, the next she wanted to fuck him.

Charlie held out his hand. "You have my help, okay? No matter how we do it, we'll find out who killed your family and why."

She just stared at his hand, overwhelmed by her emotion, overwhelmed by her body's betrayal of her mind. Tears pricked her eyes.

"Easy, Tiya." Charlie caught her up in an embrace before she could push him away.

She settled her face against his chest, hearing the beat of his heart. His body heat warmed her through and chased away the chill in her bones. He stroked his hand through her hair and rubbed strong fingers down her back. "It's all right," he murmured.

In spite of herself, she let out a shuddering sigh. With the scent and touch of him, her desire became a tidal wave of need. Want was no longer a part of the equation. She *needed* to feel his skin against hers, needed to have his hands stroking over her. She needed his touch on her body and needed to hold his cock, taste it, and bring it into her cunt.

She needed to feel alive and connected to the world. Charlie could do all that for her and more.

Tiya gasped, her pussy flooding with sexual awareness, priming itself, making itself ready to be thrust into. Her breasts felt heavy, the nipples erect and sensitive.

Charlie stopped stroking her hair. He stopped moving completely. All she could hear was their breathing in the suddenly quiet, quiet room.

She twisted up, tipping her face to meet his. Twining her arms around his shoulders and reveling in the feel of the hard muscles and the broadness she found there, she compelled his mouth down.

It came.

His hands fisted in her hair as he possessed her mouth, parting her lips and sweeping his tongue in to tangle savagely with hers. In a small part of her mind, she noted he tasted of coffee.

Tiya fought the urge to press her hips against him. All she could do was whimper at the hot onslaught of his mouth on hers. His kiss was commanding, masterful. It made every part of her body aware of every part of his body that rubbed against her. It was so, so very good. She could get drunk on the taste of him against her tongue.

He broke the kiss and pulled away from her.

"No," she murmured as he backed away.

He turned his back and pushed a hand through his hair. "What are we doing?"

"I don't care, Charlie, let's just do it."

He turned back toward her and caught her up again. Lowering his mouth, he brushed his lips across her throat. She stiffened, but he shushed her. "I won't," he said. "Never again without your permission." He laid a kiss below her earlobe and she shivered.

Gently, he moved her back toward the bed. His hands went the edges of her shirt. He pulled it up and over her head, leaving her in her silky white demi-bra. He lowered his head and brushed his lips over the swell of one breast, and swept his gaze down to note the little silver belly button ring hanging from her pierced navel. "You're beautiful, angel," he whispered. "I knew you would be."

She slid her hands down the front of his chest, undoing each button of his shirt one by one. Each bit of flesh that was exposed, she kissed and licked. Finally, she pushed it off his shoulders, revealing the solidly muscled expanse of him. God, he was well-built. Her pussy pulsed at the sight of him.

He slipped a hand to the small of her back and pulled her up flush against his chest and lowered his mouth once against to her throat, where he worked breathtaking magic with lips and teeth, kissing and nibbling until goose bumps covered her body and her clit pulsed. Tiya tilted her head back, giving him better access to her throat, and tightened her grasp on the back of his pants, hanging on for dear life at the sensation of his sensual mouth moving over her skin. It made her breath come faster. The knowledge that his fangs were close to her jugular penetrated the fog of her lust somewhat, but she found she trusted him not to bite her.

She blindly fumbled the button and zipper of his pants, finally getting them undone. His pants and boxers slipped down and he kicked off his shoes and socks. Tiya's heart pounded at the sight of his long, wide cock and the nest of dark hair that wreathed the base. God, he was any woman's dream. Her fingers curled to touch it.

He caught her up against him again and dropped his hands to the zipper at the back of her pants and undid it. Her black silk slacks slithered to the floor to pool at her feet. She felt cool air rush over her legs. His arms came around her and lifted her out of them, leaving her in her black pumps.

He pulled back, taking in the matching white thong and bra she wore. Heat suffused his gaze. "Well now, this just gets better and better."

She kicked her shoes off and dropped to her knees in front of his magnificent cock. Charlie gripped his shaft at the wide base and pumped it. A pearl of pre-come beaded on the tip of it. She licked her lips, wondering what it would taste like smoothing over her tongue. Tiya watched the slide of his long fingers over his rock-hard cock with avid interest.

She had to have it in her mouth. A dark place of lust within her hungered for it. Her pussy wept for him now, demanding she satisfy every last one of her basest urges. She stopped the slide of his hand with her own. This was one of them.

She'd lived a long time and had been with many men. There was little sexually that she hadn't done, but she couldn't ever remember needing a man like she needed Charlie right now.

Her hand slid up his cock, using his foreskin to pump him. He groaned, tipping his head back. With eager fingers, she explored every last ridge and inch of his shaft and balls, wanting both to prolong the experience and to savor it, and also to tease him a bit to build anticipation.

"Sweet mercy," Charlie murmured.

She knelt forward and licked the crown, savoring that the pearl drop. Charlie's hips jerked forward and she fought a smile. The thing she loved most about sucking a man's cock was the control she gained from it. The strongest of men could be brought to their knees by the mere brush of a woman's tongue against their shaft.

Tiya spent a rapturous minute exploring the length of his cock, tracing the tip of her tongue over every vein and tickling the knot of sensitive nerves under the crown. Every lick made him shudder. All the while, she held his balls in her hands, gently fondling them.

Finally, she engulfed him in her mouth.

Chapter Seven

Charlie fisted his hands in her hair and blew out a hard breath. The hot, velvet interior of her mouth was unlike anything he'd ever felt. She swallowed his considerable length down like it was nothing, and then pulled him back out.

He fought the urge to bury his hand in the hair at the back of her head and fuck her mouth. Hell, he fought the urge to pull her away, rip her flimsy little excuse for underwear away and sink into all that promising hot, wet satin he knew existed between her slim thighs.

He watched his cock disappear into her mouth and reappear over and over until his balls rose and grew tight. His shaft was slick with her saliva. "Ah, angel," he said. "You're going to make me come, baby."

She slanted a look up at him that had nothing to do with angels, and sucked him hard back into the recesses of her mouth. With a skilled tongue, she toyed with the extra sensitive place just under the crown.

That did it.

Charlie held her head in place as he fucked her mouth, sliding himself down her throat as she grasped his waist for balance. Hot come shot out of him and into her as pleasure enveloped his body. She swallowed down everything he gave her. He tipped his head back and gave a guttural groan. Her fingers dug into his hips.

He felt her back away and his very satisfied cock pull free from her mouth. He tipped his head forward and saw her standing in front of him dressed in that sexy bra and those damned provocative panties. His gaze traveled from her narrow feet with those ruby red toenails, up her endless, silky legs and shapely body to her face. Her eyes were heavy with need. His cock twitched at the sight of her.

"Get on the bed," he groaned. "I want to taste every last little part of you."

Slowly, moving to entice, she climbed onto the bed. This was a woman confident of the power of her body and how she could use it to drive a man insane. His gaze fixed on the sweet sway of her pretty ass and the perfect curve of her hips. He'd just come, but that didn't seem to matter where she was concerned. Already, he was aroused again. He wondered how drenched her thong was by now.

She laid down on her back on the bed, stretched like a sinuous cat, and gave him a little smile. Her long hair spread out over the pillow. Tendrils of it curled around her breasts. The minx knew how gorgeous she was and was playing it up, tempting him. She knew how damned sexy she looked in that bra and thong and she was eating up every heated inch of his gaze that traveled up and down her body.

Hell, he wanted to touch her and lick her right now, but the woman needed to be tormented a little first.

"Strip," he ordered. "Strip off that bra and show me where you most want to be touched on your breasts."

"You want to watch me touch myself?"

"Oh, yeah."

With maddeningly slow movements, she sat up and unhooked her bra. The silky straps fell down her shoulders, but she held the cups to her breasts and gave him a sultry smile.

Just as Charlie was about to growl out a command for her to drop the scrap of clothing, she did it. Tossing the bra to the side, she set her hands to either side of her on the bed and looked up at him.

"Like what you see?" she asked.

Charlie's mouth went dry. Her breasts were about a C-cup, perfectly shaped, with taut rosy nipples like little cherries on the top of creamy pastries, and he really wanted a taste. He fisted his hand at his sides. He wanted to see her touch them first. "I love it. Touch them."

She bit her lower lip and slid her hands up her sides to cup both breasts. Her fingernails were long and painted crimson. Tentatively, she plumped her breasts, acting unsure of what he wanted.

"Lay back against the pillows and part your thighs, so I can get a glimpse of your pretty pussy."

She laid back and parted her legs, bending her knees and bringing her heels up to touch her inner thighs. In this position, she was completely open to him. He saw the scant bit of material covering her mound and trailing over her plumped, creaming sex. The thong covered very little, so he had a view of her pouting labia and her perfect, excited clit. Her pubic area was bare, not a bit of hair anywhere was visible, only silken sex. His fingernails bit into his palms as he fisted his hands tighter, trying to resist leaning in for a taste of her. This was a game he wanted to see through to the end.

"You're beautiful, angel. I can see the juices glistening on your pussy. Your clit is swollen, begging to be touched and licked."

She tipped her head back, still massaging her breasts. She appeared more at ease now. "Then come over here and do it," she said breathily.

"No, not yet. Tease those pretty nipples for me."

She ran the pads of her index fingers over her rock-hard nipples, first brushing across them, then slowly circling the pebbled peaks. Her hips thrust forward and she moaned.

"Pinch them. Roll them for me."

With her crimson-tipped fingers, she did it. Charlie watched, fascinated as those little buds rolled back and forth between her thumb and forefinger. They became even harder and redder under her treatment. Her hips thrust forward again, as though looking for something to fuck. Charlie watched a pearl of her cream slide down her inner thigh and resisted the urge to lean down and lick it away.

"You're excited, aren't you, angel? You want to come so bad. Feel my cock cramming that perfect cunt so full."

"Charlie, you're killing me with this game."

"You ever touch yourself in the dead of night, angel? You ever bring yourself with your own fingers and fantasies?"

She bit her bottom lip, and then slowly let go of it. It was swollen and wet from her mouth. Charlie wanted to feel it between his teeth. "Yeah," she said breathlessly. "I make myself come sometimes."

"Show me."

She started to move her hand to her sex.

"Stop," he said. Her hand stopped midway to her pussy, hovered over her belly button ring. "Slowly, angel. Do it slow and easy. I want to see every little movement you make."

She rested one hand on her abdomen. The other still worked her breast, teasing the nipple with little flicks of her fingernail. She rolled it enticingly between her thumb and forefinger from time to time. Her breath came raspy and harsh in the quiet air of the room as she excited herself. Slowly, she moved the hand on her stomach down and let it come to a rest on her shaven mound. Tiya raised her gaze to his. Her lips were parted, the expression on her face aroused, heavy, but the look in her eyes was more a challenge than anything else.

In a way clearly meant to provoke him, she slid her finger under the scrap of the thong and ran it slowly down her pussy to her anus, then back up. "I wish this was you touching me right now, Charlie," she breathed. "Don't you want that?"

The witch was teasing him.

"Pull that bit of material to the side and let me see you sink your fingers into that creamy little sex of yours, angel."

She moved the sopping bit of fabric to the side, revealing her smooth, completely shaven pussy with its pouting, ruby lips and engorged, needy clit. Charlie licked his lips, wanting to feel her labia in his mouth as he drank her in.

She slid her hand up to her clitoris and rubbed it with two fingers. She gasped, and her back arched and her thighs closed.

"Don't close those legs," he rasped at her. "Keep them spread as far as they go. I want to see everything you're doing to yourself."

She opened her thighs back up and Charlie watched the rotation of her fingers around her swollen clit. The muscles at the entrance of her pussy pulsed and contracted, like a hungry mouth that wanted to be fed.

Tiya dropped the hand massaging her breasts to her pussy and spread her labia apart so he could see the heart of her. Teasingly, she ran her fingertip over herself. She whimpered and slid down a little in the pillows, her hips thrusting forward as if she wanted desperately to fuck her own fingers.

"You want to be fucked, angel?" he asked. "You want something to fill up that sweet cunt of yours?"

"Yes," she breathed.

"Slide a finger inside. Tell me how it feels."

His stiff cock got impossibly harder as she slid a long index finger into her pussy. He watched her swollen sex eat it up slowly inch by inch. She whimpered and closed her eyes.

"That's it, angel. That's just right. How does it feel?"

"Tight," she panted. "Tight and hot."

"Can you feel all those muscles pulsing around your finger? That's what I'll feel when I feed you my cock. I can't wait to fuck that hot little pussy, but right now I want to watch you do it. Add another finger and bring yourself. Make yourself come while I watch."

"You fuck me, Charlie," she moaned.

"Oh, I will, don't you worry about that. This first."

She pulled out her index finger. It dripped with her cream. She brought it to her mouth and licked up from her second knuckle. Every muscle in Charlie's body tensed at that erotic sight. Then she brought her finger back down to her sex and added her middle finger to the first. Her body went rigid and her back arched as she slid them both in then pulled them out. With her other hand, she caressed her clit, running the pad of her finger up and down it.

Charlie gripped the base of his cock and groaned at the luscious sight spread before him. He pumped his cock, his eyes traveling from her heavy breasts with those suckable hard nipples to her fingers thrusting in and out of her lovely little entrance.

She cried out and groaned, her back arching. "I'm coming! I'm coming!"

"Ah, yes. Come for me."

Her body trembled and the room filled with the erotic sounds of her climax. The woman made noises that went straight to his cock and balls.

Finally, she quieted and lay panting. Charlie was free to do what he'd been dying to do. He slid onto the bed and pulled that flimsy thong down her legs and off, then spread her thighs wide again and buried his mouth in her sex.

She cried out in surprise.

He didn't answer, he just groaned. The sweetness of her come spread over his tongue as he lapped her up. He licked from her anus to her aroused clit and pulled it between his lips, gently sucking. Tiya writhed on the bed beneath him, her hands threading through his hair. He pulled her labia into his mouth and massaged them between his lips. Charlie groaned again, deep in his throat. God, she tasted so good.

She whimpered. "You're going to make me come again," she panted.

He stopped sucking on her long enough to say, "Would that be so bad?" He speared his tongue into her pussy, pulling out her cream and swallowing it down. It was better than blood.

Tiya pulled herself up, away from him.

Charlie fought a growl at her sex being taken away. He looked up.

She sat with her legs spread, chest heaving. Her eyes were full of heat. She turned over and went to her knees. Her pussy glistened before him, reddened, juicy and looking like irresistible fruit. Her breasts hung to the bed, the nipples taut and brushing the comforter. "Come inside me, Charlie. Fuck me from behind. I need to feel you hard and fast."

* * * * *

Tiya had thought she'd been bored with sex before tonight. In her two hundred years, she'd done most everything there was to do. She hadn't had sex in a while because of that. But Charlie made her so hot she thought he could make her come just by the look in his eyes, the sound of his voice telling her to touch herself. Charlie standing at the end of the bed, giving her instructions on how to get herself off while he watched had been beyond hot. Her climax had overwhelmed her body and made her want even more.

She moved her hips enticingly. "Come on, Charlie. I know you want to sink your cock into me. Stop denying yourself—" He grabbed her hips, making her gasp.

His warm chest came down over her back. "You want to feel me, angel?" he rasped in her ear.

"Oh, yeah. I want to feel every inch of you."

He set his cock to the entrance of her pussy and pushed in. Her muscles clamped down around his invasion. It'd been a long time since she'd taken a man, and Charlie's cock was bigger than most.

He groaned. His fingers bit into her waist. "God, you're like a tight satin glove."

"Fast and hard, Charlie. Please."

"Impatient, are we?" he purred.

He slid into her inch by mind-blowing, delicious inch, until he touched her cervix. She felt completely possessed by his shaft, totally filled up. Every square inch of her cunt seemed touched by him.

Slowly, so she could feel every little vein of him, he slid out, and then back in. Her fingers tightened around fistfuls of comforter. "Bastard," she breathed. "You're going to drive me insane."

"You're tight, angel. I'm loosening you up." He slid a hand down and stroked her clit while keeping up that slow thrust in and out of her. "Does that feel good?"

She moaned. She could feel her clit swelling and becoming more sensitive with every stroke of his finger over it. "You know it does."

"Good," he purred.

"Faster," she panted.

He gave a low laugh, and finally, he started to pick up the pace.

She hit the mattress with a closed fist. "Yes, that's it, Charlie. That's it."

He grabbed her hips and gave her what she craved, a fast, hard fuck. He pulled back and slammed into her over and over, hitting her cervix with every thrust. It was just the perfect amount of pain, just a touch, to make her cream hard for him, float her to the razor edge of climax.

He shifted his hips and drove into her at a different angle, so the crown of his cock rubbed over her G-spot with every powerful forward thrust of his hips. She gasped and lowered her head to the bed, tipping her hips up and offering herself completely to him.

He let a finger stray to her anus. "What about here, little angel? Do you like a man's cock here?" he purred. He slid a finger inside that tight ring of nerves and she came hard. Her cunt muscles clamped down around him and her hips bucked. She gripped the comforter and cried out from the pleasure that overwhelmed her body. He thrust balls-deep into her and his cock jumped within her. He groaned. A hot stream of come filled her.

They collapsed on the mattress, both breathing heavy. "That answers your question, I guess," she said with a laugh.

"Oh, yeah."

He reached over and pulled her into his arms. She stiffened. Sex was all well and good, hell, it was spectacular with him, but she wasn't sure if she wanted any other kind of intimacy.

"Shhh, come on, Tiya. Let me hold you," he murmured as he brushed away strands of perspiration-soaked hair away from her face. "Just for a minute, okay?"

She relaxed. Lying with his chest to her back, Charlie spooned her from behind. His arms *did* feel good around her. Strong, Safe. She allowed herself to close her eyes. His fingers stroked down her arms, over her waist and over her mound. "So silky smooth, not a trace of hair."

"Fae women don't have much body hair. No pubic hair at all."

He nuzzled her hair. "It's sexy as all hell," he growled.

She smiled. Somehow, since the breakup with her last boyfriend five years ago, she'd forgotten how nice it was to lay in a man's embrace.

"So, how old are you, Tiya?"

"I'll be two hundred next year."

Silence.

"How old are you?" she asked.

"I'm one hundred and forty-three."

She snorted. "Well, aren't I just the cradle robber." Tiya paused. "I don't even know anything about you."

"What do you want to know?"

She traced her finger on the comforter. "About your childhood. Your life." She shrugged. "I'm curious, is all."

Anya Bast

"That's a nice long story." He told her about being born with the facial deformity and how his father had treated him.

When he was done, she turned toward him, still lying in the circle of his arms. She reached out and touched the side of his face, where his deformity had been. "Charlie, I'm sorry." She meant the words. The way he'd been rejected by his father was horrible. Her father had been so loving and generous with her. He'd loved her unconditionally. No matter what she'd done growing up, he'd always been there, ready to welcome her into his arms. Tears pricked her eyes and she blinked them away. Sorrow choked her throat and she swallowed it down.

"It's done and over with. My parents are long since buried," he answered.

"You know, I have fought you and I have fucked you, but I don't know a damned thing about you, Charles Alexander Scythchilde."

"What more do you want to know?"

"I don't know, really. What were the circumstances of your Embrace?"

He gave a little laugh. She watched small lines crinkle at the edges of his eyes. "I was in love with a woman."

"You were Embraced because you were in love with a woman?"

"Indirectly. Her name was Penny...*is* Penny, actually. Penelope Coddington. She's a Vampir, too. Last I heard she was living in Kentucky with her love, Aidan. Aidan was the man I lost her to, but it was right in the end. She and Aidan were meant to be together. I see that now even though it hurt like hell back then."

She laid a kiss to his shoulder and inhaled the scent of his skin. "Ah, so this is a tale of unrequited love and heartbreak."

He kissed her lips. "That's the story of my life."

She lifted her head and smiled. "Tell me."

He shrugged a shoulder. "I was taken in from the streets along with Penny, to the Sugar Jar, a House of the Embraced in New York City run by Gabriel Letourneau. One of the older female vamps was taking care of me and, in my delusion, I thought she was Penny. My, uh, —"

"Lust? Passion? Love?" she supplied helpfully.

"Yes. It triggered my mark and she Embraced me."

"Hmm…so you gained your birthright, but lost the woman in the end, huh?"

"Yeah. On the woman thing, it wasn't for a lack of trying on my part." There was a note of regret in his voice that made her wonder what he'd done.

"I think," she murmured as she laid a kiss to his shoulder. "That you have a very passionate and romantic nature."

His arms tightened around her. "That would be true. However, love keeps handing my heart to me on a platter. I really suck at it. Lust. I do lust much better."

She rolled to her back. Tiya agreed about the lust part. Her body still shivered from what they'd done. "So do I."

"Now that I told you, you have to tell me."

She cast him a sidelong glance. "Since when do you get to make up all the rules?"

He brushed his finger over her breast and stroked her nipple. It instantly tightened for him and shot a line of lust straight down to quicken her cunt. "Since I told you how to bring yourself while I watched," he murmured.

"Ah," she breathlessly. "But you know that after, roughly, 182 years of having sex, I pretty much know how to do that on my own."

He kept stroking her breast until her breath came fast and she fought the urge to writhe under the caress. "Do you remember your first time?" he asked.

She smiled. "Of course. Everyone remembers their first time. Even when it happened more than a century and three quarters ago."

"So anything I do to you has probably already been done."

"Yeah. You could say I've had an adventurous sex life. When a person is so long-lived, they get bored, you know. They have to try new things. How about you?"

"The Embraced are very sensual, so, yeah, I have. My favorite is two women at once."

"Hmmm…" She smiled. "I've had two women at once, but I prefer two men."

He groaned. "Three women at one time, God, the images. You've been a naughty girl."

She smiled and shrugged. "Mostly, I've been happy. At least sexually." Her face fell. "Mostly."

"So how does it work for the OtherKin Sidhe? Do you mature slower than a human, or—"

She shook her head. "We mature at the same rate as a human, but once we hit about twenty-five, we stay there for a very long time."

"Every woman's dream."

She laughed. "Not really. We have to move around a lot in order to keep our secret. Also, there are few OtherKin out there, especially OtherKin Sidhe. We're not supposed to become involved with humans for the long term. Overall, our lives can be…"

"Lonely?"

"Yes. Lots of great sex, few satisfying, long-term commitments. I was in this…" She paused. "You don't want to hear about this." She laughed.

"Yes I do."

"Well…I was in a long-term relationship with another OtherKin. He was a shifter."

Charlie went silent. "There are shifters?"

She laughed. "Yes. Is this blowing the vampire's mind? There are other creatures out there beside bloodsuckers, you know."

"What kinds of shifters are there?"

"Wolves are the most prevalent, but there are all different kinds. The OtherKin Sidhe are really rare. OtherKin shifters are far more common. They've done a truly fantastic job of hiding themselves, though. Their ability to mask what they are is one of the reasons we've been able to stay hidden from the bright light of humanity for so long."

"Okay, so what about this shifter you were with. What was he?"

"He was a wolf."

"You dated a werewolf?"

"Actually, I was practically married to one. They don't change with the full moon, like the legends say. They can change whenever they want. His name is Jason. He and I were together for about twenty years, but we just…I don't know. I guess we never really had that thing you have to have with someone, that spark. We were together mostly because we were both lonely and we were both OtherKin. It's not right to stay with someone just because you're lonely. You need to share love and like and respect and lust." She shrugged. "Anyway, he lives in Washington. That's where I live, usually, in Seattle. We're still friends."

"What do you do in Seattle?"

"Can you believe I own a restaurant?" She laughed. "I named it the Fancy Fae. It's food influenced by the British Isles. Plus some specialty stuff. You know, faery cakes and the like. It's doing really well. I'm, uh, supposed to be in Wales on vacation right now. The managers are taking care of the place while I'm away." She fell silent, sorrow stealing into her thoughts as she lay thinking about her ordinary life. That place was so far from where she was now that it almost seemed like a dream.

"Do you have magick?"

She nodded. "Yes, though it doesn't appear to work on you."

"You tried?"

"Yeah. See? You didn't even feel it. I didn't even brush you with it."

He rested his head on his hand and looked down at her. "Why won't it work on me?"

"I think it's your glamour. It's so strong. My magick can't penetrate it. Basically, you're a really powerful vamp. Listen, Charlie, don't tell anyone about this, okay? Not that they'd believe you anyway."

"I won't, Tiya. Do you think we ever wanted the Embraced outed? I respect the desire of the OtherKin to keep their secret."

"Thank you."

Charlie tightened his arms around her, easing her sadness. They fell silent and Tiya's eyelids grew heavy. She felt so warm and safe here in the bedroom with Charlie's arms wrapped around her. She fell asleep thinking how easy it would be to become used to it.

* * * * *

Charlie roused to a dark room, wondering what had awakened him. Tiya lay in his arms. Her warm body was still cuddled against him. It pleased him that she hadn't rolled away from him during the night. He laid a kiss to her smooth shoulder and closed his eyes once more.

"Aww, isn't that sweet?"

Charlie sat up fast and peered into the darkness. Beside him, Tiya roused and also sat up.

Charlie's gaze found and focused on two Vampir he didn't know. They were both beefy and tall. One of them was brunette, the other blond. He recognized them from Tiya's memories. These were two of the vamps who'd killed her family. The two that had escaped Tiya. Charlie's mind stuttered, trying to comprehend that they were in her bedroom right now.

"Charlie, what's—" He heard Tiya's sharp intake of breath as she, too, spotted the intruders.

The brunette vamp's grin widened. "You didn't think it was over between us, did you, beautiful? Damn, I didn't know you did vamps. Maybe we'll do you before we drain you."

Chapter Eight

Tiya shot out from the bed faster than Charlie could blink and attacked the brunette head-on. "Bastard," she shrieked at him as she punched him hard in the face.

The blond moved to help his friend and Charlie got up and rushed him. He slammed him back against the wall, breaking through the drywall. Plaster and paint hit the floor. "Who the fuck are you?" Charlie snarled. "What do you want?"

The vamp laughed in Charlie's face.

Beside him, Tiya yelled in rage as the brunette grabbed her hair, trying to pull her head to the side to bite her.

Charlie punched the blond square in the face, brought his knee up into his upper stomach, then twisted to the side, toward Tiya, and kicked the brunette in the lower back. The vamp yelped and released Tiya, who twisted away and freed herself.

He and Tiya stood in the middle of the room, back to back, and in battle stance. They were both naked. It made Charlie feel pretty stupid and more than a little vulnerable.

The blond threw them a wary glance and moved toward the door. He was young. Charlie could feel it. They were both only about twenty-five or so, more or less the same age as Vincent. Charlie was far more powerful than both them. Hell, even Tiya was likely stronger and she wasn't even Embraced. The vamps had to be aware of that fact.

The brunette spit out a tooth and wiped his bloodied mouth with the back of his hand. Apparently Tiya could punch pretty damn hard. He gave a harsh laugh. "One day, we're going to come back when you don't have a vamp to defend you, bitch. Then that cute little bare ass will be ours."

They both went for the door. *Shit.*

Tiya collapsed to her knees, breathing heavily. Charlie ran after the vamps, out the door and into the woods where they'd fled. No sound. No motion. Charlie reached out with his mind and touched the area, but felt no sign of the Vampir's passing.

He turned and headed back into the house, more concerned for Tiya than anyone or anything else at the moment. Charlie walked into the bedroom and found Tiya, still nude, kneeling on the bedroom floor. He pulled the comforter from the bed and put it around her shoulders, then went for his clothes.

"We need to get out of here, Tiya. You need more defense than this. I can't take you to Griffin House for obvious reasons, but I have a friend in town—"

"What does it matter? I caught a telepathic flash of how they found me. They can track me anywhere I go, right? The same way you did."

He paused, his hand on his pants, which hung over the back of a chair. "Did they taste your blood in Wales?"

She nodded. "Didn't you see it when you were in my head?"

He swept his pants up and started to put them on. "Fuck. Yeah, that's right. I did see it." At one point they'd overpowered her and the brunette had grazed her wrist with his fangs. She'd been able to fight free of them before he'd been able to fully sink his teeth in.

"Anywhere I go, they can find me."

"I know that, Tiya. That's why you need vamps around you who can protect you."

She looked up. Her face was tearstained. "That's how you found me, isn't it? By tasting my blood."

Reluctantly, he nodded. "I tasted your blood in the alley, remember? It was just a little, but it was enough. I could feel you after that. The closer I got the more I felt you. It was a like homing signal. It's not like that with human blood."

She wiped her face and gave a short, caustic laugh. "Well, aren't I perfect game of *hot and cold*. I'm a barrel of laughs for all the bloodsuckers of the world."

"Your blood is special, Tiya. It's milky sweet and seems to hold special…benefits…to the drinker. Once a vamp has a taste—"

"He wants another and another." She sighed, shook her head, and seemed to speak to herself. "But I've never heard of fae blood being special to the Embraced. Maybe…oh, my God." She drew a sharp breath. "*Setanta*."

"Setanta?"

She waved a hand at him. "Wait, let me think."

He hoped she didn't take too long. They needed to get out of there in case the young'uns came back with friends.

She looked up at him. "Setanta. Maybe they want the blood of my line. Maybe that's why they went after my family. Maybe it's not all fae blood that's special, just the blood of *my* family line."

Charlie reached for his shirt. "What's Setanta? Why would you think that, Tiya?"

"The only reason I can think of is that we can trace our ancestry back to Setanta. Maybe there's something special about our blood because of that."

"Okay, I'm still not following." Charlie pulled his shirt on and helped Tiya to her feet. He pulled her close and kissed the top of her head. "Who's Setanta?"

She looked up at him with wide eyes. "Cúchulainn, Charlie. Cúchulainn was born with the name Setanta."

Charlie remained silent for a long moment, stunned. "You're actually related to Cúchulainn? I thought he was just a legend."

"You with the whole thinking-everything's-a-legend thing." She waved her hand. "He was real. The stories say he was a kind of super-person, a demi-god. He was really an

OtherKin Sidhe forced to cast a few spells in the company of ordinary humans. It happened when he was in the Red Branch, while he was protecting the king. The legends grew from that incident. He *was* a kind of super-Sidhe, though. His magick was incredibly strong. Maybe…" She bit her lip. "Maybe there is something special in our bloodline, some extra little ingredient that gives vamps a little kick."

"Your blood does give vamps something special. Hell, it's like a drug." He looked into her eyes.

"A drug?"

"I know it is, Tiya. I know it because I crave it."

She looked away.

"I'll never take it. Never without your permission. I told you that already. Do you believe me? Do you trust me?"

Tiya looked back at him, finding his gaze. "I do. Now I do trust you."

"Good. Let's get going. Adam is keeping an apartment in downtown Minneapolis for his stay here. We can defend you better from there. Adam's every bit as strong as I am. Those young'un vamps would have to have a death wish to try and get at you through us."

"What if Adam craves my blood?" she asked.

"I'll knock his fangs in with my fists if he tries to take any against your will. Okay?"

* * * * *

They took Charlie's car and rolled into the parking lot of Adam's apartment building at around six in the morning. It was a tall, brown building, well-landscaped and well-maintained. The building was obviously older, but had been updated. Charlie had been here only once. That had been yesterday afternoon.

Tiya had packed a small bag. He grabbed it out of the backseat and they went into the building. As they rode to the top floor, where Adam's apartment was, Charlie couldn't help but think they were secreting a fae princess away in a tower for her own defense against marauding forces. Charlie needed to find out more about those forces, and soon.

"Hey, Charlie," said Adam when he opened the door. He wore nothing but a pair of gray sweatpants. His gaze instantly raked over Tiya in a steamy appraising sweep.

Whoa, Charlie, nice, Adam said in his mind.

I can hear you, answered Tiya in a singsong voice.

Adam gave her look of surprise. "You're not an Embraced. What the—"

"We'll explain everything, Adam, if you'll let us in," said Charlie.

Charlie pushed a hand through his sleep-mussed hair and stepped to the side. "Sorry, man," he mumbled.

When they stepped over the threshold and into the living room, a tall woman with strawberry-blonde hair and big brown eyes exited the bedroom. Her hair was also mussed and her shirt was buttoned wrong. Giving Charlie and Tiya a glance and slight smile, she moved to Adam. After giving him a lingering kiss, she said, "Last night was great, Adam. I've got to go open the shop, but stop by later, okay?" With a final sultry look over her shoulder at him, she left the apartment.

Apparently, Adam had bagged his pretty bookstore clerk the night before. No surprise there. Few women seemed to be immune to his charms.

Adam looked them, grinned and shrugged. "Life is good. What can I say?"

Tiya glanced around at the apartment. She could probably tell already that Adam was a man of hedonism and creature comforts. The apartment, with its comfy furnishings and impressively packed entertainment center showed those qualities. Adam was well-off, so he'd managed to settle himself in and make this seem like home in a short amount of time, even though Charlie knew he wasn't planning to stay here for long. Adam didn't mind throwing money around, that was for sure.

"Adam, meet Tiya. Tiya, Adam," Charlie said.

Tiya glanced at Adam and gave him a distracted half-smile.

"Hi, Tiya," said Adam. "So, does someone want to tell me why you two showed up at the crack of dawn, when most good little Vampir should still be in bed sleeping off a night of raw sex, and why Tiya, who is not a Vampir, has telepathic ability?"

Tiya glanced at Charlie. "You sure you trust him, Charlie?"

He shrugged. "Completely, but this is your show. This is your decision to make."

She stood in the center of the room and regarded Adam with a hesitant look on her face. Worry lines creased her forehead.

"Tiya?" Charlie asked. "You okay?"

Biting her lower lip, Tiya looked up at him. The uneasy look on her face vanished. "Yeah, I'm okay."

"Do you want to leave?"

She shook her head. "I'll trust him if you trust him, Charlie."

Tiya walked to the solid blue sofa and sat down. "Okay, here it goes." She told Adam the whole story, from finding the Vampir in her parent's house to how they'd tracked her to Minneapolis this morning. "It seems they want my blood and maybe the blood of my line for some reason."

Adam pushed his hand through his short blond hair again, making it stand up in little tufts. "Wow. Well, I'll tell you one thing, Tiya." His eyes grew darker than Charlie had ever seen them and he was suddenly reminded that Adam, although a mostly fun-loving and pleasure-seeking vamp, was also a *powerful* vamp. One he wouldn't want to have as an enemy. "You smell really good to me," Adam growled. *"Really good.* Ever since you walked through that door I've been thinking about—"

"Adam," Charlie said in a warning voice. Tiya had visibly stiffened at hearing Adam's words. "Lay off."

Adam looked at him. "I'm just telling you the truth. I know you, Gabe and Niccolo don't think I have a lot of self-control. You're wrong. I have it when I want to have it." He turned his gaze to Tiya. "You can trust me, Tiya. You have my word on that, but that doesn't change the fact that I want you. You're near irresistible to me, in fact. I want your body and I want your blood. I want to be inside you while I'm taking your blood. That doesn't mean I want to drain you. It doesn't mean I'm going to try anything. It just means I want you in a fundamental way."

Tiya fell silent. She licked her lips nervously.

He shrugged and smiled his Adamish smile. The dimples popped out on his cheeks. "Hey, I'm just telling you the score."

Tiya's lips parted and her breathing grew heavy, almost aroused. She swallowed hard. "Okay," she said slowly. "So now I know. Thanks for being honest with me."

A jolt of possession ran through Charlie at Adam's admission and also at the way Tiya seemed to be responding to it. What the hell? Charlie pushed it away. He had no right to a claim over Tiya. He didn't want one, either.

Adam grinned and the dark, intent look on his face vanished. "Hey, just call me Honest Adam. I just thought you should know since it looks like we'll be spending some time together."

"You said I could call on you for help, Adam," Charlie said. "I need it."

"Even at six in the morning." He spread his arms wide. "You got it. Sounds like we need to separate friend from foe around these parts. But, first, I think you two could use some sleep. You both looked stressed and tired."

Charlie ran a hand over his face. "Yeah."

Adam pointed down a darkened hallway. "Down there is a bedroom and a bathroom. I'm assuming you two are going to share a bed? I can smell you both all the fuck over each other."

Charlie glanced at Tiya. She shifted uncomfortably on the couch. "I-I'd feel better," she said, holding his gaze. "As long as it's okay with you, Charlie. I mean, sleeping with me."

Charlie let out a breath he didn't even know he'd been holding. "Come on, let's get some rest."

* * * * *

Tiya followed Charlie down the hall and into the guest bedroom. Adam trailed with her bag in hand. A king-size bed, covered with a black comforter, dominated the room. A dresser and closet lined one wall. A chair stood in the corner, next to the entrance to a bathroom.

Adam set the bag down on the chair and turned. "You need anything, you give me a holler."

Tiya watched him watch her. Oh, yeah, Adam wanted her. What the hell was going on? Was she some kind of catnip for vamps? The worst part was, she was responding to their interest. Charlie made her body do cartwheels and even Adam, who was powerfully attractive physically, made her body flare to life in all the wrong places.

Adam was tall and broad-shouldered, had washboard abs and nice biceps. The way the sweatpants draped him, she could tell he possessed a nice package between his legs. She hated herself for noticing his dancing brown eyes and the dimples in his cheeks when he smiled.

Tiya didn't find him as attractive as she found Charlie. Not on a physical or emotional level, but there was no denying that Adam was a good-looking vamp. Tiya turned away, wondering what it was that drew her to these two and what it was that drew them to her.

Hell, she was in trouble.

"Thanks," she mumbled at him.

Tiya was relieved when Adam left the room and closed the door behind him. She went to Charlie and let him enfold her in his arms. She nestled her head against his chest and took comfort in the sound of his beating heart. The old legends said that the Vampir were the living dead. How untrue. The Embraced were more alive than the OtherKin and humans, to her way of thinking. They lived directly from life force, after all. Anyway, it wasn't like they died and came back to life when they were Embraced. Their DNA simply changed. Although *simply* wasn't a good word to use to describe the process.

He laid a kiss to the top of her head and she closed her eyes. "If you hadn't been with me this morning, I'd probably be dead right now, Charlie."

He tipped her chin up, so she looked at his face. Without a word, he kissed her tenderly. His lips slipped over hers slowly, like silk. She made a little noise in the back of her throat and kissed him back. His tongue feathered against her mouth and she opened to him.

They undressed each other and curled up naked under the covers, taking comfort in the feel their skin touching and their mingling body heat.

When Charlie pulled her beneath him and kissed her lips, her throat and her breasts, she let him. When he planed her inner thigh with his broad hand, she spread her legs for him. Patiently, with his touch and his tongue, he readied her. When she was slick and swollen, he slid inside her. All the while he rode her slow, then even slower. All the while, he held her gaze steadily with his own, breaking it only once in a while to kiss her or murmur into her ear. It was intimate and arousing and made emotions swell within her and tears sheen her eyes.

He made feel protected and even…almost…loved and cherished.

Finally, she climaxed with her legs twined around his hips and his cock thrust way up inside her. Her orgasm triggered his, and she allowed her body to accept every bit of his come. They stifled each other's cries with their mouths and tongues.

When they slept, it was in a perspiration-drenched, satisfied tangle of intertwined bodies.

Tiya hadn't slept so deeply in weeks.

* * * * *

"Hey Charlie," Vincent rasped as he pushed himself into a sitting position on the bed. "Where have you been, man?"

Charlie pulled a straight-backed chair up to the side of the bed and sat down. "I've been around, Vincent. I just figured you needed some time to recuperate. You look better."

There was some color to his skin again and his eyes were brighter. His voice still sounded thready and rasping, but he looked like he was healing at a faster rate now.

"I feel better. Man, it was like we were hit by a locomotive in that alley."

"I know. They hit you worse than they hit me."

Vincent gave him a sharp look. "What do you mean, they? It was a chick. A little one, too."

"I remember. Did you recognize who it was?"

He shook his head. "Nah, I already told Anlon and SPAVA. I don't remember much after being slashed in the stomach. I remember her asking me some questions, and I remember her raising a hawthorn stake over me. That's it."

"Do you remember what she looked like?"

He frowned. "Yeah, she was pretty, long blonde hair and blue-gray eyes. I remember she smelled like violets."

"I remember that too."

Something moved in Vincent's eyes and he looked away.

"You okay?" Charlie asked.

"Great. I'm just great." He didn't sound great. Vincent glanced back at him. "Hey, SPAVA wants to talk to you about the attack. They're conducting an investigation."

Inwardly, Charlie groaned.

"They're downstairs talking to Anlon right now."

Charlie groaned for real.

"You gotta do it, Charlie."

"I know. It's just that humans investigating the crimes of the preternatural, it's a waste of time. It's better the council's Executioners do it."

"What do you think that woman was?" His voice lowered. "She wasn't a vamp and she couldn't have been human."

Charlie relaxed a little. If Vincent wasn't as innocent as he seemed, he was a damn fine actor. Charlie didn't think Vincent was award-worthy. It made lying to him feel worse, but there wasn't much he could do it about. He'd made a promise to Tiya. She was in danger right now, which made keeping that promise all the more important. "I don't know, Vincent."

Vincent looked away again. "Damn," he sighed.

Charlie stood. "Look, I'm going to go downstairs and do my duty for the local SPAVA division. You rest some more, all right?"

"Thanks for stopping by. Don't be a stranger."

"No way. I'm just glad to see you getting better. Pretty soon, you'll be up and giving the world hell again."

Vincent smiled and Charlie resisted the urge to reach out and ruffle his hair. Vincent was no kid, no matter how Charlie thought of him.

Charlie looked at him one last time before he left the room. Vincent had leaned back against the pillows and closed his brown eyes.

He really hoped Vincent was innocent.

Right now Charlie couldn't afford to trust anyone but Adam. He didn't trust anything he thought he knew about any vamp in this territory. Not even Anlon.

Charlie headed downstairs to meet with SPAVA. He felt a little guilty not letting Anlon know what was happening in his own territory. But he wasn't in Anlon's inner circle, and he didn't owe him anything. Right now, all he wanted was to keep Tiya safe and alive.

He was trying really hard not to care about her and was failing pretty damn bad.

The last thing he needed was to put his heart out there and have it handed back to him all torn up. He'd been down that road before and he was sick of the scenery.

Anlon was deep in discussion with two SPAVA agents in the house dining room. A long, polished wooden table stood in the center of the room, decorated with a large vase of white orchids. Evelyn kept the orchids fresh. Every day she tossed out the old and replaced them with new. There were vases of them all over the mansion.

The agents, both men, turned toward Charlie when he reached the bottom of the staircase. Charlie walked toward them. "I was told you wanted to speak with me."

The taller of the two agents stuck his hand out. "Hi, you must be Charles Scythchilde. I'm Agent Michaels and this is Agent Harvey." The other agent nodded at him. "We just want to know if you can tell us anything beyond what we got from Vincent regarding the attack."

Charlie shrugged. "Agent Michaels, I doubt I could give you any more insight into the event that you already have. A woman who could move faster than a human attacked us. She was stronger than she should've been, too. She and I fought and she got away. The woman is downright lethal, to tell you the truth." An image of Tiya's tear-filled eyes socked him the gut. She was lethal and vulnerable at the same time.

"You told Anlon she wasn't human."

He shook his head. "If she's any kind of human, it's superhuman."

Both the SPAVA agents laughed.

"Do you have any leads in this case?" Charlie asked.

"Right now, none. But we're working on it," answered Michaels.

Agent Harvey pulled a card out of the inner coat pocket of his blazer. "If you think of something you think we need to know, or need us in any way, give us a call."

Charlie took the card. "Thanks."

They made their goodbyes to Anlon and left the house.

Anlon watched them leave. "They're not going find out jack shit," he muttered.

"Nope," answered Charlie. "They never do. We're jumping through human hoops."

"Well, at least it makes them feel like they have a little control over things." Anlon turned. "Are you leaving, too?"

He nodded. "Yeah, I thought I'd head out for the night. I'll come back to tomorrow and check in on Vincent. He's definitely on the mend."

Anlon smiled. "He was talking some crazy stuff while he was in the throes of the poisoning."

Charlie smiled back. "Oh, yeah?"

"Mumbling about how faeries were real."

Charlie's blood ran cold as a jolt of shock went through him. He concentrated really hard on making sure his smile didn't falter. He gave a little laugh. "Really?"

"Oh, yeah. He was having delusions, seeing faeries in the room. Faeries and werewolves." Anlon laughed. "Don't tell him I told you that. He'd kill me."

"No way."

Anlon clapped him on the back. "All right, man. I'll see you tomorrow."

"See you." Charlie left the house with a million questions running through his mind.

* * * * *

Tiya sat perched on a bar stool in Adam's kitchen counter with a glass of wine in her hand and a smile on her lips. Adam stood at the stove, wearing a pair of tight-fitting jeans and black

T-shirt. That seemed to be his wardrobe for most any occasion, except for when he wore a pair of sweatpants without anything else.

Adam was a study in contrasts to Charlie. Where Adam was easygoing and carefree, Charlie was serious and reserved. Where Adam gave off a sense of being a troublemaker and irresponsible, Charlie was well-mannered and chivalrous.

But when you stripped off Charlie's clothes, all that civilized reserve came off with them. When you got Charlie hot, all those old-fashioned, gentlemanly manners went right out the window. An aroused, stripped Charlie was passionate and fiery. She shivered. Charlie was all about gentlemanly behavior, but when you got the man into the bedroom, he was one hundred percent unrestrained.

"You okay? Are you cold?" Adam said, as he stirred the mushrooms he was sautéing in a skillet. "You shivered."

She took a sip of her wine to mask her smile. "No, I was just...thinking."

He winked. "Okay, understood."

She blushed.

"Charlie's a damn fine man. He has every bit of my respect. I can't say I'm not a little jealous of him right now."

"He's a good man." Guilt flooded her, washing the grin from her mouth. "I just wish I'd known what a wonderful person he was before I slashed him. I definitely have some making up to do for that."

Adam poured a bit of cream into the concoction he was heating up on the stove. The whole apartment smelled wonderful. Her stomach growled.

"Thing with Charlie is, he won't hold a grudge against you. He'll never call in debts to be repaid. Charlie, he does what's right all the time, no matter what it costs him, no matter how bad it hurts him."

"You make him sound like a doormat."

"A doormat?" Adam turned toward her. "Hell no! Charlie's not a man you can take advantage of, far from it." He pointed the spatula at her. "In fact, Charlie's a very powerful vamp. He's powerful enough to hold his own territory. Hell, he's probably stronger than Anlon."

"So why doesn't he fight for a seat on the Council of the Embraced?" Every Vampir who had a territory had a seat on the council, thus a vote in what passed for the government of the Embraced.

Adam shrugged. "I don't know, never asked him. Up until last year, he seemed happy enough to be in Gabe's inner circle with Niccolo and me. Then he up and took off without a word." Adam spooned up a mushroom smothered in cream and brought over to her. "Here, take a taste."

She opened her mouth and took it from him. Tiya noticed Adam watching her mouth. Purposely, just to tease him, she closed her eyes and went, "Mmmm."

When she opened her eyes, Adam was still standing there, staring at her. She laughed.

"Anyone ever tell you you're a minx?" he asked.

She smiled. "Sure. Though, mostly, I get called a tease."

"Yeah, I can see that."

She leaned against the counter and sipped her merlot as Adam went back to the stove. "So, what happened with that woman back in Newville really threw Charlie for a loop, huh?"

"Yeah, that's for sure. He got out of Dodge faster than Gabe could ask, 'Ou est Charlie?'. Niccolo lit out, too. We still don't where he ended up."

"I'm sorry Charlie got hurt, but I have to say I'm happy I met him. I'm growing to really like him a lot."

Adam turned and winked. "Are you now?"

"Yeah. I mean, I don't know him that well yet, but I already want good things for him."

Adam put three steaks on a hot skillet. They sizzled and snapped. Looked like it was going to be a heart attack on a plate tonight. Good thing clogged arteries weren't an issue for any of them.

"Well, you know that's good to hear, because Charlie could really use someone who wants good things for him."

"Don't you?"

"I mean someone of the female persuasion." He grinned and his dimples popped out. "I like Charlie and all, but not like that."

She laughed. "Uh-huh. Understood." Adam turned back to the stove to tend the meat and Tiya watched his very nicely shaped male posterior. Adam was drop-dead gorgeous. Like, stop-the-female-heart beautiful. Yet, she didn't have the same reaction to him as she had to Charlie. She could admire Adam's form, wonder what he'd be like in bed, but she didn't have that base, primal reaction to him as she had to Charlie.

That very same reaction she was having right now.

She swallowed hard, sensing Charlie at the front door. The key turned in the lock, and her whole body tightened. The door swung open and her nipples hardened. She saw Charlie step into the room, wearing a pair of dark tailored pants and a finely woven black shirt, and she got wet between her thighs. Tiya met his chocolate-brown gaze and was lost. Utterly and completely…gone.

Damn, she cursed herself. Damn. Damn. Damn.

She was an idiot. This kind of attraction was the last thing she needed right now.

"Whoa, baby," said Adam, turning toward her from the oven, "Did the sexual tension in here just get thicker than the mushroom sauce, or is it just me?" He grinned.

Tiya swallowed hard and ignored him. "Hey, Charlie."

"Hey," said Charlie as he took off his duster and hung it in the closet. "It smells good in here, Adam."

"Uh-huh." Adam looked meaningfully at Tiya. "It just got a whole lot better, too."

Charlie and Adam shared one of those completely masculine looks. They both knew exactly what Adam was talking about and so did she. Tiya wished she could control her body better around Charlie, but it seemed impossible.

Charlie crossed the floor, snaked a hand around her waist and pressed his mouth to her ear. "Good enough to eat, in fact, and I'm starving." He kissed her earlobe and backed away.

Tiya practically broke into a cold sweat. She turned around and drained her wineglass.

Adam filled her glass again. "So, now that we've established that we're all horny, er, hungry." He grinned and fixed his gaze on Tiya. "And I do mean, *all* of us…let's eat."

Tiya shuddered under the perusal of both their gazes and slid from the stool. "Okay. I'm famished," she said with forced levity.

They sat down at the small dining room table and Adam served them thick steak smothered with mushrooms and cream sauce. A tossed salad, potatoes and a nice red table wine completed the meal. Tiya picked at her food, and ate more than she really wanted because she knew the only reason Adam had cooked was because of her. Obviously, the vamps didn't need the food.

After she'd thoroughly chewed a bite of steak and swallowed, she asked them both, "So, did you guys, uh, feed, today?"

A part of her feared Charlie's answer. After all, normally the Vampir fed from the Demi and the Demi required sustenance from the Vampir in return. It was kind of a reciprocal thing — sex for blood. Stupidly, the thought of Charlie giving his wonderful body to another woman was…disturbing.

"I have a Demi coming over tonight," said Adam. He grinned. "They do delivery. Just like pizza."

"Ah." She pushed a piece of steak around in the cream. "How about you, Charlie?" She forced a smile. "I'd hate to think you guys were more concerned with feeding me than yourselves."

Charlie took a drink of wine. "I fed at Griffin House."

Tiya's heart sank. "Oh, good." *Fuck.* For a moment, she truly hated herself for caring. She hated herself even more for asking. "I feel better, then," she murmured.

"Karina was more than happy to quickly donate to me from her wrist." Charlie commented before taking a bite.

Tiya relaxed and cussed herself out in both English and Welsh in her mind.

After dinner, the three of them cleared the table. Every time she passed Charlie, Tiya could feel the heat of him radiate off him and warm her. The scent of him, that blend of spice and man teased her nostrils until she didn't know her left hand from her right and nearly dropped the salt and pepper shakers.

When the kitchen was almost clean, on Tiya's last trip to the table, Charlie grabbed her around her waist and pulled her up flush against him. She gasped in surprise, but when his mouth came down on hers, it became a soft moan. Her fingers curled into the shirt covering his upper arms.

His tongue swept into her mouth and tangled with hers. The taste of him went straight to her sex, making her pulse with need.

When he pulled away from her, she buried her face in his shoulder, saying, "I'm sorry," over and over.

He tipped her chin up and she saw the question in his eyes.

"I'm sorry I hurt you in the alley, Charlie," she said. "I'm so, so sorry. I was sorry I had to hurt you when I did it, but I'm even more..." She shook her head, helpless to find the adequate words.

He trailed his fingers through the loose length of her hair. "I know you are."

She looked away. "And if Vincent is innocent, as you think he is, I'm profoundly sorry I hurt him, too."

His hand fisted around a tendril of her hair. "I'm still working to determine that."

She nodded.

"Tiya, I know you're not a bad person, okay?" he said. "You did what I would've done, what lots of people would've done, in rage and grief over a heinous act."

"I wish we could've met before all this happened, Charlie."

He kissed her. "I'm just glad we met."

Someone knocked on the door and Adam, who'd retreated into another part of the apartment to give them some privacy, answered it.

A tall redhead in a long gray skirt and a black silk top entered the apartment. You could see her black satin bra beneath the shirt.

"Maria," Adam greeted. "Meet Charlie and Tiya."

Maria pulled her long gray coat off and laid it on the couch and sauntered straight to Tiya.

Tiya watched her approach with fascination. Her hips swayed in a way that said sex. Her beautiful heart-shaped face held an expression of interest, fixed on Tiya. Her mouth was full, her ruby red lips slightly parted. Her eyes were green and slanted like a cat's. This had to be the Demi who'd come to allow Adam to feed.

Maria approached Tiya with so much single-minded intensity that Tiya stepped backward until she came up flush against the kitchen counter. Maria reached out and laid a cool hand to Tiya's cheek. Her cat eyes closed and the woman made a noise not unlike a purr.

Tiya felt her magic coalesce and strengthen in her stomach and start to rise as a defensive, instinctive reaction.

"Uh, Charlie…" Tiya said.

"She can smell you, too, Tiya," Charlie answered. His eyes were dark and heavy with lust. "To every last one of us in the room, you're a powerful temptation."

Great.

Maria glanced at Adam. "You never told me you had a beautiful human in your apartment," she cooed. "She has so much lovely lust in her, for—" she pointed at Charlie, "—that one."

Frowning, Tiya glanced at Charlie. How did the Demi know that?

Maria closed her eyes and inhaled. When she opened those exotically slanted green orbs again, it was to find Tiya's wide blue-gray gaze. "I could lick your skin and be full for a week," she murmured.

Well, at least Maria had finally deemed Tiya worthy enough to address directly. Tiya couldn't respond to the passionate look in the other woman's eyes. "Can-can you feed indirectly that way?" she finally managed to ask.

Adam spoke near her, startling her. "Maria is very old, Tiya."

Maria raised an arched eyebrow. "I'm five hundred," she answered. "Old enough to have gained strength and learned a few tricks." She reached out and ran a finger over Tiya's forearm. "Many…*different* kinds of tricks."

Little did this Demi know that Tiya was also old and had also learned many sexual tricks, not all of them for use on men.

"Like this, for example," said Maria. She held out her hands, about an inch away from Tiya's collarbone.

Chapter Nine

Tiya felt a light pressure on her skin and a comforting warmth. It was as though Maria touched her without really physically touching her. The Demi slid her hands down and Tiya's breath caught in her throat as she felt invisible hands caress her breasts, stroke her nipples into stiff little points. Her nipples poked through the material of her bra and shirt, giving away her arousal.

Charlie and Adam's gazes were on them, watching avidly. Tiya had put on a low-cut plum-colored cotton shirt that morning, along with a lacy demi-bra that accentuated her cleavage. Tiya found Charlie's gaze. He stared at her breasts and clenched his hands loosely at his sides as though he wanted to be touching them. Her breathing grew heavier, knowing the sight was exciting him.

Maria moved her hands down further, over her stomach to her mound. Tiya grabbed the counter behind her as the sensation began. Though her legs were closed and her panties and jeans remained on, it felt like Maria ran her fingers over her sex. The feeling of those phantom butterfly brushes drew moisture from her pussy and plumped her clit. Her hips thrust forward, toward Maria's hands, as if on a string. Her head tipped back on a moan. It was like Tiya's body wasn't even hers to control anymore.

"Let me kiss you," the Demi murmured. "Just a little kiss."

Tiya licked her lips and gave a slight nod. Women weren't really her thing, but what could a kiss hurt? It was arousing Charlie to watch her with Maria, and that's what counted. It was arousing Adam as well.

Every single bit of it made Tiya hot.

Maria pulled Tiya into her arms and pressed her mouth to hers. They were about the same size and height, so they fit together well. Maria rubbed her breasts against Tiya, drawing a ragged sigh from her throat. Maria's tongue played against Tiya's lips and she opened for her. Maria tasted like mint and smelled of roses. Their mouths crushed and their tongues tangled together softly. Tiya gave into it with a little sigh and twined her arms around Maria's waist.

Tiya slid her hand up Maria's side and cupped one of her heavy breasts in her hand. She ran the pad of her thumb over her nipple and felt it harden. Maria moaned into Tiya's mouth. Tiya's breath caught in her throat as Maria returned the favor by bringing her own hand up and palming Tiya's breast through her shirt.

"Oh, God," groaned Adam from somewhere close.

Tiya felt Maria smile a little against her mouth and then pull away. "Come on, cowboy," Maria said to Adam. "You want to kiss her with me?"

Adam looked at Tiya and Tiya looked at Charlie. At what point had she started thinking Charlie had any kind of say in what she did sexually? Had it been when they'd slept together a couple times? Or had it been when she'd slept with him and actually found she cared about him?

No matter. Now she looked to Charlie to see what he'd do. Would he step in and lay a claim to her?

Charlie locked gazes with her and heat flared to life between them. Tiya thought at that moment he could make her come just by looking at her like that—like he was on death row and his execution was the next day. Like she was the last woman he'd ever sink himself into. Like she was everything to him in that one moment.

Two strides had him across the kitchen and her in his arms. He kissed her hard, most definitely laying a claim.

Somewhere to the side of them, Maria laughed softly. "I thought so," she murmured. "I thought that one was feeling a little jealous."

Tiya hardly heard Adam's low voice, murmuring a reply. She was too consumed by Charlie's kiss, by his hands roaming over her heavy breasts, teasing her taut nipples. She was too enraptured by the feel of his fingers kneading the muscles of her back and the slide of his hands down to cup her buttocks. She was too consumed by the way Charlie tasted on her tongue, how his hips thrust against her stomach, showing her that the hard ridge of his cock was all for her.

Her hands roved the muscles of his shoulders and back, then traced down to curl needfully over the waistband of his pants in front.

"Come on, angel," he growled in her ear. "Wanna give them what they want?"

She glanced at Maria and Adam, who both seemed avidly consumed by their every movement. Adam idly palmed Maria's breast.

"What do you think they want?" she murmured back.

"A really, really good show."

She drew his earlobe into her mouth and gently bit, raking her teeth over it. He shuddered against her. "I'll take you any way I can get you, Charlie," she whispered.

"Then come on." He led her into the living room. Adam and Maria followed.

Not wasting time, she stepped forward and unbuttoned Charlie's shirt to expose all that wonderful, hard, muscled chest that she loved. Once he was free of the shirt, she leaned forward and licked over one flat male nipple. Charlie's hands tightened on her shoulders.

"Slip your shoes off," she murmured.

He did it and Tiya's hands went to the waistband of his pants, but not before she rubbed along the length of his shaft from the outside and made him groan. "I can't wait to get these off," she whispered as she unhooked the buttons and slid his pants down. Her hand wrapped around his cock and she teased the underside of it through his boxers with skillful fingers.

Adam and Maria now sat on the couch. Maria rested in front of Adam, between his spread legs. Adam was unbuttoning Maria's blouse slowly. Her skirt was already hiked up high on her thighs. Obviously, they were enjoying the presentation.

Well, then she'd give them one they wouldn't forget.

She sent out a tendril of magick to the stereo system that sat in the entertainment center in Adam's living room, and found a CD with music that suited in the five-disk changer. It was low, sexy blues tune that set the mood. She made sure the volume was set fairly low, but high enough to mask the moans and cries that were about to fill the apartment. She felt sure Adam's neighbors would thank her.

Tiya flicked a glance at Maria to see if she suspected what Tiya had just done. Either of the vamps could've been responsible for flipping the stereo on from afar. Hopefully Maria assumed it had been Charlie or Adam. It appeared that Maria's thoughts were nowhere near the stereo or magick. Adam's strong hands were kneading her beautiful bare breasts. Maria's lips were slightly parted and her gaze solely centered on Tiya. She suspected Maria had a preference for women.

Shooting a coy glance in Maria and Adam's direction, she stepped toward Charlie who now wore nothing but a pair of silky black boxer shorts. Extending her index finger she traced it over Charlie's chest. He tried to grab her wrist and draw her close, but she wagged her finger at him.

"No touching me," she said. "Not yet."

Charlie gave her a look of warning in response.

"You'll get to touch me all you want soon."

There had been a time in her life when she'd been an exotic dancer. She remembered how to move in order to entice. They wanted a show, she could sure as hell give them one.

She lifted her hands over her head and swayed with the slow, sensual music. Tipping her head back and closing her eyes, she slowly brought her hands down to smooth over her long hair, her throat, over her collarbones and breasts, all the way to her waist and the hem of her top.

"Oh, yeah," Adam yelled playfully from the couch. "Take it off, sweetheart."

She winked at him and turned her back to him, teasing him by pulling her shirt up just enough so he could glimpse a little skin, then pulling it back down. All the while, she moved her hips to the beat with slow, sensuous snaps and twists. She caught Charlie's half-hooded, dark gaze and pulled her shirt over her head.

Heat flared in Charlie's eyes as he raked his gaze over the black lace demi-bra that plumped her cleavage so exceedingly well. He curled his hands at his sides as though resisting the urge to rush out and touch her.

She gave him a look of warning, before she turned toward Adam and Maria, still letting her hips and shoulders find the beat in the soft, sultry music coming from the stereo.

She cupped her hands on her breasts, delving a finger under the material of her bra to brush over a hardened nipple. She missed a beat in her dance as pleasure poured through her, centering between her thighs. Pulling the material away from her nipple, she flashed it at Maria and Adam.

"Beautiful," murmured Adam.

Her fingers dipped to find the button on her jeans. She undid it and pulled the zipper down slowly, peeling enough of the material away so that the room could see the front of the matching black lace that covered her mound. Instead of peeling her jeans off, she pranced behind Charlie and peeked around him.

"Awwww, come on," yelled Adam. "You're just a tease!"

"The whole room wants to see that pretty little body stripped, angel," said Charlie. "There's going to be a mutiny soon."

Tiya just laughed. It felt good to feel a little lighthearted again. With two murderous vamps on her trail who could track her anywhere she went, she needed a little light. She needed a little fun. Narrowing her eyes at Charlie, she realized she needed a whole lot of him.

Using Charlie as a shield, she peeled her jeans off and tossed them aside. Luckily, she'd been barefoot already. Tiya rubbed her almost nude body up and down against Charlie's back like she was a cat. She laid a kiss to his shoulder. He groaned.

Tiya stepped out from behind Charlie wearing nothing but her soaked black thong and bra. "Ah, baby, yes," said Adam.

Adam had hiked up Maria's skirt up even higher and slid her underwear off, baring her pussy. Her legs were hooked over Adam's knees and Adam slowly slid two fingers in and out of her sopping sex and flicked her clit with his thumb as they watched her. Maria had a nearly drugged look on her face.

For a moment, Tiya watched the glide of Adam's fingers in and out of Maria's cunt. Tiya's body reacted as if it was being done to her. She bit her lip and fought back a moan. Her poor body needed attention very soon.

But Tiya's show wasn't finished yet.

Tiya sauntered up to Charlie and kissed him. When he tried to enfold her in his arms she pushed them down and away. She did allow him to run his big hands over her buttocks. He shuddered.

"Fuck, I knew you'd be wearing one of these sexy little bits of nothing again," he murmured. "They're enough to stop a man's heart."

Almost every piece of underwear she owned was a thong. This one was black lace and matched her bra. Having nice lingerie had always been a priority for her.

She smiled and backed away a little, then circled him, running her hands over his body and twisting her body up and down against his to the low music that filled the room. Tiya ground her hips against him, kissing and touching him as she went.

As she passed in front of him, laying a lick to his pectoral, he made a grab for her. With a light laugh, she twisted away from him and pranced a few feet away. Another faux innocent glance over her shoulder and she spread her legs and bent at the waist, showing everyone in the room her thong-clad derrière and pussy.

"Take them off," Charlie rasped behind her. "I'll come over there and do it for you, if you don't."

"Not yet," she sing-songed back at him. "Waiting for it makes it all the better." Smiling, she wiggled her ass at him.

Tiya had learned over the years how to excite a man, or a woman, to the point of breaking. The sexual tension in the room was now so thick you could breathe it in. Maria seemed to be doing just that. This evening was probably a feast for the Demi.

Slowly, Tiya hooked her thumbs under the scrap of material at her waist and pushed down. Adam groaned from the couch. With half her ass exposed she pulled them back up again.

"Angel, you don't get those off now, I'll come over there and give that sweet ass a spanking you won't ever forget," Charlie growled.

From between her legs, she winked. "Oooh, threats." She pulled her thong down to her ankles, leaving her dripping pussy exposed to the air and everyone's view. Tiya dipped her hand between her legs and fingered herself.

"Awww, baby, that's it," said Adam. "Let's see you push your finger into that sweet little cunt of yours."

"You mean, like this?" The words came out breathless. She was at her own breaking point by now. She sunk a couple fingers into her pussy, closing her eyes and biting her lip at the sensation of it. It felt good, but she wanted Charlie's cock there and nothing else.

Movement behind her told her she'd breached Charlie's limits of control. She straightened, stepped out of her thong and sauntered over to him. She made sure the lust she felt for him infused her gaze and the look on her face and in her eyes stopped him dead in his tracks.

Tiya came to a halt in front of him and kissed and licked his chest, then walked around behind him, but this time, instead of dancing, she hooked her leg around and used him like a pole on a stripper's stage. She ended up sitting on the floor in front him, both hands on his hips. Adam hooted and Maria clapped her hands and laughed.

Charlie looked down at her. "Holy shit, Tiya."

She just grinned up at him and pulled his boxers down.

Holy shit was right. He was so beautiful, he took her breath away every time she saw him.

His cock was ramrod-straight and hard. She bit her lip and looked up him with both eyebrows raised. Her mouth watered.

"Suck it, angel," Charlie rasped. "I want to see your pretty mouth wrapped around it."

She grasped it by the base and pumped him once up and down. Charlie tipped his head back and groaned.

"You want this?" she asked. She shifted to her knees and licked the head. "Are you sure?"

His hands went to her hair. "Tiya," he said in a warning tone. "I'm dangerously close to just...oh, yeeeah."

Tiya had decided to get down to business. She stuffed as much of that thick length into her mouth as possible. She groaned at the taste of him, the thick, hard length of his cock on her tongue and between her lips. This was a shaft she'd never tire of, not ever, she thought on a sigh.

Vaguely, Tiya became aware of motion coming from the direction of Adam and Maria, but didn't pay attention. Her whole world was Charlie's cock in her mouth. He'd fisted her hair in his hands and was fucking her mouth slowly. Her hands played over his hips and ass. Her pussy was sopping, engorged and needy.

She felt warmth at her back and the gentle pressure of a hard chest. Adam pushed her hair to the side and laid a kiss to her throat and a gentle brush of lips to her shoulder.

"Let us touch you," Adam said. He put his hands to her waist and slid them over her stomach, over her little belly ring and up to cup her breasts through her bra. "We both want to make you feel good, Tiya, all right?"

Tiya knelt in front of Charlie with her legs spread and her swollen, achy sex exposed. She groaned around Charlie's cock at the feel of his big hands massaging her breasts through the material of her bra.

"All right?" he whispered in her ear. "All in the name of pleasure. Just for tonight."

She hesitated, and then nodded.

"I've been dying to get a look at these pretty breasts." He unhooked her bra and pulled it off her.

Tiya had to cease the slide of her lips over Charlie's cock for a moment and pant as Adam palmed her breasts from behind and rolled her tight nipples between his fingers.

"Mmmm," Adam growled near her ear. "As sweet as I thought. I bet they taste even better." Tiya felt another hand on her. Soft, feminine fingers toyed with her belly ring, then trailed down to slid over her mound.

"She's got a pretty pussy, too," cooed Maria. "Smooth and pink and excited. Just the way I love them." Tiya's hips jerked when Maria stroked her clit. She dug her fingers into Charlie's hips as Maria sank a finger up inside her and glided it in and out.

Tiya groaned around Charlie's shaft at the overload of sensation, at having all these hands working her body all at once. It made her want to scream at the pleasure of it.

In a move that seemed almost orchestrated, Adam pulled her back away from Charlie to lie between his legs. She could feel the jut of Adam's cock at the small of her back. Adam palmed her breasts, then slid his hands down her inner thighs and spread her sex open wide for the view of both Charlie and Maria. "Someone want a taste?" asked Adam. "If no one does, I'm taking one."

Both Maria and Charlie moved down on her, one on each side. Two tongues licked over her at once and Tiya nearly lost it. Her back arched against Adam and she let out a long, low moan.

Charlie pulled her clit into his mouth and sucked on the aroused bit of flesh, tonguing over it. Beneath him, Maria toyed with her labia and licked down to her anus and back up. All the while, Adam palmed her breasts and played with the hard, excited nipples. The sensation of having all these tongues and hands touching her at once was indescribable.

Adam kissed her earlobe. "You are so sexy, Tiya," he murmured. "You don't know how bad everyone in this room wants a piece of your luscious body."

Charlie tongued her clit and Maria slid her tongue up inside her as far as she could push and started to fuck her with it. Tiya cried out as a climax hit her hard and fast. She dug her heels into the carpet and curled her toes as the waves racked her body until she could hardly see straight. They licked her until the orgasm finished pulsing through her body and all Tiya could do was lie there in Adam's arms and pant.

Maria backed away, her eyes heavy with lust and Charlie moved between her legs. Maybe the almost choreographed moves had been arranged on telepathic back channels they'd locked her out of. Tiya didn't know, and with Charlie crawling up her body with that dark, possessed, most uncivilized look on his face, she didn't care. Every part of her body tightened at the intention in his dark brown eyes.

"I need to be inside you now, Tiya," he murmured. He ran a hand up the outside of her leg, up to rest on her hip.

Behind her, Adam settled her against his chest, letting his arms come around to run over her stomach to play with her belly ring and then come up to caress her breasts and tease her nipples. Finally, Adam dropped his hands down to her inner thighs and spread her labia for Charlie.

Charlie dropped his hand to her pussy and stroked from her anus to her clit. Fissures of pleasure rocked through her, bowing her spine. Adam's hard cock stabbed into her back and his hard body braced her from behind. His groan reverberated through her body. "You're killin' me here, Tiya," Adam rasped.

Charlie dipped his head and pulled her swollen clit into his mouth and tongued over it. Tiya's eyes widened at the delicious sensation of having one man spread her pussy wide for another to lick. He toyed with her clit with the tip of his tongue and another climax ripped through her. Charlie dragged her shuddering orgasm out while Adam held her close, murmuring into her ear about good she felt against him, how sexy she sounded when she came.

Finally, the tremors ceased, leaving her body more excited than it had been before.

She levered herself up, away from Adam, and pushed Charlie onto his back. Giving him a look as dark, aroused and wild as the one he'd given her, she slowly crawled up his body. She locked her gaze with his and for that moment it was like they were the only two people in the room. Tiya felt the man's soul intertwining with hers in that instant. Two trembling spirits finding a match in each other during the most unexpected times and under the strangest set of circumstances.

Tiya wanted to take him inside of her any way she could.

She positioned her pussy over his rigid cock and slid herself down the hard length. She was so wet and turned on that her pussy took his huge shaft with no trouble at all. She tipped her head back and moaned at the sensation of him filling up every little part of her. Slowly, she lifted up and slid back down, slow, so slow, so she could feel every single ridge and vein of him.

Charlie's hands clenched on her hips and he groaned low. "You're driving me crazy with this pace, Tiya," he gritted out.

In the space of a heartbeat, she found herself flipped onto her back and staring up into his intent face. He pulled out and rammed himself back inside her. Pleasure suffused her body. "I need to move," he whispered.

He rose up above her, hooking her legs over his upper thighs, and then started to shaft her hard and fast.

Tiya reached out, wanting to find something to hold onto and groped air. Climax flirted hard with her body, and all she could do was pant and moan at the onslaught of pleasure at having Charlie slam into her so hard and fast. Finally, she found flesh as Maria moved in by her head. Her hands stroked over her breasts, teasing the nipples as Charlie slammed his cock into her over and over.

Adam leaned in on her side and stroked her clit.

Tiya's body seemed to explode in her climax. She screamed out Charlie's name as her pussy pulsed and contracted around his length. Her vision darkened from the intensity of it.

Charlie thrust himself as far as he could inside her and groaned out his own climax. He came down on her, kissing her cheeks and mouth.

Panting, they both lay for a moment in the sweet aftermath. Then Charlie pulled out of her, rolled to the side and pulled her close, spooning her back.

Maria and Adam were at each other, kissing each other like they wanted to eat each other's mouths off. Tiya let her gaze roam Adam's body. He was built solid, with muscles in all the right places. His cock was wide and thick and even his nicely shaped buttocks had dimples.

He and Maria were both on their knees, facing each other. Adam's hand trailed down between Maria's thighs. Tiya watched Adam's wrist twist and his hand move on Maria's cunt as he sank his fingers into her and start to finger-fuck her slowly, then faster and harder.

Tiya watched his broad fingers, wet with Maria's juices, appear and reappear over and over. Maria's moans grew louder and louder as she hung on under the treatment Adam was giving her.

Tiya felt her own breath catch in her throat at the erotic scene before them. Her heart rate increased.

Charlie ran his hand over her breasts, tweaking her nipples. He murmured in her ear, "You like to watch, angel?"

She nodded.

"You like to be watched, too, don't you? It gets you off."

"Uh-huh."

He slid his hands down and pulled one of her legs over his hips, then stroked over her sex. It was slick with her cream and his come. He rubbed their mingled moistures over her, circling her swollen clit.

"God," he groaned in her ear. "I can never get enough of you."

In front of them, Maria was coming. Her body shuddered as Adam's fingers worked her sex, then she tensed and moaned. "Come on, baby," Adam crooned. "Come all over my hand."

With a wail and a shudder, Maria did.

Adam hardly waited for her tremors to cease. He went around to her back and pushed her down on all fours. Scooping up all that cream she'd made for him, he coated her anus in it.

Tiya's pussy tensed at the way she knew Maria was about to be taken. Charlie slid his wet fingers down and rubbed over her labia until Tiya moaned. Then he slid two fingers into her dripping cunt to leisurely work them in and out.

She watched as Adam grasped Maria's hips and eased the head of his cock into her ass at her urging. Maria had her legs apart as far as they'd go, obviously wanting Adam's cock within her.

Charlie kissed her throat, making Tiya shudder. "You want to take me back here some time, sweetness?" He circled her anus with fingers, making all those little nerves leap to life.

"Uhnn," was all she could say.

"You want me to fuck you here?" he whispered as he slid what felt like his middle finger into her ass.

She moaned her approval.

In front of them, Adam was now taking Maria from behind in long, driving strokes. The muscles of his buttocks worked as he pulled out and pushed back inside. From this angle, Tiya could watch his shaft appear and reappear as he fucked her ass.

"How about here, too," Charlie murmured. He pressed his index finger into her pussy while his middle finger was still in her anus. His voice sounded strained now and she could feel his cock pushing against her again. "How about both places at the same time, angel? Would you like that?" He started to drive his fingers in and out of her.

"Oh, oh, God," said Tiya. She watched Adam fucking Maria in front of her, while behind her Charlie possessed her body once again, driving her hard and fast toward another climax.

"Is that good, Tiya?" he whispered. "Do you like what I'm doing to you now?"

The sensation of her pussy and anus being stimulated at the same time was beyond anything she could handle right now. She came in a pulsing, moaning frenzy all over Charlie's hand.

In front of her, both Adam and Maria keened out their own climaxes.

"Ah, Tiya, you gave me another hard-on," Charlie said behind her.

"Let's take care of it, then," she murmured back.

Charlie rolled her onto her back and mounted her, coming down over her body and pressing his hard cock into her pussy. She doubted she'd ever been so wet in her life. He worked his cock into her and took her slow and easy, kissing her lips and throat as his shaft glided in and out. Finally, he shuddered and came, bringing her with him on another orgasm. She'd lost count of how many she'd had.

They collapsed in a tangle on the floor.

Near them, Adam and Maria had also collapsed.

Sweet, satisfied lethargy stole over Tiya's body and she slept.

* * * * *

Charlie lay on his side, watching Tiya sleep. Her pink lips were parted and her dark lashes were swept down over her pale cheeks. She really did look like an angel, even if what she'd just done in the living room proved she was anything but. He pushed a tendril of her hair over her shoulder and fingered its softness before letting it fall.

She still tempted him beyond belief. Not only sexually, but every time she was near, the *sacyr* twisted and bucked in his stomach. Adam had the same instant, base reaction to her, but had controlled himself. Maria had also reacted to her, though it had been more from a place of lust than a thirst for her blood.

After their encounter in the living room, Maria had been as full as a kitten after a saucer of milk. As Tiya had slept, both he and Adam had fed from the Demi. Charlie almost never fed twice in one day, but with Tiya around it was necessary to keep himself sated. As it was, it was all he could do not to bite Tiya when they had sex. Considering the trauma she'd been through, that was the last thing she needed.

Earlier at Griffin House, he hadn't fed the Demi blood donor with sex in return, and he hadn't done so with Maria either. Right now, he simply didn't want to have sex with any woman but Tiya.

After Maria had gone, Charlie had lifted Tiya from where she'd curled up on the floor and carried her to bed. There had been envy in Adam's eyes as he'd watched him carry her away.

But Adam just wanted her for her blood. For Charlie, it went deeper than that. His feelings for Tiya seemed to grow more complex with every passing heartbeat.

Charlie leaned forward and kissed her smooth forehead. Damn, he was falling for her hard. It was the last thing he needed or wanted. It figured he'd fall in love with the first woman to try and kill him after the last one had pummeled his heart.

He let the tendril of hair fall.

No.

He wasn't going to do this again. He'd aid Tiya out of this mess and figure out what the hell was going on with Vincent, if anything was going on. Then, once things were squared away, he'd let this woman go. He couldn't afford to allow his emotions to get all tangled up and confused again.

With one last look at her face, he turned his back on her and settled down to go to sleep.

* * * * *

When Tiya heard Charlie's breathing fall into an even pattern of sleep, she flipped onto her back and stared up at the ceiling.

God, she was falling in love with him.

Chapter Ten

"Charlie," said Anlon as soon as he'd cleared the threshold at Griffin House. "Man, you will not believe what happened here last night."

"Hey, Anlon. How's Vincent?" asked Charlie. He'd masked the scent of Tiya on him using glamour. Charlie really hoped it held.

"He's better today. Every day he gets a little better."

Charlie took his coat off and gave it to a Demi to hang up. Evelyn stood near the pocket doors that led into the living room. Her brown eyes were wide and her normally dark-toned face was a shade paler. To Charlie's right a fresh bouquet of white orchids stood in the crystal vase on the dining room table. "What's wrong, Evelyn?" Charlie asked.

She gave a half-smile and waved her hand at him. "N-nothing. I'm fine."

She really didn't seem fine.

Charlie turned to Anlon. "What happened last night?"

Anlon motioned for him to come further into the house. "It was late, around midnight, and couple vamps came calling. They were looking for Vincent."

Instantly, an image of the Vampir who'd come calling on Tiya a couple of nights ago entered his mind. "What did they want with Vincent?"

"Come with me."

Anlon led him down the hallway, past the stairs that led to the upper floors of the house, to a door that opened to the basement. Charlie suddenly had a bad feeling about this.

Anlon opened the door, switched on the light and led Charlie down the stairs. "They were looking to kill Vincent," said Anlon. "But Colin, Harlan and I got them first."

Charlie stepped off the last stair into the dank, unfinished basement of Griffin House. Lying neatly against one wall were the two Vampir he'd fought with Tiya. They'd been killed with hawthorn by the looks of it. Charlie walked close enough to ascertain that they both had wounds made by a hawthorn baton, then backed away. They'd bled to death.

What the hell was going on? He really needed to have a private conversation with Vincent. Charlie turned toward Anlon. "Do you know why they wanted to kill him?"

He shook his head. "As of now, it's a mystery. One of them talked about enchanted blood as he was dying. Blood of the Fae. They talked about having to find a woman."

"So, these two just barged into an entire house of Embraced, set on taking one of them out?"

Anlon shrugged. "They were rogue. We were well within council law to kill them. It's like they were in bloodlust, crazy from it."

Vampir could go into bloodlust and start killing if they were denied blood for a time long enough to enrage the *sacyr*. When that happened, an Executioner usually had to be called in to prevent the rogue from injuring or killing anyone. The vamps he'd encountered in Tiya's house had seemed a bit crazy, but hadn't been in bloodlust. Things were getting stranger by the minute.

Charlie pursed his lips. "Strange. Usually a vamp in bloodlust goes after humans, not after one specific Embraced."

He nodded. "I know. I need to have a nice, long conversation with Vincent. Maybe he's involved something we don't know about. Maybe—"

"—It's related to what happened in the alley," Charlie finished for him.

"Yes."

Charlie walked to the stairs, but turned before ascending. "Anlon, do you want me to talk to him alone first? I mean, there's less pressure where I'm concerned. I'm not the territory keeper, the one he really wants to earn the respect of."

Anlon rubbed his hand over his chin. "That's probably a good idea, Charlie."

"I'll go up now." He turned and started to climb the stairs.

"Hey, Charlie, man," said Anlon.

Charlie turned.

"Do you know anything you're not telling me? I'm not accusing you or anything, but you've been gone a lot lately and I know you were pretty revved up by the attack. I didn't know if, maybe, you know, you'd been investigating the whole thing on your own or not."

Charlie hesitated and licked his lips. He didn't like withholding information from the keeper of this territory, but at the same time, he couldn't afford to trust anyone right now with Tiya's safety. Not even Anlon. "I don't know anything about it, Anlon," he answered. "I'm as confused as you are right now." That last part wasn't even a lie.

Vincent was sitting up in bed when Charlie entered the room. A board balanced on his lap, spread with cards for a game of solitaire. Vincent set it to the side and smiled when Charlie walked in.

Charlie flashed a smile back. Dammit, it was looking more and more like Vincent had something to do with the murder of Tiya's family and Charlie hated it.

He pulled up a chair and sat down. "Hey, Vincent, rough night, huh?"

"Yeah, so I hear. Lots of action around the house lately, I guess."

"Did the vamps get in here?"

"No, I never even saw them. Colin, Harlan and Anlon took care of the whole thing downstairs. I never even heard them come in."

"Really. Well, that's good for you, I guess. You have any idea what they wanted?"

Vincent reached over and played with the deck of cards. "Anlon already asked me." He looked at Charlie. "I have no idea, Charlie. I don't know anything about the fae being real or supercharged blood, or anything like that."

"Supercharged blood?"

Vincent looked away quickly and played with the deck of cards again. "That's what Anlon told me the vamps were talking about. Supercharged fae blood. I have no idea what they thought I had to do with anything like that." He gave a short laugh. "I mean, what the fuck? They think faeries are real? What have they been smoking?"

"Vincent, look at me."

Vincent kept playing with the cards.

"Vincent," Charlie infused his voice with steel.

Still, he didn't look at him.

Charlie reached over and slammed his hand down over Vincent's to cease the flip of his thumbs over the cards as he shuffled them.

Vincent looked at him.

Charlie removed his hand and felt his jaw lock. Anger unfurled in the pit of his stomach. He was sick of being played and being lied to. "Vincent, Anlon told me you talked about faeries being real when you were in the throes of the fever."

He frowned. "Huh?"

"I like you, Vincent. I don't want you to lie to me. I want you to think of me as a friend, okay? I have no reason to rat you out to Anlon if you've become involved in something bigger than you can handle. Just tell me what's going on so I can help you." *And protect Tiya.*

"Charlie, man, I'm telling you the truth. I don't know what the fuck is going on."

Charlie sat and stared into Vincent's wide eyes for several long heartbeats. "Are you lying to me, Vincent?"

"Are *you* lying to *me*?" Vincent looked down at the card deck. "I can smell her all over you," he gritted out. Vincent glanced up at him, his eyes snapping with rage. "You've been shielding hard, masking it, but I have a particularly good sense of smell and I can pick up a trace."

"Of what?"

A muscle worked in Vincent's jaw. "Violet. I smell fucking violet on you. I smell *her*." He picked up the deck with shaking hands. More from rage than anything else, judging by the hard tremor in his voice.

Charlie pushed a hand through his hair. "Yeah, okay, Vincent. You caught me out. I found her. I found her because I really wanted to kill her for what she did to you but—"

"But what?" Vincent spat out under his breath. "Did you make friends with her, Charlie? Have you fucked her? Are you sleeping with the woman who tried to kill me now?"

"She told me a story, Vincent, a damned compelling story. Now I'm wondering what exactly you've been into lately…and who you've been hurting."

"I have nothing to more to say to you," Vincent said coldly.

"Vincent, I'm asking you one last time. Please, help me get to the bottom of this. I want to protect you just as much as I want to protect the woman."

"Get out," Vincent ground out in a low, angry voice.

Without another word, Charlie left the room.

* * * * *

Charlie pulled Tiya into his arms when he entered Adam's apartment and inhaled the violet scent of her. She wrapped her arms around him and buried her face in his throat.

"You have news," she murmured. "You have something to tell me. I can tell."

Adam was gone for the evening and that was probably for the best. Charlie pulled away from her and headed for the kitchen. "Want a glass of wine or something?"

She looked at him suspiciously. "Why? Am I going to need to be drunk to hear what you have to say?"

Charlie pulled down a wineglass and a shorter glass from the cabinet. He poured merlot for her and made a bourbon and branch for himself. It was more like he wanted her nice and relaxed to hear what he had to say. The last thing he needed was to have her jump to a conclusion they couldn't make yet and do something rash. Tiya was one of the most impulsive people he'd ever met.

He handed her the wine and took a sip of his bourbon, studying her over the rim of his glass.

"Charlie, tell me whatever the hell it is you have to tell me already," she said.

"Take a drink of the wine first."

She looked down suspiciously. "Why, did you drug it?"

He gave her withering look. "Just take a drink."

Eying him carefully, she sipped it.

He pulled the glass from her hand, took her by the waist and kissed her long and deep. "Mmmmm," he said as he pulled away. "That's the best kind of wine tasting, in my book. I love the taste of merlot on your tongue."

"Charlie. As much as I love it when you kiss me…"

"Okay, I want you to stay calm, all right?" He told her everything.

She stood staring at him. "So, it doesn't seem complicated to me. Vincent is lying to you about not knowing what's going on. It's obvious he's the one with all the information. Hell, maybe he's even the ringleader of this group of fae-seeking vamps."

"*Calm*, I said." Charlie just couldn't imagine Vincent as a "ringleader".

Her eyes flashed dangerously. "I *am* calm, Charlie. I'm also pissed as hell. Whose side are you on anyway?"

"Yours, Tiya. Completely on your side, but I want to make sure we know the truth before we take any action."

She walked away from him, set the wineglass on the counter and hugged herself. Tiya turned toward him. "So, why don't you want to take things at face value here? The vamps seemed crazy enough when they came to my house the other night. I wouldn't doubt they'd be stupid enough to break into Griffin House and try to kill Vincent. The question is why they'd want him dead."

"Yes, that's one question."

"There are more questions than that one?"

"Maybe. I'm not trusting anyone at this point." He walked toward her. "Tiya, if you don't really trust me, I understand. We haven't known each other very long."

She shook her head. "No, I do trust you, Charlie. I do." She looked up at him. "I've been sleeping beside you every night, haven't I? Sleeping in your arms, in fact. I wouldn't do that if I didn't trust you."

He nodded. "Please trust me a little longer. Let me try and sort this all out."

She tried to push past him, but he took her by the shoulders. "What choice do I have?" she mumbled. "It's not like I can bust into Griffin House and question Vincent at hawthorn point."

"That's what you want to do, isn't it?"

She looked up at him. "Yeah, that and more. Unfortunately, Vincent is protected there. I wouldn't even make it to Vincent's room before Anlon's vamps had me and what would they want to do to me?"

Fear gripped Charlie at the thought. If other Embraced reacted to Tiya the way he and Adam did... "Promise me you won't do anything on your own, Tiya."

The expression in her eyes was bitter. "I can't make that promise, Charlie. I can promise I'm not going to go after Vincent as long as he's in Griffin House. That would just be suicide. I might want revenge, but I don't want it bad enough to sacrifice my own life."

It would have to be enough for now.

Charlie.

Charlie set his glass down on the counter and stepped away from Tiya, hearing Anlon open the telepathic communication thread between them. It was so much faster and easier than a phone.

Yes, Anlon?

Pause. *I just thought you should know that Vincent is gone.*

Gone? What do you mean?

He left Griffin House tonight.

Do you have any idea where he might have gone?

No. He just took off. Look, Charlie, we know about the woman. We know everything. Vincent spilled before he took off.

Charlie fell silent for a few heartbeats. *What* exactly *did he tell you?*

Anlon's voice went chillingly cold. *Why? Are you afraid he revealed something you wanted kept secret?* Pause. *Something you don't want me to know?*

Maybe. You're not my keeper, Anlon. I keep the secrets I want to keep.

Silence. The coolness that stretched between them seemed to deepen. *Come to the house tomorrow and I'll tell you all I know. Bring the woman.*

No. I won't bring her to Griffin House. Hell, I know she won't go anyway.

Anlon sighed. *We can keep her safe here, Charlie. Vincent has closed down all communication pathways with me. I don't know what his intentions are. Bring the woman here and she'll be safe.*

Charlie paused. *I'll think about it.* He broke the thread.

Charlie turned and looked at Tiya. "I have more news."

She took a step toward him. "What is it?"

For a moment, Charlie considered not telling her, making up some story that would ensure she wouldn't go rushing into the night after Vincent, but he couldn't do that. She deserved all the information he could give her, no matter the result.

"What?" she asked again.

"Anlon told me that Vincent left Griffin House, that he spilled everything he knew and ran away."

She halted in the middle of the room. "And you believe him?"

"At this point, I don't know who or what to believe. I know that when I was there, Vincent wouldn't tell *me* anything. He may have been more at ease telling his keeper about the situation than me." He shrugged. "Anlon has given me no cause to distrust him. On the contrary, I think he's a good keeper who cares about his people. He said to bring you to Griffin House tomorrow for your protection and he'll tell us everything. He said he doesn't know Vincent's intentions and wants to keep you safe."

She folded her arms over her chest. "Bring Vincent on. I hope he does come for me."

"I figured you'd feel the way."

She gave her head an empathic shake. "No way am I running away to hide from Vincent. On the contrary, I can't find him so I can only hope he'll find me."

Charlie loosely fisted his hand as he walked toward her. When he reached her, he cupped her cheek in his palm. Tiya closed her eyes and sighed. "I don't want you anywhere near

Griffin House right now. Not before I can figure out what's going on…maybe not ever."

She opened her eyes and rubbed her cheek against his palm. "Why, Charlie, you actually sound as if you care about me." She gave him a slight, coy smile and batted her eyelashes at him.

He pulled her close and murmured, "Imagine that," right before he took her mouth in a hot, possessive kiss. She wrapped her arms around him and opened her lips for him. He slid inside and stroked his tongue against hers, tasting wine and sweet Tiya.

She shuddered against him. "Why do I want you all the time, Charlie? What is it about you that makes me so hot twenty-four/seven?"

"Does that mean you want me right now?" he growled into her ear.

"Always," she answered breathlessly.

He slanted his mouth over hers and slid his hand under her ass to pick her up from the floor. She wound her legs around his waist as he bore her backward to the wall bordering the kitchen and living room. They hungrily consumed each other's mouths as they went. They reached the wall and Charlie pressed her against it. Instantly, they started pulling each other's clothes off.

Chapter Eleven

"What if Adam walks in?" she asked as she pulled his shirt over his head.

He worked to get her panties down and off. "He can watch, but he can't touch. I'm not sharing you again. I'm sorry, Tiya. You're mine."

She smiled and it went straight to his heart and squeezed. "That's fine with me, Charlie."

Charlie raised his gaze from her slender feet, up her long legs to her perfect mound. Unable to resist, he dropped to his knees, spread her upper thighs and snaked his tongue in for a taste.

Above him, Tiya gasped.

He gazed up her gorgeous body. All she wore now was a lacy, dark green bra. "Open for me. I want better access."

She spread her thighs and he licked as far back as he could get his tongue and drew it forward, feeling her soft, smooth labia and the lovely little aroused nub of her clitoris. He laved over her clit, teasing it with the tip of his tongue. Tiya shuddered and moaned. God, she tasted good. He closed his eyes and savored it. Charlie continued to play with her clit, feeling the bit of flesh grow larger, engorging with blood, readying itself to climax. Back and forth he licked it, focused on one goal.

"Charlie," she gasped, "you're going to make me come. Oh, God, I'm coming!" She cried out and he felt her pussy spasm. He snaked his tongue in while her climax racked her body and stuck his tongue up into her hot little cunt. He thrust in and out as deep as he could, lengthening her orgasm. Above him, she shuddered and clenched her hands on his shoulders. He groaned and closed his eyes at the musky scent of her and the lovely cream that spread over his tongue as she came.

"God, Charlie," she panted.

He kissed his way up her body, stopping to worship the gentle bulge of her breasts at the top of her bra, before claiming her mouth once again and letting her taste herself on his tongue. Tiya trembled in his arms from the force of the climax. It didn't stop her hands from straying to his cock, however. He was hard and ready. The feel of her strong fingers closing around his base and stroking up his shaft made him groan into her mouth. The feel of her hands on him, the taste of her mouth on his tongue, it was ambrosia.

"Come on, Charlie," she whispered. "Take me. I want to feel you inside me. I can't wait for it."

And she wouldn't have to. He couldn't wait to feel the slick, hot muscles of her sex gripping his cock, her soft breasts against his chest and her moans and sighs ringing in his ears. He slid his hands down her back, cupped her ass and lifted her to impale her on his cock. The difference in their heights wouldn't allow him to take her against the wall with both of them standing.

Tiya bit her lip and grasped his shoulders, helping to slide him into her welcoming body. "Ah, yes," she hissed as he thrust himself home. He pressed her against the wall behind her, pushing all the way into her hot depths. Then he pulled back out and thrust back in balls-deep.

Tiya moaned and set her teeth to his shoulder as he took her a little bit harder, a little bit faster. He spread the cheeks of her ass where he held her and toyed with the sensitive nerve endings around her anus.

He pulled out, and then thrust it all back in, every last inch of his cock. He pummeled her hard and fast until she squeezed her eyes shut and bit her bottom lip. She drew blood and he couldn't resist. He caught her bottom lip in his mouth and drew on it, sucking out every bit of blood he could get.

"Open your eyes." The words were harsh and guttural. "I want you to see me while I make love to you."

She opened her eyes and gave him a little smile. "Make love, huh?"

"Oh, yeah." He captured her lips and slanted his mouth over her, driving his tongue deep into her mouth over and over until she moaned.

"Ah. God, that's good," she murmured between kisses. She moved her mouth to his ear, and drew his earlobe into her mouth to tug at it with her teeth.

"You like that, huh, Tiya?" He slid his fingertip into her anus and Tiya bucked in his arms, threw back her head and cried out.

Oh, yeah, she liked that.

He wanted more from her, though. In this position, he really couldn't play with her the way he wanted to. He didn't have the freedom of movement for that. Charlie backed away from the wall, still holding her, and sank to the living room floor to lie on his back. His extra vampiric strength definitely came in handy at times. Now she straddled him, giving him unlimited access to her pretty little anus.

Tiya rose up until she almost pulled his cock out of her, and slid back down slowly to impale herself. Charlie groaned at the feeling of her hot pussy eating up all the inches of his shaft so slow and easy. She held his gaze with an intensity that deepened the sexual pleasure, made him realize how hard he was falling for her.

He closed his eyes. God, he didn't want to.

Once she was all the way down, she reached back and unhooked her bra. Those lovely, full breasts tumbled from the lacy cups and Charlie caught them in his hands to knead. The small pink nipples were erect and so very, very suckable. "Let me taste," he murmured.

She leaned forward and he caught one in his mouth and worked the other in his hand. With his tongue, he worshipped every hill, every valley with exquisite thoroughness. Tiya whimpered and fucked him slowly, rising up and coming back down on his cock as if she wanted to drive him insane with the torment of the pace.

Two could play at that game.

He switched breasts, giving the other the same careful treatment. She whimpered again and picked up the pace. Her juices trailed down over him from her body. Her cunt practically cried out for a hard, fast fuck.

She pulled her breasts away. "You ever make a woman come just by sucking their nipples?"

"Once or twice."

"Oh, God. I'm not surprised."

He smoothed his hands down her sides to cup her buttocks. "I make more women come by playing back here." He skated his fingertip over her anus and she shuddered. He scooped up some of the cream from her pussy and slid his finger inside. Her hips bucked and she moaned. "Lift up a little, Tiya."

She elevated herself a bit higher, so he could move. He thrust his hips up and down, driving his cock in and out of her while he slid his index finger in and out of her anus. Tiya closed her eyes and bit her bottom lip. "It's so good, Charlie. God, it feels so good."

He added a second finger and felt her muscles relax for him. Her body was excited, ready for anything. He thrust three times and she came all over him. Her muscles pulsed and rippling around his cock and she cried out.

Panting, she leveled her gaze at him. "I want *you* back there. *Now*."

He pulled his fingers free of her and rolled her over, so he was on top. Hard and fast, he worked his cock in and out of her pussy until she was keening for him. She was wet enough, open enough, that they wouldn't even need any lubricant. He pulled his cock free. He wanted use some anyway to be sure he didn't hurt her. "Get on your hands and knees. I'll be right back." He went into the kitchen and found a glass jar of olive oil.

When he came back, she was on her hands and knees presenting her luscious swollen, already well-loved sex up to him. It hung like ripe fruit and he couldn't suppress a growl as he fell to his knees behind her and ran his fingers up it.

She wiggled her ass and moaned and he couldn't wait any longer. He coated the head of his cock in some of the olive oil and covered her back with his chest, pushing the crown of his shaft against her beautiful pussy. He grasped the base and teased her with the slick head a little before he set it to her anus.

Beneath him, her body tensed. "It's been a while, Charlie."

"Are you sure you want to do this?"

She nodded her head. "Oh, yeah."

He kissed her shoulder. "Relax, Tiya. Just relax. You're open and wet enough for this not to hurt a bit."

She laughed and murmured, "That, coming from a man hung like a Mexican bull. Easy for you to say." Still, he felt the tension ease out of her body.

He thrust his hips forward and breached her entrance easily. All those tight muscles gripped the crown of his cock, making him groan. "Fuck, Tiya, you're so damn tight. Are you okay?" he asked.

Tiya moaned before dropping her head down and pushing her hips up at him for more.

He took that as a yes. Charlie eased himself in another inch and grasped her hips, fighting the urge he had to pound straight into her. "God, you're hot and tight, Tiya. So fucking sweet."

She whimpered and rocked her hips back, forcing him another inch. "More, Charlie. Goddamn it! Give me more."

"How do you want it? You want it fast and hard?"

"Yes! Please, Charlie."

Still, he didn't want to hurt her. She might think she could handle it, but she'd said it had been a while for her. He pushed himself in at a slow and steady pace as far as he could go. Tiya balled her fist and hit the floor, moaning and thrusting her hips back at him. It was almost enough to drive him insane.

He slipped his hand around to her front and dragged his fingers up her dripping cunt and stroked her clit back and forth. "Tiya, calm down," he purred. He caressed her clit relentlessly, holding her hip with his other hand in an effort to keep her still so he could shaft into her. Finally, she relaxed and went still.

He gripped her hips with both hands and held her still while he pulled back out and pushed back in, grunting at the way her ass gripped him. God, he *was* going to go insane. He stroked in and out of her a few more times.

He was going to come, too.

"Ah, Tiya, you feel so fucking unbelievably good," he murmured as he slipped his hand down around her front once more to stroke first her lovely, suckable clit and then to slick over her wet labia to her slit. "How ready are you to come for me, baby? How far can I push this sweet body of yours?" He teased her opening and she shuddered.

"You want me in here, too, Tiya?" he asked. At the same time, he rubbed his fingertip through the heavy cream at the entrance of her cunt, stroking over her silken skin.

"Charlie," she moaned. "You're going to make me crazy."

"Then that'll make two of us." He slid his finger inside her tight, wet slit and she moaned. His cock jumped inside her at the feel of her silken muscles gripping at him. He found her G-spot and caressed it and she cried out.

"Take me hard and fast, Charlie," she begged. "Please."

Still rubbing that magical bundle of nerve endings way up deep within her, he braced himself on the floor with his other hand and set up a punishing pace behind her, thrusting in and out of her in long, easy strokes.

"I'm coming, Charlie. Oh, God, don't stop, I'm coming!" Tiya cried out. A second later, her body trembled and shuddered as her climax hit her. The muscles of her pussy pulsed around his finger and the muscles of her anus tightened on his cock.

It sent him over the edge. Feeling ecstasy tighten his balls and spill up and out, his own climax ripped through his body. His cock jumped in Tiya as he spilled his come into her.

Panting, he folded Tiya into his arms and they tumbled to the carpet together. He smoothed her hair away from her forehead and scattered kisses wherever he could. Her hair was tangled across the carpet in long gold skeins, and her beautiful face was flushed and perspiration sheened her skin, making her appear made of satin. All he wanted was to hold her, keep her, care for her, protect her.

Damn if he wasn't doing the one goddamn thing he didn't want to do.

Fall in love with her.

* * * * *

Later, in bed, Tiya tucked herself as close to Charlie as possible. They were both freshly showered and naked and she wanted as much of her skin touching his as possible. The feel of his body against hers was becoming a deep contentment and she really needed a balm for her troubled thoughts and emotions tonight.

Somewhere beyond the door of their room, Tiya picked up the sound of Adam coming through the front door of the apartment. He dropped his keys on the counter, softly whistling some old little song. The hallway light switch snapped on and light spilled under the door. A few seconds later and Adam had entered his room. The light switched off, dousing the guest room in darkness once more. It seemed so cozy to be cuddled up against the man she cared for, hearing sounds beyond their room and knowing she was safe in his arms.

Charlie pulled her close to him and kissed the top of her head. Tiya closed her eyes and inhaled the scent of his skin. It had taken no time at all for her to link her life with his, for her to start caring deeply about him. She had no idea where any of this was leading...not the Vincent situation, or whatever it was that was happening between herself and Charlie. Right now all she knew was that she wanted him to hold her for the entire night. She wanted to feel his breath on her skin. She wanted the scent of him rubbed into her flesh, marking her.

Tomorrow could take care of itself. She wouldn't think of it now.

"I wonder where Vincent is laying his head tonight?" she murmured into Charlie's shoulder. "Probably nowhere near as good as where I'm laying mine." She smiled and rubbed her cheek against his skin.

He rubbed her back. "No way to know. I don't think he'll come after you tonight."

She lifted her head a bit. "Why not?"

He lowered his head and kissed her, then gathered her close. "Okay, I'm hoping he doesn't."

"What? You don't think we can take one young Vampir ourselves?"

"It's not that I don't think we can do it, it's that I don't want to do it."

She stiffened in his arms. If it came down to a choice between her and Vincent, who would Charlie choose? She closed her eyes against a sudden prick of tears, realizing she didn't like being unsure of the answer to that question.

Charlie bussed his lips across her cheekbone. "What are you going to do when all this is over, Tiya?"

She opened her eyes. "I guess I'll go back to my old life, go back to Seattle. I have a business there that the managers can't run alone forever." She traced her finger over his chest, where the moon spilled silver on his skin. "What are you going to do?"

He sighed. "I have unfinished business with Gabriel. I'll go back to Newville and we'll take care of it. I'll stay there for a while, maybe not permanently."

"Where would you go if you didn't stay in Newville?"

"I have money in the bank. I can go anywhere I want to go. Truth is, I don't know."

"Have you ever thought of trying for your own territory? Adam says you're strong enough to hold one."

"Adam's strong enough to hold one, too. He hasn't tried for one, either."

Tiya rubbed her cheek against his warm chest. "You know that wasn't even close to an answer."

"Yeah, I know."

Tiya let it go. She sighed and snuggled so close to him, it was like she was trying to crawl inside him.

Yes, tomorrow could take care of itself.

* * * * *

"Before I leave for Griffin House, I want to move you, Tiya," Charlie said calmly as Tiya took a sip of orange juice.

"Move me?" She set the glass down. "Move me where?"

"Somewhere other than here. He hasn't ingested your blood, but Vincent can easily guess where you are. Let's move you to a hotel, maybe."

Tiya stood. The gray shirt she wore today complemented her eyes, eye that snapped with sudden anger like thunderstorm through a blanket of snow and ice. She was even more beautiful when she was pissed at him. "I'm not going anywhere."

He sighed. "Tiya, I'm afraid that in a fight, you might not come out the winner in a one-on-one with Vincent."

She crossed her arms over her chest. "Oh, really? I did in the alley."

Damn. He was in trouble now. "That was an ambush. Not a fight Vincent initiated. Not one he was ready for. And I might not be there to help you."

"And whose side would you take in that fight, Charlie?"

"What kind of a question is that? I might not be there *for* the fight, Tiya. That's my concern."

"It's my choice and I choose to stay here."

"I'll stay home with Tiya while you go to Griffin House," said Adam from behind him.

Charlie turned toward the hallway and saw Adam leaning against the wall, barefoot and shirtless, wearing only a pair of jeans.

"I can be protector number two. Vincent can't do anything on his own," said Adam. "He'd never be able to get through both Tiya and me together. She'll be safe."

"That would be good, Adam," answered Charlie.

Tiya threw up her hands. "Great, now you guys are thinking I need a babysitter. I'm pretty sure I've proven that I can take of myself in a fight."

Charlie took a step toward her, hand extended. She stepped back, drawing away from him.

He dropped his hand. "Tiya, I only want to keep you safe."

"I can keep myself safe." Her voice had a harsh edge to it.

He believed her, but it didn't stop him from feeling protective of her.

When he left the apartment five minutes later, she still wouldn't look at him.

On the way over to Griffin House, it was her face and her angry eyes that danced in his mind. It was her backbone, her stubbornness that made him clench his hands on the steering wheel.

Charlie knocked on the door of Griffin House, not bothering to hide the scent of Tiya on him. Now there was no need.

Evelyn opened the heavy red door with a wide smile on her lips and looked around expectantly. Her face fell. "You didn't bring her?"

Charlie shook his head.

"I was hoping to meet her. I've never seen a fae. When I was a little girl I used to hunt them in my garden." She sighed. "Oh, I did so wish to meet her."

Charlie entered the house, wondering at her reaction. After all, Tiya was responsible for the attack on Vincent. He'd been expecting more hostility toward someone who'd tried to kill a friend of hers. Maybe Vincent's confession last night had tipped the scales of sympathy in Tiya's direction. He really needed to find out the whole story.

A familiar scent wafted to his nose. He inhaled deeply. Violet hung in the air. He followed the source of the aroma and saw that Evelyn had abandoned her traditional white orchids in the vase on the dining room table. Today, there were violets.

Evelyn followed his gaze. She smiled. "I decided to do that in honor of your friend."

He frowned. "They're beautiful." And strange.

Evelyn led him through the living room, past a set of polished wooden pocket doors and into the study at the back of the mansion. It appeared most of the house vampires had left for the day.

Anlon collected old books. Here the built-in bookshelves that lined the walls were filled to the ceiling with the fragile, ancient spines of everything from Shakespeare to Voltaire. Anlon turned from the window, one hand tucked into the pocket of his dark blue trousers. His long dark hair was swept back and secured at his nape. "You didn't bring her."

Charlie shook his head.

"Why not?" Anlon took a step toward him. "Don't you trust us with her?"

"No, actually, I don't."

Anlon's eyes snapped with rage for a moment, then it was gone, replaced by weary sadness. "I'm so sorry you feel that way, Charlie. I really am."

"I'm sorry, too, Anlon."

He turned back toward the window. "So, faeries, huh? The fucking Tuatha Dé Danaan." He shook his head. "My childhood in Ireland was filled with stories about them. I can't believe they're real."

Charlie stopped in the center of the room. "Yes."

Anlon glanced at him and sighed. "Vincent said he'd been trying to catch a faery. Told Evelyn they were real, a race like any other. Said they'd been hiding from mankind for centuries. He says their blood is sweet, like a drug, and some faery blood bestows certain powers to the drinker. He told me that he'd hoped it would make him more powerful, powerful enough that I'd catapult him into my inner circle." Anlon laughed. "I thought he'd lost his mind, but Evelyn believes him."

"He hasn't lost his mind."

Anlon whirled on him. "Yeah, you know that because you've got one, the very one we've been looking for. You've been hiding the woman who tried to kill you and Vincent, both. What are you, crazy?"

Charlie shrugged. "Maybe."

"Darling," said Evelyn from the door of the study. "I'm going out for a bit, let you two talk in private."

Anlon nodded and Evelyn smiled at Charlie before she disappeared and closed the pocket doors to the room.

"You smell like a woman's been crawling all over you. Is that the fae? Is that the Tuatha Dé Danaan?"

"Yes."

"She doesn't smell any different than a regular woman. Touch of violet, maybe." He inhaled and closed his eyes. "That must be her perfume."

Charlie shrugged. "I'm not sure if it's a part of her actual scent, or if it's perfume. I suspect it's the former."

"It's haunting."

Charlie nodded. "*She's* haunting." He wasn't about to reveal the strange attraction that Embraced seemed to have for her. "So tell me what the hell is going on, Anlon?"

He narrowed his eyes. "I hoped you could tell me that, Charlie. You're the one sleeping with the enemy." His Irish accent, long washed away from years of living away from his home country flared when Anlon was angry. Charlie could hear a trace of it now.

Charlie raised a hand. "She's not the enemy. She's been wronged, Anlon. Her family was slaughtered before her eyes by a group of vamps with ties to *this* territory. How would you react, Anlon, if Evelyn was murdered in front of you? Wouldn't you want to go after the people who did it?"

He looked offended. "Of course."

"Tell me what Vincent told you before he took off."

Anlon pushed a hand through his hair. "He talked to Evelyn, not me. According to Evelyn, Vincent told her he was sorry for bringing trouble to our territory. He said he'd discovered that faeries were real and some of them had blood that would bestow random abilities on the Embraced when they drank it. He said he'd tried to organize a group of Vampir to go collect some of these faeries, but everything had backfired."

Charlie fisted his hand. "Did he say how he found this out?"

Anlon nodded. "He told Evelyn he'd come across a woman in uptown one night. He'd been out for fun and so had she, and he'd taken her blood. He'd noticed something strange about it, so he started researching to figure out the secret. You know Vincent is a researcher. You saw his room. It's filled with books and he's always on his damn computer. He ferreted it out, somehow. He found out the woman had been a fae. That led to more research which uncovered the information about certain Tuatha Dé Danaan having supercharged blood."

So, according to the information he was now receiving, Vincent really was the mastermind. He'd discovered Tiya's special family line, and then he'd found some vamps to help him gather them and things had gone awry. Seeing as how Tiya was tempting to even the older vamps with more control, Charlie could see how a younger Vampire might go a little crazy. Apparently, Vincent had done it all to gain strength and gain respect in Anlon's eyes. He'd always been ambitious.

It all made sense, but Charlie just couldn't believe it. There was something off. Something just didn't seem right. He was an excellent judge of character and Vincent simply wasn't the kidnapping type.

Charlie turned away from Anlon and walked to the large window that overlooked the rolling back yard of Griffin House. Deep in thought, he stuck his hand in his pocket and played with his key ring as he surveyed the mature trees and privacy-providing bushes. Behind him, he heard Anlon pour himself a drink.

Vincent wanted more than anything to impress Anlon and convince him to bring Vincent higher up the management of the territory. Typically, Vincent got to Anlon through Evelyn.

Charlie turned toward Anlon. "You said Evelyn saw Vincent last."

He nodded.

Evelyn.

Charlie remembered the violets when he'd come in, remembered her disappointment that Tiya hadn't come with him. It was probably just as she'd said. She was probably just excited to meet a faery, still…

Charlie ran and hand over his jaw and walked for the door. "I have to get going."

Anlon set his glass on his desk. "You just got here, man. We still have things to talk about."

He shook his head. "We'll talk later."

Anlon took him by the shoulder and spun him around. What showed in his eyes was less than friendly. "I'm the keeper of this territory, Charlie, not you. If you know something I don't about what's going on in it, I *will* get it out of you."

Because Charlie only had a suspicion and no concrete evidence, he didn't want to tell Anlon he suspected his wife might be into murder and mayhem. Somehow, Charlie just didn't think Anlon would handle the accusation well. Evelyn was his world. If Anlon suspected Charlie meant her any harm, it wouldn't be pretty and he didn't have time to play right now. He had to get out of here to investigate his hunch.

Hell, what was he thinking, anyway? *Evelyn?* She seemed sweet as sugar. She seemed even less likely than Vincent to be a kidnapper. Likely, he was grasping at straws. Nonetheless, he felt compelled to follow up.

Charlie shook off Anlon's grip. "I owe you nothing and I'm leaving now," he said in a steely voice. He turned and came nose to nose with Colin and Harlan, house muscle. Two more vamps stood behind them.

"Sorry, Charlie. You're not going anywhere," said Anlon. "You might as well take a seat and settle in."

Chapter Twelve

Tiya was reading a book and sitting on Adam's couch with her legs curled under her when someone knocked on the door. She lowered her book to her lap as Adam came down the hallway and into the living room.

"A vamp," he said under his breath. "I can feel one."

"So can I," she answered. She put her book down on the couch beside her.

"Tiya, go in the back."

She slid off the couch and went down the hallway toward the bedroom. It wasn't to hide, it was to get her hawthorn stake and malchete in case she needed it.

Just as Tiya reached into her purse and pulled out her weapons, she heard Adam open the door. "Hey, Evelyn," he greeted in a loud, friendly voice.

Evelyn. Tiya's mind searched to put an identity with the name. She was Anlon's wife and a friend to Vincent. Her hands tightened on her weapons.

Low voices came from the living room. Adam laughed. Holding the stake in one hand and the malchete in the other, Tiya inched toward the bedroom door.

"Tiya," Adam called. "Come on out here. Someone would like to meet you."

Tiya quickly crossed the floor and dug her wrist holsters out of her bag. She snapped them on and slid the hawthorn stake up the inside of one sleeve and the malchete up the other. She could draw them easily this way. She only had to be careful how much of the inside of her wrists she flashed. Luckily, she'd worn a loose, long-sleeved shirt today. She pulled the sleeves down to cover her weapons, leaving enough give in the cuffs for her to draw them if she needed to. There, now she could even shake hands, though she wasn't feeling very friendly.

Tiya smoothed the sleeves of her black button-down shirt over the wrist holsters once more for safe measure and walked into the living room.

Tiya took stock of the tall, slender woman who stood near Adam as soon as she hit the threshold of the living room. The woman wore her dark hair loose and almost to her waist. It was thick, heavy hair, like the kind you see in the shampoo commercials. Except shampoo commercial hair is almost always digitally enhanced and this was natural. Her face was heart-shaped. Her eyes were large and dark and glimmered with intelligence. The woman wore a long black dress with a stylish, sheer shawl around her slim shoulders. She looked like a model or an actress.

So, this was Evelyn.

Suddenly Tiya felt mighty frumpy in her worn pair of blue jeans and manly button-down shirt. When was the last time she'd had her hair trimmed?

The lovely Evelyn spotted her and her smile grew wider. She took several steps toward her. "You must be Tiya. I just couldn't wait to meet you. Oh, I've been so excited ever since I heard."

"Uh." Tiya crossed the floor toward her. "And you are?"

"Tiya, this is Evelyn Markam. She's—"

"I'm Anlon's wife," Evelyn finished with a huge smile. She had really, really white teeth and a charming English accent. Her smile faded. "You do know who Anlon is, don't you?"

Tiya took the hand she offered and squeezed it briefly, before she dropped her arms down to her sides to hide her weapons as best she could. "Of course, I do." She forced a smile. "I'm surprised to find you so...friendly, I guess. I mean, at the way I entered your territory."

Evelyn gave her a quizzical look. "Oh! You mean because of what you did to Vincent and Charlie?"

"Uh, yes." What was with this chick? Was she being sincere in her friendly vapidness, or was it just an act?

"Well, if Charlie can forgive you, I certainly can. And Vincent...well, Vincent appears to be quite guilty, doesn't he? I can't blame you for what you did to him. Frankly, I would have done the same in your position."

A measure of calm settled within Tiya, but she still wouldn't let her guard down. She licked her lips and tried not to sound eager. "Do you know where Vincent is?" she asked gently.

Evelyn reached out and took her hand. Tiya hesitated, and almost flinched away, before allowing her to take it. "No, I don't know where he is, but on behalf of all the Vampir in the territory and Anlon, himself, I came to tell you how very sorry I am for your loss."

As politely as she could, Tiya pulled her hand from Evelyn's grasp. "Thank you."

Evelyn abruptly made a high-pitched squealing noise. Tiya took a step back and put a hand to the handle of the malchete.

"You, uh, okay?" asked Adam.

Evelyn covered her mouth with her two perfectly manicured hands. She laughed. "Oh, I'm just so excited to meet a real, live faery!"

Tiya relaxed and dropped her hand from her wrist. Shit. What should she say to this woman? "I'm really glad to meet you, too."

Evelyn lurched forward and Tiya resisted the urge to back up. "You simply must tell me everything," she squealed. "I want to know it all. Where the faeries came from, where they live now...*everything*!"

Okaaaaay.

Evelyn pulled her over to sit down on the couch. All Tiya could do was follow behind and sit down beside her. "Uh, you know, you shouldn't even know we exist. I shouldn't really elaborate," Tiya said.

"Oh, please!" She clasped her hands together in front of her as if in prayer. "I'll keep your secrets, I promise."

"Well..."

A stricken look passed over her face and she looked quickly from Adam to Tiya. "I'm being so rude. I'm sorry. I just burst in here all excited and demanded you tell me all." She stood. "I'll go. You were probably in the middle of something and I interrupted. Charlie should be home soon and I should be leaving." She started for the door.

Tiya hesitated, then reached out and caught her forearm. "No, it's fine." She laughed. "Really. Stay." What the *hell* was she doing?

Evelyn turned toward her with a childlike, happy smile on her face and sat back down. "Thank you."

Tiya managed to smile a real smile back at her and they began to talk.

* * * * *

"Anlon," Charlie said patiently. "You really need to let me out of here."

"First, tell me why you're leaving so fast. What's going on, Charlie?"

Charlie turned from the solid wall of Vampir in front of him to spear Anlon with his gaze. It appeared that he wasn't going to be able to keep his suspicions secret, after all. "Do you believe Vincent could be the mastermind in a ring of Vampir set on kidnapping or murdering a line of OtherKin Sidhe descended from Cúchulainn?"

"Cúchulainn? What?" A confused look passed over his face. "What does Cúchulainn have to do with any of it?"

Of course, since Anlon was of Irish decent, he was familiar with the legends. "Just answer me. Do you think Vincent capable of organizing a worldwide ring of Vampir bent on murder and mayhem?"

"He's too young now, too weak. No, of course I don't think that."

"Okay. Who is Vincent constantly trying to please?"

"Me." He laughed. "Oh, so you think I'm behind it all now?"

"I don't know." Charlie walked into the room a bit, staring at the glass window separating him from freedom. At his back, he could feel the heavy gazes of the four house vamps. He turned. "Okay, tell me straight out. Are you in on this, Anlon? Are you friend, or foe?"

Anlon's eyes narrowed. "Friend. Why do you even have to ask, Charlie?"

Charlie still wasn't completely sure of that, but his gut told him that Anlon wasn't lying. He really hoped he could trust his instincts on this one. "Who else is Vincent always trying to please?"

"Evelyn." A look of surprise quickly followed on the heels of the puzzled expression on Anlon's face. He gave a bark of laughter. "You think Evelyn's the mastermind? You really have lost your marbles."

Charlie shook his head. "I don't know what I think. I know Evelyn just took off, though, and that Tiya and Adam are at Adam's place alone right now."

Another bark of laughter. "So, you think Evelyn went over there to, what, kill her? Kidnap her? Feed her to the demon she's keeping in the basement of Griffin House these past five years without my knowledge?"

Charlie shrugged.

"What drugs have you been taking lately? Evelyn wouldn't hurt a fly. She might go over to drag her shopping, Charlie. Maybe to make her tell her everything she knows about the fae over a cup of coffee, but Evelyn doesn't have a sinister bone in her body."

Charlie smiled sadly. "You'd be surprised how much people can surprise you."

"I've been with Evelyn for *fifty* years, Charlie."

His smile faded. "Even so. Sometimes people hide their true natures from those they love, or those they love simply can't see the truth…even after fifty years."

Anlon grimaced. "You're wrong about her. It's completely absurd, and I won't let you hurt Evelyn. I won't allow you to scare her."

"I don't plan to do either. Just let me go, so I can investigate my suspicions."

Anlon shook his head sadly. "No, Charlie. We're going to stay right here and wait for Evelyn to come back. You can tell her what you think of her to her face. After that, you can get the hell out of my territory. Take the little fae with you. *We'll* deal with Vincent and whatever he's done. It's our business."

Inwardly, Charlie chuckled at the image of Tiya sedately leaving this territory under Anlon's orders. That would only happen if he drugged her to within an inch of her life. "It's Tiya's business."

"Whatever, you're not leaving here right now."

Frustrated, Charlie pushed a hand through his hair and flopped down in Anlon's office chair.

* * * * *

Tiya peeled off her shirt and the wrist holsters and set them beside the sink. Then she leaned over to regulate the water of the shower.

She and Evelyn had talked of her family and the history of the Tuatha Dé Danaan for a long time. It had been nice. Tiya had even come to partially regret strapping her weapons on, since she hadn't needed them.

The rush of the water in her ears and steam clouding the bathroom mirror, Tiya peeled off the rest of her clothing and turned to draw the blue shower curtain back and step into the bathtub.

Charlie would be home soon. Tiya couldn't wait to hear what he'd found out from Anlon. Right now she felt relaxed and almost happy. Evelyn was an intense, strange woman, but overall, Tiya had liked her.

The door opened and Tiya heard commotion. Her heart jolted in her chest. At the same time she felt them — *Vampir in the room.*

Several of them.

She lunged out of the shower, toward her weapons, but something slammed forcefully into her before she could even clear the shower curtain. Strong arms wrapped around her, encasing her in the plastic curtain, which the man ripped from the rod. Sopping wet, madder than hell and naked, Tiya flailed and kicked, but those arms wouldn't let go. They were like bands of iron around her midsection. She screamed and the man clamped a hand over her mouth. She bit him.

"Damn little whore," the man yelled as he tore his bloody hand from her mouth. Other hands. Other people. She couldn't see them well because the shower curtain kept flapping into her line of sight.

She calmed so she could see and at the same time she coiled her energy up inside her, ready to fire.

In front of her stood Evelyn with a cold smile on her face. Beside her stood another vamp. In her hand she held a roll of duct tape. In her other hand she held a cold iron collar.

Tiya let loose with the fastball of energy she had ready. Evelyn stepped out of the way just in time and it hit one of the goons behind her in the hallway. He groaned and slumped to the floor, clutching his stomach.

The vamp to Evelyn's left snarled and lunged forward. He forcibly held her arms down, as Evelyn wasted no time leaning forward and snapping the collar around her throat. "There," Evelyn said. "Now we can train you to heel like a nice bitch."

Tiya spit in her face. She tried to reply but the cold iron made her throat close up. Cold iron always made her feel like she was being suffocated.

Evelyn calmly closed her eyes and wiped her spit away. "I firmly believe in the element of surprise," she said as ripped a length of duct tape off and placed it over Tiya's mouth. "Are you surprised, duckie? Were you nice and relaxed? Did you let that formidable guard down for me? Considering the work you made of my vamps in Wales, I figured a full frontal attack was out of the question. Not with all that powerful Cúchulainn blood running through your veins. I needed to psych you out a bit first." She laughed and clapped her hands. "It worked!"

Tiya stared at her with death in her eyes and breathed heavily in and out of her nostrils.

"Get her out of here," Evelyn commanded.

The vamp holding her hefted her and began to walk. She made an enraged sound in the back of her throat and whipped her wet hair in his eyes as she kicked and flailed. She wasn't going down without a serious fight. He stumbled and fell against the doorjamb of the bathroom. A quick glance told her that the weapons she'd set on the bathroom counter had been removed. Tiya kicked hard, connecting with a kneecap. The man holding her grunted, but didn't let go. He just picked her up as he cursed her out loudly and brought her into the living room.

When they entered the living room, her struggles ceased and her blood ran cold as she spotted Adam lying in the middle of the living room floor. He lay facedown and pools of blood came from his head area and somewhere in the vicinity of his stomach.

Had they used her hawthorn stake on him? Her stomach roiled at the possibility. Black spots dotted her vision as images of her family's deaths rose up to greet her. Breathing deeply in and out through her nose, she fought to retain consciousness.

Evelyn came to stand in front of her. The Vampir bitch from hell perused Tiya from head to toe. Tiya was wrapped in the shower curtain, wet and barefoot. Again, she felt defenseless in the face her attackers because she was naked. Tiya's hard breath blew a tendril of damp hair back and forth. All Evelyn did was smile.

The instant after the shock of seeing Adam had worn off, she started to fight again. The vamp who restrained her hardly blinked an eyelash, however. He just bore her out the door. Evelyn and the rest of her muscle followed. They were probably counting on glamour to mask her, so they could get out of the building without being noticed. Once outside in the hallway, Tiya started to struggle harder. She'd make masking her as difficult as possible.

Evelyn snarled at her and hit in her the head. Blackness consumed her.

Chapter Thirteen

"Where the hell is Evelyn, Anlon? She's been gone a long time."

"She's shopping. She'll be back. You stay put."

Charlie sighed, sick of the little power game Anlon was playing. *Adam?* Charlie opened the telepathic channel that stretched between himself and Adam. *How's Tiya?*

Nothing. No response.

Adam?

Again, nothing.

Well, hell. That wasn't good. Something cold settled in the pit of his stomach.

Charlie moved from where he'd been leaning against a row of bookshelves and walked over to stand behind Anlon's desk. He curled his hands over the top of the expensive leather office chair. "It's too bad you feel you have to keep me here, Anlon. I think it's time for me to leave."

"Too bad for you, you mean," said Anlon.

"No. Too bad for you." Charlie pulled the office chair out and hefted it up and over as hard as he could toward the large picture window. The heavy chair slammed through it under the force his vampiric strength, shattering the glass.

Charlie was right behind it. As he leapt out onto the grass, a shard of broken glass tore through his black leather jacket and into his forearm. Pain ripped up his arm and his blood gushed, but the wound didn't slow him down. Charlie rolled to his feet and shot toward the street, wishing like hell he could shift into a raven like Gabriel right now. Instead, he had to get to his car.

His strength manifested in the power of his glamour, not in shifting.

Behind him, he could hear Anlon and the four house vamps scrambling out the window behind him. He had no time to play with them. He needed to get over to Adam's and move Tiya somewhere safe, despite her protests, then he needed to examine Evelyn more closely. Hopefully, he could rule her out.

Why the hell hadn't he considered her before? She'd simply flown under his radar with her sweet, unassuming smile and her white orchids. Those who appeared sweet and innocent could get away with murder sometimes.

Charlie reached his car and got in. A large black panther, Anlon in his shifted form, hit the driver's side door with a thump that rocked the vehicle as Charlie started it up and revved the engine. He slammed on the gas and squealed away from the curb, forcing the panther to back up quickly and get out of the way.

In his rearview mirror, Charlie watched Anlon shift back and crouch in the center of the street, staring at Charlie's car as he sped around the corner at the end of the block. The last image he had was of the keeper with his dark head bowed.

Charlie tightened his grip on the steering wheel and guided his car toward Adam's place. As he drove, he wondered why Anlon would try to hold him like that. Did Anlon know more than he was letting on, or was he legitimately worried about how Charlie would treat Evelyn?

Christ, Evelyn was probably as innocent as she looked. If so, he was going to owe Anlon a new window.

Finally, Charlie reached the apartment building. He parked his car outside and left it idling, though he cast glamour over it to make the vehicle appear shut off and locked up. Last thing he needed right now was a stolen car.

He took the elevator up and burst into Adam's apartment. Before he could draw a breath to call for Tiya, something slammed him hard up against the wall beside the front door, knocking the breath out of him. The world dimmed for a moment before he could focus. He blinked. A square-shaped face with dark eyes and hair came into view. The face wore a grim expression. It was the expression this particular face always wore.

"Niccolo, what the hell are you doing here?" Charlie asked.

The brutal lines of his face didn't move. His forbidding expression didn't flicker. Niccolo could do stoic like nobody's business. "Looking for you and Adam." He released him and backed away. "I found Adam first."

Why did that sound so ominous? At the same time, he spotted a large spot of blood on the thick tan carpeting. He hadn't smelled it when he'd come through the door. Maybe his mind had been so focused on Tiya that it hadn't registered.

Charlie lifted his gaze to Niccolo's. "Where is he?" he asked hoarsely. "Did you find a woman here?"

Niccolo gave his head a tense shake. "Come."

Charlie followed Niccolo down the hallway and into the bedroom he'd been staying in with Tiya. Her violet scent infused this room even when she wasn't in it. It rocked Charlie back on his heels for a moment.

Adam sat bent over on the end of the bed, his elbows on his knees and his head between his knees. Charlie couldn't see his face. His hair looked wet and his skin pale. A crumple of bloody clothing formed a pile in the corner of the room.

"Adam?" Charlie asked. "What the fuck happened? Are you okay? Where's Tiya?"

Adam raised his head to look at him under the peppering of questions. His throat had been slashed. Charlie could see the line the knife had made from ear to ear. It looked like a macabre smile. His face was taut and pale. "I couldn't protect her, Charlie. I'm so sorry. They fooled us, overwhelmed us, and took her." His voice sounded rough, raspy.

Charlie's blood ran cold. He'd known it, of course. Known it as soon as he'd breached the entrance to the apartment and hadn't scented her within. He'd known the instant he'd seen the pool of blood on the carpet.

"It was Evelyn, wasn't it?"

Adam dipped his head in a slight nod. "She blindsided both of us this afternoon, Charlie."

Charlie ran a hand over his face. "All of us."

"We'll get her back," said Adam.

"Are you all right, Adam? What happened?"

He shrugged. "Evelyn came over all friendly like, pretending she wanted to know all she could about the OtherKin Sidhe and wanted to pal around with Tiya. Tiya had her weapons strapped on and I was alert, aware and ready, but she never made a move. They were talking, Evelyn was laughing. Evelyn spent a couple hours here, and then left. About a half hour after she was gone, when Tiya and I were just starting to relax, they stormed back in. She had five vamps with her. They slashed my throat and cut me stomach from sternum to crotch, almost. I don't remember anything after that." Adam flicked a glance to the bathroom door. "From the looks of the bathroom, they got Tiya when she was ready to take a shower."

Charlie instantly went to the bathroom. The shower curtain had been ripped from the rod and was missing. Water had pooled on the floor and bathmat. A container of bath beads had been knocked over and the contents were scattered everywhere. For a moment, Charlie forgot to breathe. She'd struggled hard against her abductors.

"You must've had Niccolo's blood to be healing so fast." Charlie said hoarsely when he came back into the bedroom. He pushed a shaky hand through his hair.

Adam nodded weakly. "Niccolo let me drink from his wrist. His blood is so old and powerful, it's healing me right up. If he hadn't shown up when he did—" Adam grinned weakly, "—I'd probably be starring in the big rodeo in the sky right about now. They meant to kill me. I was damned lucky."

Charlie turned to regard Niccolo. He'd almost forgotten he was in the room since Niccolo was usually a man of few words. He was leaning up against the wall, his arms crossed over his massive chest. "Why are you here?" Charlie asked him.

Niccolo shifted and glanced away. "The council contacted me. Said there was a rogue here responsible for masterminding about ten deaths throughout Wales, Ireland and Scotland. Told me to find out who it was and execute him. Turns out the *him* is a *her*."

For a moment, Charlie wondered how the council could still employ Niccolo, since he was wanted for murder. That was really strange, but he'd ask him later. There were more important things going on right now. "Do you know who contacted the council?" asked Charlie.

"A woman in Scotland. Said her family was being targeted by a group of Vampir and were being murdered one by one. Said they were connected to this territory. She said she didn't know why it was happening."

Vamps were likely targeting the rest of Tiya's family. Maybe another family member had also discovered the Vincent connection, but instead rushing into the fray herself, she'd done the sensible thing and called the Council of the Embraced, omitting the OtherKin Sidhe part of the story. "Is that all you know?" Charlie asked.

Niccolo pushed off from the wall. "That's all the council had for me."

Charlie nodded. "Okay, I've got more information for you. After I tell you all I know, we've got to get going. We have to find Evelyn and her vamps before they drain Tiya."

If they hadn't already.

About the second Charlie had finished telling Niccolo everything he knew, the sound of splintering wood, like a door being ripped from its hinges, met their ears.

"Ah, good, Anlon's here," said Charlie.

* * * * *

Tiya struggled to open her eyes. The first thing she noticed was that was she was cold. Her hands and feet felt like blocks of ice. The second thing she noticed was the dull vibration in her body, almost as if her magick was being stifled or snuffed out. That made her eyes open.

She blinked, letting the room come into focus. Instantly, she realized she was standing. Trying to move her arm gained her the knowledge that not only was she standing, she was chained to a wall in cold iron shackles at her wrists and ankles. The cold iron...that's what was making her feel like her magick was slowly being siphoned away. At least they'd taken the collar off her.

They'd dressed her...slightly. She wore a silky red nightgown that hit her about mid-thigh. The thing had spaghetti straps and showed a lot of cleavage. She was still barefoot and they hadn't bothered with underclothes, which was worrying to her. As if she needed more worry than what came with waking up a prisoner, chained half-naked to a wall by a bunch of vamps who wanted to drain her blood. She felt like a hunted deer, ready for slaughter. Actually, she kind of *was* a hunted deer, ready for slaughter. She swallowed hard.

Yeah.

She suddenly felt like a virgin sacrifice to a dragon. Except, of course, she was far from a virgin.

She raised her head and peered into the large, dimly room they'd put her in. It wasn't a dungeon, thank God. It appeared to be a normal room. Hardwood floors, neutrally colored walls. No windows. One door. Expensive-looking furniture scattered the room—a sofa, a few easy chairs, even an entertainment center. It looked like a great room in a mansion. Upon each table sat a flickering candle. They guttered in their containers, ready to extinguish, and cast shadows over the walls and floor.

Experimentally, Tiya tried to wrench her wrist free and got only pain for her effort. Hot blood trickled down her inner arm, where the cuff dug into her flesh.

Tiya froze, remembering how Charlie's pupils had dilated, how his entire body had noticed it when she'd drawn blood from her lip that day. She was stupid. Stupid. Oh, God, that had been so, incredibly...

The door opened.

Tiya's head snapped up at the sound. Beautiful, cruel Evelyn walked into the room. She still wore her outfit from that afternoon. From that, Tiya deduced she probably hadn't been unconscious for too long. Finally, some good news. Evelyn had twisted her dark hair up into a sleek chignon. Maybe she didn't want it trailing in her food. Tiya's breath caught in her throat at that last thought.

"The fae princess is finally awake," Evelyn said with a smile. She walked to her in a slow, slinky pace. "And she even brings me an offering," she purred as she eyed the trickle of blood from her wrist.

"Back off, sister. I'm not offering you anything."

Evelyn paused and raised an eyebrow. "Those are bold words from someone in your position. I don't know if you've noticed, but you're shackled and defenseless. Sass isn't a way to earn points in your favor, duckie."

"Points?" Tiya laughed. "What do points matter when you're just going to kill me?"

"Kill you?" Evelyn said in surprise. "Darling, that's the last thing I want. If we kill you, you won't be able to produce that lovely blood for us anymore. No, we want to keep you nice and healthy. You *are* a fae princess as far as I'm concerned, one who has the blood of a demi-god running through her veins. A human is worth one pint of blood every eight weeks. I figure you're worth at least two during that same period, since you're Tuatha Dé Danaan. Why should we slaughter the cow when we can have her milk for life?"

Tiya really didn't like the cow analogy. If her ankles had been free, she would've kicked her for that one.

"What about my family," Tiya gritted out in a shaky, enraged voice. "You slaughtered *them*."

Evelyn's eyes snapped suddenly with irritation. She turned. "Yes, well, the vamps I sent to collect your family couldn't resist the temptation you and your line represent. The ones you didn't kill that day have been duly punished for that slip." She laughed. "In fact, they're all dead." Evelyn turned toward Tiya. "They were supposed to bring all the fae of Cúchulainn's line here...*alive*. Instead they went into bloodlust. Never send a man to do a woman's job, hmmm? You know that as well as I, duckie. They're weak to the pleasures of the flesh and can't be trusted."

"So killing my family was a pleasure of the flesh?"

Evelyn gave her the look of a predator and walked toward her. She reached out and placed her hands on Tiya's waist and leaned in until Tiya could smell her intoxicating breath. It didn't work on her. Only Charlie's breath seemed to calm her.

Evelyn brushed her lips over Tiya's cheek and then laid a careful, lingering kiss to her lips. Tiya grimaced and tensed her mouth into a flat line. Evelyn laughed softly and pulled away, trailing a finger over Tiya's jutting collarbone.

"You're like sunlight and roses to Vampir's senses. So alluring. So tempting," Evelyn murmured. She closed a hand around Tiya's injured wrist and squeezed until Tiya winced. Blood welled and trailed down her forearm. Evelyn dipped her head to lick up Tiya's arm, gathering every drop of blood that had dripped down. Tiya tensed at the feel her silken tongue tracing over her flesh.

Evelyn stepped back with a heavy look in her eyes. Her fangs were extended. They flashed white in her mouth when she spoke. "I can't really fault my men for going crazy, I suppose. You're *awfully* irresistible."

"And you're a Vampir bitch from hell," Tiya shot back, her voice shaking with rage.

Evelyn laughed. "Oh, my dear Tiya, you don't know the half of it."

"Charlie can feel me. He'll know where I am."

"Don't you think I haven't thought of that? We've planned for him and we're ready for him. I hope he shows up. I'd like to keep him alive. I don't need Gabriel on my back, but Charlie needs to be taught a lesson for intervening in the affairs of a territory that isn't his own."

"You taught that lesson to Adam, I guess." Tiya's voice broke on his name. Sorrow rose up at the mental flash of his body on the living room floor and threatened to overwhelm her.

"That was unfortunate. I didn't want it to happen. It complicates things, but he got in the way and it couldn't be avoided. Adam's dead by now, duckie. We're immortal, but if we're wounded bad enough, we die."

"And Anlon? Is he in on this, too?"

"Ah, Anlon, he's a good man. He really is. He's been trying to save me from myself for a long time now. He's never succeeded."

Tiya swallowed hard. That hadn't answered her question at all.

Evelyn threw her head back and sighed. "Ah, God, your blood in me feels so good, Tiya. You're incredible. Drinking from you is better than sex. Just that one little taste has enhanced my senses. I can smell and hear more acutely than I ever could."

"Great. Listen up, then. What are you going to do with me?"

She tipped her head forward to spear her with a confused look. "I thought that was clear. You're ours now. Our little pet cow, our blood slave. We keep you well, feed you, and bathe you." Evelyn smiled. "Pet you. Most of all, we'll drink from you." She smiled and spread an arm to encompass the room. "We now have fae blood on draft right in our living room."

Not if Tiya had anything to say about it. First chance she had, she'd try to escape. If that didn't work, if she really was going to be stuck here and forced to cater to their whims, well, prisoners used bedsheets for more than just sleeping, didn't they? More than one kind of escape was available to her.

The door behind Evelyn opened and a man walked in, his face was obscured by flickering shadows. He wore a pair of dark dress pants and an expensive-looking white button-down shirt. His dark hair came down to his collar. He walked out of the shadows and Tiya saw his face.

"Vincent," she stated in a flat, monotone voice.

"Hello, Tiya." His polished black shoes clicked on the wooden floor as he approached her. "It's so good to finally know your name."

"Yeah, it's a real pleasure to meet you formally."

He took two more steps toward her. "I have to say that seeing you all helpless and splayed out like a hooker takes a little of the bogeywoman aspect from you. You almost killed me, you know."

Tiya smiled sweetly. "I know."

Something violent and savage flashed through his eyes. "One wrong move and you're mine, Tiya," Vincent said in a deceptively soft voice. "I'm not as forgiving as Charlie. One good fuck won't turn me to your side."

Tiya's smile faded. "Charlie really believed in you, Vincent, right up until the end. He didn't want to think you were cruel enough to mastermind the abduction of OtherKin Sidhe."

Vincent spread his hands. "What abduction? We haven't abducted anyone yet. You practically came to us. No kidnappings, only murders. Those were unfortunate." He took another step toward her and she flattened herself up against the wall as much as she could. He inhaled. "But not unexpected. You really are tempting."

"Back away," said Evelyn. "Back away from her, Vincent." She sounded worried.

Vincent leveled an evil look at her before backing up. "You want her alive, so she'll stay alive, Evelyn." The look in his eyes when he glanced at Tiya seemed to add the words *for now*.

Chapter Fourteen

"Goddamn it, Anlon," Charlie yelled as he threw one of the Griffin House vamps across the room to slam into a dresser. "Will you please fucking listen for a minute?"

Anlon grabbed Charlie's lapels and pulled him to meet him nose to nose. All around them swirled chaos as Adam and Niccolo fought Anlon's house vamps. "Listen to what, Charlie?" he snarled into his face. His Irish accent was heavy now because he was so pissed off. "Listen to you accuse my wife of murder?"

"Where is she right now, Anlon, huh? Have you contacted her lately? What's she doing right this very minute?"

Anlon pushed him backward hard. Charlie caught himself before he toppled to the floor. Somewhere behind him a vase crashed against the wall. "She's getting a manicure," Anlon growled at him.

A manicure. Charlie fought the absurd urge to laugh. Instead he surged forward and punched Anlon in the jaw. He felt the split of skin and crush of bone under his fist. Anlon looked surprised at the force of the punch. He staggered back and sat down hard on the floor by the side of the bed.

"Fuck, Charlie," Anlon yelled as he put a hand to his face. "That hurt."

"Anlon, listen to Adam," Charlie yelled. "He saw the whole thing. We're losing time here. An innocent woman is about to die because you're blind, Anlon, blind! Evelyn is behind all this. *It's her.*"

Anlon just glared up at him. One of Anlon's vamps plowed into Charlie's side as he fought Adam. Niccolo picked up the vamp and tossed him out the door. Suddenly everything went silent. Apparently, Adam and Niccolo had been able to beat back the others.

"I can still feel her location," said Charlie. "But it's growing fainter by the heartbeat. I don't know if that means the power is wearing off, or—" he snapped his mouth closed. He didn't want to follow that thought.

"Evelyn didn't do this."

God, the man was in deep denial. "Great, then let's prove it by finding Tiya." Charlie reached down and offered Anlon his hand.

Anlon cradled his jaw in one hand and glared up at Charlie, Adam and Niccolo each in turn. "Fuck you."

"Come on, Anlon. You know we're going with you or without you," said Adam. He produced some handcuffs from behind his back. "But without you means we're going to have to restrain you. We can't afford any more delays, regardless of how fun it was to kick your vamp's asses."

Anlon spit out a bloody tooth and shot Adam a look to kill in reply.

"Sooo...handcuffs or the possibility of clearing your wife's name in front of a council Executioner," continued Adam. He motioned to Niccolo. "Yup, there's the Executioner right there. Hmmm...choices, choi—"

"Fine!" Anlon roared. "I'll go." He took Charlie's hand and Charlie helped him to his feet. "I'll gather up some muscle and we can get going."

"Uh, didn't we already render all your muscle pretty much, er, you know, useless?" asked Adam. He still looked pale to Charlie, but he definitely looked better. Niccolo's ancient blood was helping him to heal swiftly.

"I have more," answered Anlon tersely.

"I have a feeling Evelyn might have some of her own," said Charlie.

"Hey, man, I know she does. Remember? They almost killed me," answered Adam.

"What are you talking about?" Anlon snarled.

"*Dio*." Niccolo turned and walked toward the door. "Save it for the car. We have to collect some weaponry and get going. Adam, you can tell Anlon what happened on the way." He turned toward them at the doorway. "Where are we going, Charlie?"

"I feel her somewhere west."

"Come," commanded Niccolo.

* * * * *

If she could just get these cuffs off, she'd be able to punch Queenie Vampir in the head with a magickal fireball and get the hell out of this place, wherever she was. She had a feeling she could probably take boy wonder with her bare hands.

Evelyn sidled up close to her and ran her hand down Tiya's silk-encased waist, making Tiya stiffen. Her breasts brushed Tiya's breasts—deliberately, Tiya was sure—as she leaned in toward her throat.

Evelyn had decided that the taste of blood she'd had before wasn't enough. She wanted a deeper taste this time…directly from the vein. Actually, Evelyn had used the terms *teat* and *cow* in the same sentence, but Tiya didn't want to remember the exact wording. It was too enraging.

Vincent and three other vamps stood nearby. Just in case she miraculously managed to break her shackles and threaten their evil queen, maybe. Or maybe this was a pull-the-train kind of thing. Maybe they meant to go for a joyride on her veins as well.

Oh, happy day.

Evelyn's breasts brushed her once more, making Tiya grimace. "I'm not especially attracted to you, Evelyn, so you can quit with the ham-handed seduction."

She recoiled. "Ham-handed? I do believe I'm insulted. No one has *ever* called my seduction ham-handed." Evelyn gave a throaty laugh. "You were attracted to Maria, weren't you?"

"Yeah, well, she didn't want to chain me to a wall and keep me as her pet blood cow, either. That's not a real turn-on to a girl, you know."

Evelyn slid her hand to the small of Tiya's back and laughed softly. "You're chained now because you're not used to the idea of serving us. We'll treat you very well, Tiya. Soon, you'll elect to stay here with us. And, who knows, maybe I can find a way to turn you on as a bonus. There's nothing that says this situation has to be unpleasant for us."

Tiya laughed. "You are one crazy bitch."

Evelyn twined a hand into Tiya's hair and forced her head to the side, exposing the long line of her neck. "I'll be whatever you want me to be, duckie." She ran the tip of her tongue from the sensitive spot under her earlobe all the way down to the place where her shoulder and neck met. She kissed her skin once, and then...

She bit.

Tiya gasped. Evelyn didn't use any glamour to mask the pain and, goddamn it, it hurt. Tiya closed her eyes and panted as Evelyn drew blood from her body in a series of short hard tugs. Did she not use glamour deliberately?

A particularly hard pull made Tiya cry out. Images of her parent's murders rose up in her mind's eye, choking her. *The sound her mother's body hitting the floor. The blood...* Tiya made a mewling sound in the back of her throat and darkness started to consume her mind. She panted and swallowed hard, fighting to stay aware.

Instantly, she felt Evelyn's glamour roll out and cover her over. Tiya slumped in the shackles, relieved that the pain was gone. Warm pleasure coursed over her body, suffusing every pore. Tiya knew it was Evelyn's glamour and fought it. She was grateful for the removal of the pain, but the last thing she wanted was to feel pleasure at Evelyn's bite.

As quick as the rush of glamour came, it was gone. Evelyn raised her head from her throat and Tiya cried out as the pain from the wound overwhelmed her. "Ow! God, your glamour sucks!" she yelled.

"Shhh," Evelyn hissed as she backed away. "Everyone be quiet." She walked around the perimeter of the room, looking skyward.

Had she gone nuts, or what?

Blood trickled down her collarbone from the wound Evelyn had made at her throat and Tiya fidgeted uncomfortably in her restraints at the pain. She glanced up and stilled, realizing first that the scent of her blood hung heavy in the air and second that Vincent and the heavies behind him all had intense stares focused on that dribble of blood Evelyn had left behind her. Their hands were fisted at their sides. Their nostrils were flaring. They looked ready to pounce on her.

Ooooh, shit.

Here she was, all trussed up and nowhere to go, and her catnippy blood was currently trailing down between her breasts. Was Evelyn powerful enough to put down a mutiny?

That was the question.

One veeeery good question.

Tiya was unsure of the answer.

One of the guards behind Vincent was the first to break rank. "Just a taste," he muttered as he stepped toward her.

Vincent grabbed him by the shirt and pushed him back. "She's mine before she's yours," he snarled. "I'm *entitled*."

One of the other guards pushed Vincent to the side to get to her and all hell broke loose. All four of the vamps in the room started brawling over her.

Out of pure, base fear, Tiya started pulling at the shackles.

"Quiet!" roared Evelyn in a voice that chilled Tiya's blood. She sounded every inch a commanding queen. The force of that voice seemed to go straight through her bones. Evelyn's power rose like heavy smoke in the room. Wow, had her blood done that for her? Had Evelyn gained that much power from the recent feeding at her throat?

The vamps instantly froze in mid-punch, mid-sprawl, whatever. They all gave Evelyn their undivided attention.

"Someone's in the house. I can smell them," said Evelyn.

Tiya raised an eyebrow.

"Fee fi foe fum. Give me a fucking break," came Adam's muffled voice through the door. Someone kicked it open. Wood splintered and cracked. Charlie came through the door first, pistols in both hands, Adam second. Even more vamps she didn't know poured through after them.

A wash of relief went through Tiya at the sight of Adam. God, she really thought they'd killed him back in the apartment. Two other vamps she didn't know stuck close behind him. One vamp looked to be maybe of Italian descent, with dark hair and dark eyes. He had longish hair and was a big, muscular guy. He was gorgeous, of course. Most of them seemed to be. The other was also dark of hair, but had blue eyes. Her gaze caught Charlie's and euphoria filled her.

"Are you okay?" Charlie asked her from across the room.

"No, no. I'm really not okay. Get me the hell out of these chains, so I can kick some ass, please?" she answered, and then smiled. "God, I'm so happy to see you."

She only had a split second to be happy, however, because all hell broke loose...again. Evelyn's vamps rushed Adam. Charlie, Adam and the two other vamps leveled their guns at them. The Italian-looking one drew a sword that was strapped crosswise to his back.

Uh. She blinked. A sword? Then she realized the blade of the sword was flecked with little bits of hawthorn, making it a kind of long malchete.

Evelyn's vamps came to skidding halt in the face of all those gun muzzles and that long, wicked blade backed by a vamp who sure the hell looked like he knew how to use it.

Adam stomped his foot. "Goddamn it," he said. "Weren't you boys born with any sense at all? You give a man with a gun some respect. Especially when the guns are loaded with pure hawthorn bullets." He motioned to the sword-wielder. "Give Niccolo here some respect, too, okay? He's a little old-fashioned, but we'll forgive him for that since he's so lethal. Meet a real-life council executioner, boys." He turned toward Evelyn and waggled his eyebrows. "Guess who he's here for?"

Evelyn took a step back.

"Release Tiya," said Charlie in a voice that boomed through the room much the same way Evelyn's had. Tiya jerked, startled, and then remembered he'd tasted her blood, too. He had added power as well. "Unlock the cuffs, Evelyn."

"No!" she cried petulantly.

The vamp with the long black hair and blue eyes stepped forward. "Evelyn, what are you doing? I thought we agreed not to play these evil games anymore, princess."

Okay, that vamp had to be Anlon. Tiya took heart that he currently had his gun trained on Evelyn.

Evelyn smiled coyly as she tilted her head to the side and batted those long, dark lashes. "I know, my love, but I couldn't resist." She motioned to Tiya. "Once Vincent told me about what he'd discovered, about the fae being real and how those of Cúchulainn's line could bestow such wonderful powers...well, I had to do it." She batted her lashes again, and looked at Anlon through them. "*For us.*"

"Ah, princess," Anlon said sadly.

"You understand, don't you, baby?" Evelyn said. "I know it's wrong, but I wanted us to have all the advantages possible in this evil world." Tears sheened her eyes. "I-I just love you so much."

"Evelyn, my darling. What am I going to do with you?" Anlon cooed.

"I know things got out of hands," blubbered Evelyn. "But I had only good intentions."

Good intentions? Rage made Tiya literally see red for a moment.

The muzzle of Anlon's gun dropped a bit.

Oh, no.

Niccolo must have seen it, too, because he raised his sword higher and took a step toward Evelyn. Instantly, Anlon whirled to face him, targeting Niccolo's chest.

"Back off," Anlon said with threat in his voice. "I don't care if you are almost two thousand years old, one of these bullets could kill you."

Niccolo stilled.

"Men, protect Evelyn," Anlon commanded, without taking his gaze from Niccolo. Anlon glanced at Evelyn. "It's going to be okay, baby."

Tiya watched in horror as some of the gun muzzles behind Charlie, Niccolo and Adam shifted. Anlon moved forward and pressed his gun muzzle to Charlie's temple. Tiya's breath caught in her throat. No…not Charlie. She'd rather die than see Charlie be killed. She wouldn't be able to take it.

"Damn it, double-crossed again," muttered Adam.

Evelyn laughed. "Good job, baby," she purred. "Excellent. We'll get this mess all cleaned up and end up the better for it."

"Drop your weapons," said Anlon. "You're surrounded and defeated." He flicked a glance at Niccolo. "Even the great Niccolo is defeated."

No one moved. No one made a sound. Everyone had guns pointed at everyone else. Charlie locked gazes with Tiya. They both understood. It was a Mexican standoff.

"Oh, good God!" Evelyn screeched. She grabbed a gun out of one of her men's holsters and stalked to Tiya. She leveled the muzzle of the gun at Tiya's heart. The cold metal pressed through the thin nightgown and into her ribs. She winced. "She won't survive a bullet to the heart at this range, lover boy," she said to Charlie. "Be it hawthorn or not. Drop the damn weapons."

Something in Tiya's throat clamped and tears pricked her eyes. They were going to kill Charlie before this was through and she was going to have to watch. She couldn't watch one more person she cared about...no, *loved*...suffer and die at the hands of these vamps. Rage and sorrow built within her until she couldn't contain it any longer. "Don't do it, Charlie! Don't do it!" she cried.

"You won't do it, Evelyn," said Niccolo in a low, commanding baritone. "You want her blood too much to waste it that way. You've already proven the fae of her line are too hard to take alive. You won't waste this one. You're bluffing."

"Wait," said Vincent. "Let me hold the gun. The bitch tried to kill me. It's only fair."

Evelyn hesitated a moment. She glanced to Tiya and Vincent and back again. Finally, she stepped back. "All right, you've earned it, Vincent."

Vincent walked over and took the gun from Evelyn. He held it under Tiya's breast, rubbing the muzzle back and forth along the underside of it. "You know I'll do it." He raked his gaze down her body. "I have a score to settle, after all. I don't care about her blood or hard the fae are to take. Drop your weapons!"

"No, don't—" Tiya started.

Charlie, Niccolo and Adam all dropped their weapons to the floor with a clatter and raised their arms.

"—disarm yourselves," Tiya finished weakly.

Suddenly, Vincent moved. He grabbed Evelyn around the waist, making her scream and put the gun to her head. "Okay, Anlon, this is it. Let them go, or I'll let her have it. I'm sick and tired of being your little toady. I'm sick of Evelyn using me as the scapegoat for this scheme she has going."

Chapter Fifteen

"Vincent?" Anlon breathed.

Vincent looked at Niccolo. "You tell the council that I discovered this information, but I never meant to act on it. Evelyn acted on it. She used me as her cover. She figured out how to place the blame on me so I couldn't back out. I had to go through with it or risk the council finding out and hunting me down. Now is my chance to end this."

Tiya blinked. Okay, *that* had been unexpected.

Evelyn whimpered and Anlon looked stricken at the sound, the blind, evil bastard. "Vincent, what are you doing?" Evelyn whined. "I promised you power if we pulled this off. If we can capture enough fae of Cúchulainn's line and drink enough of their blood, we could rule the entire council together, you, Anlon and I."

Vincent shook his head. "I decided I'm not cut out for mayhem. I've just been biding my time until I could free Tiya, then I was going to join with Charlie and take you out."

Anlon's face hardened. "That doesn't show much loyalty, Vincent. I don't agree with what Evelyn has done here, but I'm not going to let her take the fall for it. We'll clean this up, cover it up. We're a family."

"Fuck this family! Let them go, Anlon," said Vincent evenly.

"No. They'll ruin everything," cried Evelyn.

"Everything's already ruined," Vincent answered.

Anlon cocked the gun pointed at Charlie's head and straightened his arm as if to fire.

Tiya screamed.

Chaos freed itself from the tensed air within the room like an explosion. Charlie dove to the floor in hyper-speed as Anlon's gun fired. Thank God for the power of her blood. Charlie grabbed his gun and lunched to his feet in one smooth motion. He trained his gun first on the vamp holding a gun on Niccolo and fired, then shot the one threatening Adam. Tiya cringed at the sharp sound of gunfire in the small room. Niccolo and Adam scooped up their weapons at the same time. It had all seemed to happen between one breath and the next.

Tiya watched Evelyn wrench herself away from Vincent's grasp with a strength she could've only gained from drinking her blood. She whirled and struck Vincent in the head, sending him to the floor in a clean knockout. Vincent's gun flew from his hand and slid across the floor. Evelyn scrambled after it.

Guns fired and Tiya cringed. She was exposed this way, completely vulnerable to the bullets flying around in the room. If she could free her hands from the iron cuffs... she'd have her magick.

Instead, she watched helplessly as Charlie and Adam took out Vampir after Vampir, evening the odds in the room a little. Niccolo cut a bloody swathe through them with his sword, working his way over to her slowly.

Finally, he reached her. They locked eyes for a moment in silent understanding. His blade cut through the iron like it was butter. He sliced through with an unbelievable precision and the cuffs came free from her wrists without leaving even a scratch to her skin. Maybe he knew she not only had to be freed from the wall, she needed the cold iron off her skin for her magick to work.

Freed, she stumbled forward, mumbling her thanks and sinking down just as a bullet hit the wall right where her head had been. Plaster rained down on her and she flattened herself to the floor.

The room was smoky from the gunfire and smelled of hot metal. Her ears rang from the continual *pop, pop* of it. The furniture was smashed and destroyed.

She couldn't see Charlie anymore.

Protecting her head with her hands, she crawled on her stomach behind an overturned sofa and closed her eyes, focusing inwardly on her magick. It coalesced in the pit of her stomach like a warm blanket, the embrace of an old friend, the kiss of a lover. Her power swelled, pressed against the walls of the room like the flex of a large metaphysical muscle. She gathered it, cemented it, and readied it to fire like a nuclear weapon.

A tickle of another magick had her opening her eyes. It smoothed along her skin, teasing her. It was strong…so strong…and it felt familiar. What was that?

She opened her eyes to find Evelyn and Charlie facing off in the center of the room. In the smoke, she couldn't see much. There were a lot of bodies lying around, but she couldn't see Adam, Niccolo or Anlon, though the door to the room was open. All was quiet now. In the time it had taken to gather her magick to full strength, the battle had ended. Now there was only Evelyn and Charlie, staring each other down in a battle of metaphysical wills.

Magick sizzling through the room again, but this time it was Evelyn and Charlie. Their power pushed at each other in a tug of war. Evelyn used largely borrowed power, borrowed from *Tiya's* blood, from her family line. Tiya sensed that most of what Charlie wielded was his own incredibly strong glamour.

She had power of her own and she wanted to use it. This was her fight, ultimately.

Tiya stood and walked toward the woman responsible for the death of her family. "Oh, Evelyn," she called in a singsong voice.

Evelyn turned from Charlie and cast an arm out toward her. A blast of magick pushed at her like a wall of icy cold air. Tiya raised her hand pushed it back at her easily. Evelyn gasped and stumbled backward under the force of that magickal barrier.

Charlie backed away, letting her fight her own battle. Tiya was grateful for that.

"Oh, *duckie*," Tiya purred as she pressed her magick down at her. "Do you feel how strong I am? Just think how powerful you would've been if you'd succeeded in keeping me as your own personal little cow. What a shame."

"I still will succeed," she spat. "Give me time. I'll gather more of your line."

Tiya shook her head sadly. "I think not. Your antics have come to an end." She flattened her magick down on top of Evelyn's body, making her eyes widen at the power.

"No! Please!" Evelyn cringed. "I'm unarmed. I'm begging for mercy. You can't! You wouldn't!"

"I can and, more importantly, I *want* to." She felt the rest of her magick climb up her back from where it sat coiled like a snake at the base of her spine. It spilled out in a sudden, violent burst and hit Evelyn straight in the chest.

Evelyn shrieked.

The exertion dropped Tiya to her knees. Her head pounded from the depletion of her magick. She wouldn't be able to use any of it for days now. She'd nuked it all in that one act.

Tears filled her eyes as she realized it was finally finished. She'd managed to avenge her family. Her shoulders shook as weariness and sorrow enveloped her. Sob after sob racked her body.

Why didn't she feel better?

She felt arms come around her shoulders. Charlie pulled her into his lap and stroked her hair. "Baby, baby, are you okay?"

Breathing heavily, she turned toward him and fisted her fingers in his shirt. She could feel his enhanced glamour coursing through her, easing the rough edges left within her body from the explosion of her magick. He tightened his arms around her and rocked her back and forth. She let out a shuddering sigh.

Now she felt better. His arms brought her peace when nothing else could.

She nodded. "I'm fine…now. I'm fine." She opened her eyes and spotted Evelyn lying on the floor in front of them.

"Is she dead?" asked Charlie.

She shook her head. "No. She's just incapacitated for a while. I thrust her into the astral, into a secure place where her deepest fears will be reflected back at her. It's a temporary state. Like a prison for her mind. It'll wear off. I just needed her restrained so we could get her to SPAVA and to the council. Death was too easy for her. She needs pay for what she's done…for a long, long time."

"I agree."

She glanced at Anlon, who lay sprawled over two of his henchmen. "What about him?"

"I guess great minds think alike. He's knocked out, angel. I wanted you to have the privilege of deciding what to do with him."

She wiped her cheeks with the back of her hand. "Prison," she said coldly. "For life. That's a very long time for an immortal."

Charlie helped her stand. "Come on, we need to go and see where Adam and Niccolo ended up. They ran out of here after some of the fleeing vamps."

Someone groaned from a corner of the room. Charlie walked over and helped Vincent up. Vincent struggled to his feet, holding a hand to his head. He cast angry eyes at Tiya. "This doesn't mean I like you," he snarled.

She raised her hand in a gesture of surrender. "That's fine. I don't like you, either. Thank you for what you did, all the same."

"You're welcome." He nodded at her. They were in accord. The three of them limped toward the door.

From Charlie, Tiya discovered that they were in an old Victorian mansion on the west side of Minneapolis and she actually *had* been chained in the basement. It was just a very *nice* basement.

Battered, bruised and covered in blood, they inched up the stairs and came out in a large, elegant kitchen. It looked fit for a four-star chef with a stainless steel double door refrigerator and a large island in the center over which hung copper pots and pans. Maybe they'd planned to entertain a lot and make her an appetizer.

Voices and the sounds of an altercation came from what appeared to be the living room. Carefully, since they didn't know if there were any more vamps lurking around, they made their way over there.

* * * * *

Charlie came around the corner and into the graceful, rich antique-furnished living room. His body was tensed for more fighting, but he took a step back at the scene that greeted him. Several Vampir he recognized as council because of the Celtic knot emblem they wore on their shirts, and a swarm of SPAVA officers had Niccolo surrounded. Two council vamps were holding Adam back by grasping his upper arms.

Adam looked over at him. "They're taking him, Charlie. They're taking Niccolo."

Confused beyond belief, Charlie stepped into the room with Tiya and Vincent trailing. "What the hell is this about?" he asked to the room at large.

One of the officers turned Niccolo forcefully toward the wall and cuffed his hands behind his back. Tiya grasped Charlie's upper arm to hold him back, and Charlie realized he'd started to walk over there to stop what was happening without even knowing he'd moved.

Agent Michaels, the SPAVA agent he'd met at Griffin House, walked toward him, holding a clipboard. "Mr. Scythchilde, nice to see you again."

Charlie glared at him.

The agent's eyes widened at the unfriendly look on his face.

"What's going on here, Agent Michaels?" Charlie ground out.

He cleared his throat nervously and immediately launched into an explanation. "We got notification from the Council of the Embraced that a fugitive—" he glanced at his clipboard, "—one, Niccolo Romano, had obtained classified council information about an ongoing investigation and traveled here without council authority to intervene. This individual had previously worked for the Council of the Embraced but, as he is wanted in Newville for his connection in the slayings of one, Dorian Cross, and one, Cynthia Hamilton, he has been released from his duties as an executioner and has a warrant from the council for his apprehension. SPAVA, in conjunction with the Council of the Embraced tracked him here to complete the arrest."

"But he didn't do it," Adam yelled.

Charlie shook his head. "Niccolo is not responsible for those murders, Agent Michaels."

"The council and the courts will determine that, Mr. Scythchilde," he answered. "It is not for us to say. Mr. Romano is cooperating with us and we appreciate his lack of resistance."

Charlie's mind sputtered as he wondered why the council would do this. They knew as well as anyone that it had been the Dominion who'd killed those humans, not Niccolo.

"Let them take me," said Niccolo from across the room. "I'm being sacrificed on the altar of public relations, Charlie. Think about it."

Charlie went still. That was probably true. The Embraced were always fighting to retain their rights in human society. A murdering Vampir on the loose, one of their own peacekeepers, no less, it wouldn't look good. They wouldn't want to appear as though they couldn't control their own people. The murders of Dorian Cross and his assistant had been big news because it was suspected a Vampir had killed them. It had been even bigger news that the Vampir had gotten away and was still at large. Hell, it had made the national networks, and there had been a corresponding nationwide manhunt for him.

But Niccolo was *innocent*.

Charlie's glamour and his power flexed in a gut reaction to that final thought, that *truth*. In the room, all the Vampir went very still as it rippled through the air. It was pure, barely leashed power with a lot of rage behind it.

The words Tiya had uttered downstairs came back to him. *Prison. For life. That's a very long time for an immortal.*

"I'm not letting you arrest him," Charlie said in a deceptively quiet and gentle voice. He felt angry enough to take on every man in the room at the moment. Tiya tightened her grasp on his arm.

"Well, Mr. Scythchilde. It's not up to you," said Agent Michaels. He turned away to signal his men to guide Niccolo out to the detainment vehicle.

Charlie took a step forward.

"Stop!" yelled Niccolo. "I'm going of my own free will, Charlie. Let them take me. I might not be guilty of this crime, but I'm guilty." He turned toward Charlie, wearing a weary expression. "I'm guilty and I could use a rest."

"Niccolo," Charlie said. "Goddamn it. Why'd you come here? You must've known they'd track you down."

He smiled. "I heard about what was going on here through council back channels. I knew you were in this territory in the middle of it. I couldn't let a friend down. I had to come."

"Jesus," Charlie breathed.

"Adam?" Niccolo asked.

"Yeah?" Adam answered sullenly.

"Check your apartment when you get back, all right? I left you something important to take care of." He walked toward the door. The Vampir who'd cuffed him followed behind. "Come on, let's get going." Niccolo gave an uncharacteristic laugh that sounded a little like water running through a rusty pipe. "I can't wait to be judged for my crimes."

Charlie watched, mute, as they shuffled Niccolo out the door. Agent Michaels walked over to him. "So, I guess there's a mess down there, huh?"

Charlie nodded absently, his gaze still on the door that Niccolo had gone through. "Yeah. Come on, we'll show you who else you need to arrest."

* * * * *

Charlie pushed the half-smashed door open to Adam's apartment four hours later. It had taken a while to get everything sorted out at the house. Then they'd all had to go into SPAVA headquarters to be questioned. They'd avoided being arrested for anything because several of Evelyn's vamps who'd lived through the battle had fessed up to everything in front of the council vamps and the SPAVA officers.

Vincent had been charged with conspiracy and Charlie figured he'd probably be convicted, but his sentence would be reduced because of what he'd done in the end. Even Tiya had admitted that they probably wouldn't be alive now if Vincent hadn't turned on Evelyn.

The council had cut a deal with SPAVA to keep the situation under wraps. Luckily, with all the ranting about faeries being real, the council and SPAVA had written the whole thing off as a cult affair, with Anlon and Evelyn the deranged leaders who'd been able to convince their followers to believe in faery tales.

Tiya and her people were still safely hidden from the bright light of humankind's awareness. That was fortunate. It was more than the Embraced could say.

As soon as they opened the door, Kara, Niccolo's cat, came running up to them from the bedroom.

Tiya knelt and scooped the fat brown tabby up into her arms. "Kitty! What are you doing here?" She was dressed in clothes donated by a SPAVA officer — an oversized blue sweater, a pair of men's gray sweatpants and a pair of too big sneakers.

She still looked gorgeous.

"Bastard came in here, left Kara, knowing all along this was going to happen," muttered Adam as he pushed past them. "Goddamn bastard," Adam muttered again with a hitch in his voice.

Charlie passed a hand over his weary face. "The cat's name is Kara, Tiya, she's Niccolo's cherished familiar."

"A familiar? Wow, that's a rare thing for a vamp," she answered.

Adam walked into the living room and plunked himself down on the couch. "Yeah. Some vamps find out they have familiars, but not many. Niccolo's been alive for a really long time, so he's had time to find Kara."

"So, she's what? Like an immortal cat?" asked Tiya. Her voice was muffled because she was currently cuddling Kara, and Kara was purring loudly in response.

"Yes," answered Charlie. "Gabriel and I have long suspected that she might be only thing keeping Niccolo sane. She's keeping him connected to his soul."

She looked up and frowned. "What do you mean?"

"Niccolo is an ancient Vampir, Tiya. He's among the oldest of us. He was born in Rome in 54 A.D. He was a soldier at first, and started killing really young. Later on, he was a real, live gladiator. Later still, he was an executioner. Niccolo has been taking life almost since he was born. That's a lot of years of killing, for whatever reason."

"Well," she said quietly. Kara nudged Tiya's nose. "I can see where that might get to a person."

"Yeah," said Adam. "We've been worried about Niccolo for a while now. When he disappeared after that deal in Newville, man, we thought we'd lost him for good. Thought he'd disappeared forever."

"And now you have lost him, maybe," she softly.

"We'll get him out," said Adam forcefully. "There's got to be a way. This is just wrong. We'll go back to Newville, get Gabriel and we'll—"

"I'm not so sure Niccolo wants to be sprung," interrupted Charlie. "If Niccolo doesn't want it, it won't happen, Adam."

Adam stood up, walked over to the wall and put his fist through it. "Fuck!" He turned around and leaned back against the wall. "I don't want Niccolo to be stuck in some jail cell for a crime he didn't commit."

"I don't either, Adam, but it's not what we want that matters here," answered Charlie.

The room went quiet.

"But," said Tiya at last, "what will Niccolo do without his soul?" She looked down at Kara.

Charlie sighed. "I don't know."

More silence.

Adam surged toward the door, startling Tiya. Kara jumped free of her arms and ran back into the bedroom. "Well, I'm out of here," he said.

"Where are you going?" asked Tiya.

"I'm weak after all I went through today. Baby, I need blood. The *sacyr* is screaming at me. I'm going to head down to Griffin House and see if any willing Demi survived before I go ahead and bite you out of pure hunger."

Tiya took a step forward. "Bite me. I'll let you. After what you did for me, Adam, I'll let you take my blood."

He shook his head. "Don't tempt me. You're as weak as I am. Anyway, you need some time alone with Charlie." He headed out the half-ruined door, but turned before he left and winked. "I have a kick-ass bathtub. Check it out."

Tiya turned to Charlie. He stood watching her with a heavy gaze. As soon as Adam had mentioned the bathtub all he'd been able to think about was Tiya stripped and wet and rubbing up against him. His *sacyr* was screaming, too. He needed blood, but he wanted Tiya more. He *needed* her...and not for sex. He needed to feel her body against his, smell her hair. After what had happened that day, he needed to lose himself in her.

She was like his refuge.

She glanced down the hallway, in the direction of Adam's bedroom and bathroom, and bit her bottom lip.

He hadn't wanted to think about tomorrow, about what would happen when all this was over, but now it was here. This might be his last chance to ever be close to Tiya. This could be his last chance to feel her skin rubbing on his, her mouth on his mouth.

"You game?" she asked him.

He walked toward her and pulled her into his arms. He bent his head and kissed her tenderly, thoroughly. His voice rumbled through her when he finally spoke. "I'll go run the water."

Chapter Sixteen

A minute later they stood next to Adam's bathtub. It was big enough for four, Charlie mused. Decadent Adam.

They undressed each other slowly as hot water filled the tub and the mirror steamed up. Charlie nipped and kissed every bit of skin that was exposed on Tiya's body as he pulled off the ridiculous sweater and the men's sweatpants. He had her panting in his arms by the time he was through.

Her sex was plumped. Slick, ready for him. Her suckable nipples stood up like small cherries, wanting to be worshiped. He obliged them each in turn as he found her pussy and slid his fingers into all that delicious, soft, moist heat.

This would the last time he'd ever be this close to her. This would be the last time he'd feel her skin rubbing over his. Tomorrow had finally come and he'd have to let her go. She'd go back to Seattle. He'd go back to Newville...at least for a while. Already he'd been approached about taking this territory by one of the council vamps who'd come for Niccolo. Maybe he'd do it.

Goddamn it. That's the way it had to be. He wasn't going to open himself back up for more heartbreak.

She kissed him and he caught her gaze. It speared him to his heart. She looked at him like a woman in love. She looked at him like he was going to break her heart.

He looked away.

Yeah, he was going to break her heart. That was the way this was going to end.

He pulled her into the water with him. Their hands and mouth were everywhere at once, exploring and petting. Her pussy muscles clenched around his fingers when he slid them in and out of her. She gasped as he flicked his thumb over the little bud of her clit.

He had to taste it.

He hoisted her up onto the side of the bathtub, spread her thighs and lowered his mouth to her delicious pussy. She was wet with her own juices and the bath water. Her back arched as he went down on her like she was a gourmet feast. He laved and licked over her like he'd never be able to taste her again, because he knew he wouldn't.

He pulled her sweet clit between his lips and sucked at it while he thrust a finger within her to rub and tease her G-spot.

"Oh, God, Charlie, I'm coming," she cried.

He made a satisfied growling sound in his throat as her muscles convulsed around his fingers and her back arched. She moaned and cried his name and he lapped up every bit of her cream he could.

Tiya slid into the water with a look of a nymph on her face. "Stand up," she said.

He did it and she went down on her knees to return the favor. Pleasure coursed through his body as she engulfed the head of his cock in her mouth and swallowed him down to the base. He tipped his head back on a groan of ecstasy and fisted his hands in her hair.

The woman was a menace with her tongue and lips. She worked him in and out of her mouth until his balls contracted and he was ready to spill himself. She worked his cock like she meant for him to come in her mouth, but he didn't want that. He wanted in her sweet, hot pussy.

Just one more time.

He forced her to her feet, turned her over and delivered a smack to her ass. She squealed in surprise and then laughed. "What are you trying to do to me," he growled in her ear. "Spread your legs, angel."

She bent over a little more, offering her nicely rounded ass to him and spread her legs. "What do you think, I'm trying — oh!"

He surged balls-deep into her wet, suctioning cunt, cutting her sentence off. "God," he groaned. "God, you're so damned sweet, Tiya," he said thickly.

Tiya made a breathy, incoherent sound and grabbed onto the edge of the tub as he began to shaft her. He pulled the entire length of his cock out and then thrust back in slow and easy. He did this until she was begging for him to pick up the pace, until she was clawing at the porcelain. Little by little, he increased the speed and force of his thrusts until he was holding her by the hips and slamming into her and they could hear the slap of wet flesh on flesh.

Tiya screamed out and her muscles clamped down on his cock. He felt the rush of her cream all over his cock as she came again. "Charlie," she cried, once the rippling of her pussy had calmed. "Charlie, take my blood," she rasped. "Bite me in the throat and take my blood."

His thrusts faltered. "What?" She'd never invited that and he'd never asked.

She swallowed hard. "Turn me around and bite me, Charlie, please. I want you to have my blood once more."

Once more.

"You're too weak," he said.

She shook her head, sending the wet tendrils of her hair flying. "I don't care. Please."

He stopped, turned over and pulled her close. He kissed her deep before murmuring, "You're sure?"

"Completely." She spread her legs for him and he slid inside her. At a gentle, easy pace, he glided in and out of her.

He liked this position, having her face-to-face with him. It allowed him to smooth his hand over her cheek and down her body, caress the gentle curve of her buttocks, the silky skin of her back. It allowed him to kiss her beautiful lips and look into those smoky gray eyes, where, if looked closely enough, he could almost see his future.

He looked away.

She guided his jaw back gently stare once again into her eyes. "Charlie, I love you."

"Tiya—"

She shook her head. "No, you don't have to say anything back. I just wanted you to know. I love you, Charlie. Somewhere, in all of this, I met a man who makes me feel safe. He makes me laugh and he holds me when I cry. Sometime within the last week, impossibly, I met a man with whom I have that elusive spark." She shrugged. Unshed tears made her eyes shine. "A man I love." She arched her throat. "Take my blood, Charlie. Consider it a parting gift. Please."

Charlie didn't know what to say in response.

Did he love her? *Yes.*

Was he ready to tell her that? *No.*

Instead, he dipped his head and nuzzled her throat. At the same time, he thrust his cock in and out of her until she moaned. He licked and kissed her throat and glided in and out of her until he couldn't think straight anymore and neither could she, most likely.

His gaze focused on the pulse in her finely veined throat and his fangs extended down into little points. He thrust as far up inside her as he could get himself and lowered his mouth to her throat. When he finally sank through her flesh with his fangs, he rolled his glamour over her hard, forcing them both into climax right away. Tiya gave an animalistic moan. Her sweet, milky, *powerful* blood coursed into his mouth at the same time his come poured into her body.

When it was over, he held her close and stroked her hair, her skin. They stayed in the water until it grew cold, wordlessly embracing.

Chapter Seventeen

Tiya sat at gate B10, staring at her airline ticket back to Seattle. She'd left that morning while Charlie was still sleeping. She'd managed to catch Adam to say goodbye, but saying goodbye to Charlie wasn't something she could handle.

She could have a real estate agent sell the house she'd purchased. The few possessions she'd accumulated when she'd been in St. Paul, she really didn't care about. She'd just needed to get away from the promise of heartbreak that had been on Charlie's face the night before. Nothing else mattered.

Tears welled over the rims of her eyes and coursed down her cheeks. She dashed them away. Damn Charlie and his fears. Her heart felt like mashed pulp right now because of him.

At least she'd managed to avoid the awkward goodbye in which Charlie would've chucked on her on the cheek and told he'd had a good time and that he had feelings for her but he just wasn't ready for a commitment right now.

The night before, when she'd told Charlie she loved him, she hadn't expected him to say it back. Hell, they'd only known each other a short time and not under the most normal of circumstances. No, she hadn't expected him to say it back, but she had to admit there was a part of her that had hoped he might.

More tears.

God, she was so pathetic!

She looked up to find a little girl staring at her. The child clutched a doll to her chest. "Are you sad?" she asked.

Tiya tried to smile. "I'm okay, sweetie."

The little girl's mother came over and admonished the child for talking to a stranger and pulled her away, apologizing to Tiya.

Finally, they announced boarding for her flight. Wiping her eyes, she got up and got on her plane.

Tiya slumped down in her first-class seat and stared out the window at the tarmac. God, she felt miserable. More tears coursed down her cheeks. And *so* sorry for herself, she admonished inwardly.

Someone sat down beside her, but she didn't turn her head. No sense in letting the whole world know what a wuss she was.

"Something to drink?" asked the flight attendant. Tiya continued to stare out the window. They could think her rude if they wanted.

"A bourbon and branch for me and the oldest, finest merlot you have for the lady."

Charlie? She turned to find Charlie looking at her.

"Where are you going, angel?" he asked.

Shock rippled through her. "Uh, home, Charlie."

He sighed. "That's a pity. I guess I'll just have to go with you then."

"Charlie?" she asked, sitting up a little straighter in her seat. "I thought you—"

He leaned forward and kissed her hard, cutting the rest to her sentence off. "I feel you all through me, Tiya. I felt you when you got up and left me like a thief this morning. I felt you take a taxi to the airport. It will kill me to feel you fly away from me, angel," he murmured. "Every mile this airplane flies you away from me will hurt. I love you. God, I love you so much."

Euphoria suffused her. She twined her arms around him and kissed him deeply. "I thought I was going to lose you," she said softly.

"I'm yours, Tiya. I tried so hard not to be, but I am, body and soul. It's hard for me to admit my fears. You scare me. The possibility of losing you scares me even more. But laying in bed this morning and smelling you in the pillows made me realize I was losing you before we ever really got started."

The plane jerked backward and started to back up. "But what about this territory? I thought they wanted to you take it?"

"I'm a candidate for it, but I won't take it if you're not in it. It's empty without you."

She smiled and leaned back to allow the flight attendant to serve their drinks. "Hmm...well, a franchise of the Fancy Fae might do well in Minneapolis. I've been thinking of starting another restaurant anyway." She raised her glass. "To new beginnings."

He clinked his glass against hers and leaned forward. "To love."

They kissed.

Enjoy this excerpt from

Blood of the Rose

© Copyright Anya Bast 2004

Chapter One

Twigs and dry leaves snapped and crackled under Penelope's polished black riding boots as she marched toward the stables.

"Aidan," Penelope snapped when she strode through the double doors. "Saddle Daisy. I fancy a ride before dinner."

Aidan O'Shea looked down at her a fraction longer than a servant should before moving to take the chestnut mare from her stall. "Yes, miss," he drawled out, casting her a dark sidelong glance. "You know I live to do your bidding."

Penelope's lips tightened into a thin line. It was always so with him. He could never remember his place. It was as if he thought that just because they had been childhood chums, he could take liberties in the way he talked to her. "Thank you," she bit off.

She took her black riding crop from its peg on the wall and dangled it from one finger while she watched Aidan lead Daisy from her stall. His features had always been well formed—his jaw strong, his lips full and nice...when they weren't quirked with sarcasm. He looked less like a servant every day. Indeed, ever since Penelope had grown old enough to notice those of the opposite sex, she'd noticed Aidan. She knew well how scandalous that was, but she couldn't help herself.

He tossed a saddle blanket over Daisy, and Penelope watched as his back muscles worked under his shirt. A hank of glossy brown hair fell over a dark blue eye as he turned toward her, his attention focused on his work. Small curling tendrils of his thick hair brushed the collar of his tan shirt as he moved.

His pants molded to nicely muscled thighs. As a lady, she shouldn't notice the impressive bulge between his legs, but as a woman she couldn't help but let her eyes linger and her mind wonder what he'd look like without his pants. She lifted a brow.

Yes, overall, Aidan was an exceptionally good-looking man. He did not put one in mind of a servant when one gazed at him.

And it was not only his physical appearance that made him appear more like a member of the upper class than a servant; it was his composure and confidence. While the shoulders of the other servants always sagged, his were broad and squared. While a proper servant lowered his gaze when speaking to a member of the Coddington family, Aidan's intense eyes never failed to find hers.

Even now, his midnight blue gaze met hers over the saddle he was cinching around Daisy's midsection. A dark brow rose. "Your father know you're going for a ride?"

"I am not a child anymore, Aidan. I can go riding if I choose." She glanced away. "Anyway, you know he doesn't care if I ride or not."

Aidan nodded while slipping the horse's bit between its teeth and adjusted the thin leather straps over the animal's head. He handed the reins to her. "Your horse, Miss Penny," he said, while looking straight into her eyes just as a good servant ought not.

"Call me Penelope!" she scolded.

At one time, Aidan had called her Penny and she'd liked it, but those times were long past. When she'd been a child and had been lonely, she'd adored Aidan and trotted at his heels. Indeed, when she'd been young she'd been inexplicably drawn to him. She was *still* drawn to him, though she fought it.

Thank goodness for Horatia. She'd taught her to be respectable. Indeed, over the years Horatia's sharp tongue had cut and shaped Penelope into a proper English lady. The bond Penelope and Aidan had seemed to share was quashed before it grew out of control and she sullied her reputation with such foolishness. But their early familiarity had affected Aidan in bad way. Now it was as if he fancied himself an equal. He was never suitably courteous to his betters. Even when he spoke in a pleasing manner, satire always simmered beneath his words.

It just wouldn't do.

She regained her composure and lifted her chin a degree. "You know, you would be better served to address your superiors with care, Aidan. My father was quite charitable in keeping you on after your parents passed away. It is not often we employ the Irish."

His eyes got that dangerous dark glint in them. The look that made her stomach do flip-flops. She pulled her gloves from her pocket and pulled them on to distract herself.

"And isn't that ironic seeing as how you got a wee bit o' the Irish in you," Aidan responded, exaggerating his accent simply to irk her, she knew.

Penelope's attention snapped from her gloves up to Aidan's face. One fat sausage curl that had caught on the button of her jacket pulled free and bounced against her chin. "I most certainly do not!"

He smiled lazily, showing the dimple in his cheek. "Then what of the bit of red in your hair then, or the green of your eye? How do you explain those away, miss? Other than the possibility that one of your ancestors dallied a bit with one of their servants and you inherited their characteristics?"

Penelope's mouth opened in a silent 'O' of surprise. Aidan had hit a sore spot with her. Both of her parents were exceedingly tall, with dark hair and eyes. She was exceedingly short with reddish blond locks and greenish blue eyes. "I am not Irish! How dare you! I will have you know that every drop of blood in my veins is English! Every drop!"

Aidan scratched his clean-shaven chin. "Odd. I do recall a story...oh, a lovely, romantic story, told by old Katy McGuire about how her great uncle had caught the eye of a particular great grandmother of yours when they were young." His blue eyes twinkled. "How they seemed to have gotten along, too. Seeing as how that story is floating around I'd say it's possible you might be more mutt than English. In fact, my blood may be purer than yours." Aidan's lips spread in that slow, infuriating smile again.

"Mutt?" she screeched. "What impudence!" She stomped her foot and sputtered in an effort to get her enraged thoughts out of her throat. "My family name is Coddington. A good, sound, very English name. Not Irish, and not even a trace of mutt!"

"Or, I suppose it could be on your mother's side."

"Oh!"

"And I do remember you having a taste for potatoes."

Penelope jerked Daisy's reins and started past Aidan, toward the door of the stables. "Really, Aidan, you act as though your station is equal to mine. Your familiarity is more than can be borne at times!" She shook her head. "Whatever could be the matter with you?"

"Ah, Penny. I just wanted to see your pretty eyes light up in fury one last time. I'm leaving the estate this morn, never to come back here again."

Penelope stopped dead in her tracks. A curious blend of emotions swirled inside of her. "What do you mean? Where could you go?"

"Anywhere I choose. The whole world is waiting for me. It's time I made a life for myself. I feel pulled away for some reason. It is time for me to travel."

Penelope turned, knowing surprise shone on her face. Aidan, leaving? But he had always been there. Been there to banter with her and tease her when it seemed that no one else cared even to talk to her. Of course, the possibility of his leaving had always been there. Aidan was not an ordinary servant. He seemed to want more than the others.

"Where will you go?" she asked.

"America. First to Boston, then out west. Mucking out the stalls of other men's horses was never really what I had in mind for myself. I maybe want some horses and stalls of my own to muck. I hear in America even a poor Irish boy can make a good life for himself."

That he would have such aspirations had never occurred to Penelope. Rapidly, she blinked away a sudden wetness in her eyes. Ridiculous! She wouldn't cry over a stable hand!

"I'm a strong man. I'll be making my way just fine. I suppose Ethan or one of the others will ready Daisy beginning tomorrow."

He really did want to leave her here then. Leave her alone with her father's eternal absence, the memory of her dead mother, Horatia's iron hand. Penelope hoped her tears were not visible. "Well then, I wish you luck in your new life."

Aidan stepped forward, clasped her hand in his warm one, and squeezed lightly. "And I wish you luck in yours." When he dropped her hand, she noticed it felt very cold. "You'll be marrying soon, Penny. Don't let your husband doll you all up. Don't let him use you as some bought and paid for mannequin to display his wealth upon. You're more than that. I can see it there, shimmering just beyond all your posturing."

"What do you mean?" She sensed a compliment somewhere inside all that ambiguity. Wasn't that one of the reasons why men took wives, as a way to demonstrate their wealth to the world? She turned her nose up at him. "Really, Aidan, you act as if you have the right to pass judgment on us."

"Don't play the snob with me, Penny. You're not that way. Not really, I remember."

Another half compliment, half insult. She didn't know what to say so she didn't say anything. Daisy stomped and tossed her head beside her, eager to leave the stables. Penelope no longer felt like riding, however. All the joy had been sucked out of the day.

"My mother told me something right before she died," he continued. "I just want you to be careful, all right? No matter what, you fight. I know you can because you're a scrapper, Penny. Under all those silken flounces, you're a fighter with a will of iron."

She frowned. The servants had always said his mother had possessed second sight. Not that Penelope believed in any of that rubbish. "What are you talking about, Aidan? What did your mother tell you about me?"

"She said — "He gave his head a shake. "No. I won't say any more. Don't scowl at me that way, Penny. I'll be leaving you now. Remember what I said, about you being more than frills and expensive lace work," he smiled. "Besides I always thought you looked better natural." With that said, and one last squeeze to her hand, he turned and left the stable.

"Gone," she whispered to herself after he'd left. She stroked Daisy's nose absently. Suddenly the stables, which she had known all her life, seemed oddly cold and foreign.

Aidan strode back through the doors and her heart leapt with a joy that neared pain. "I'm not leaving here without doing something I've been wanting to do for a good few years now," he muttered as he strode toward her.

Before Penelope could react, or even simply draw a breath, Aidan's arms came around her and his lips pressed against hers. His tongue swept into her mouth and mated with hers. She stiffened, and then melted against him. This was not a chaste, safe kiss, like the ones her suitors had given her. It was hot, passionate and unrestrained. This was the kind of kiss she dreamt about.

Amazed, honeyed pleasure licked its way up her spine, leaving a tingling in its wake. God, hadn't this been what she'd always wanted? Wasn't this what she thought about in the dead of night while her hands strayed to parts of her body meant only for her future husband?

He withdrew a little and searched her eyes. She let out a sigh and inhaled his scent—leather and man. He spoke so close to her mouth, his lips brushed hers. "Somebody needs to kiss you right, before you marry one of those half-dead suitors and you never get kissed proper again."

He lowered his head and his smooth lips brushed hers. He kissed her top lip, then her bottom with exquisite care, sending another jolt up her spine. He covered her mouth with his and Penelope kissed him back. His warm tongue slipped between her parted lips and branded the inside of her mouth.

Penelope felt her knees weaken and he held her around her waist, pressing her against the small of her back and tight up against him. The swell of her breasts brushed his hard chest, sending a fast lick of fire shooting through her and making her nipples tighten into hard little points. How good would it feel to have his mouth on them—laving his tongue over them, and finding every little ridge and hollow.

Dropping Daisy's reins from her already lax grip, she wound her arms around his broad shoulders. Her fingers found the hair at his nape and threaded through it. She cursed her gloves. She wanted to feel his silky hair against her skin. She wanted to feel every inch of him against her.

Once she'd come upon a couple of the servants in the stables. From the shadows she'd watched them copulate in several different positions. They'd used a wealth of crude words she'd never heard while they went at each other. At the time she'd been both aroused and disgusted. Now Penelope couldn't help but envision Aidan doing the same things to her while they used the same forbidden, naughty words aloud to each other. Just the thought of it made her throb with want.

If anyone came into the stables right now and found them, her reputation would be savaged beyond repair. Strangely, the desire coursing through her blood made her not care in the least.

She dropped her hand to the outside of his pants and rubbed at the hard length of him. "Touch me," she said into his mouth.

He tensed and hesitated at her demand, and then relaxed as though surrendering. Dropping his head, he kissed the swell of her breasts where they bulged from the top of her gown. A gasp of pleasure escaped her throat when he licked the mound of one, as close as he could get to her nipple. Her awareness of her femininity and his masculinity shot up to a near painful level.

He returned to her mouth and spoke against her lips. "You don't know how much I've wanted to touch you, or for how long," he murmured. He kissed her again, his tongue delving in to dance against hers. At the same time, he hitched her skirt up with one hand, keeping the other at the small of her back. He hunted through the complicated folds and layers of her clothing, pulling here and untying there, finding her sex with a practiced ease that gave her pause. He cupped her damp pussy and she held her breath. She'd never been touched so intimately before.

Any thought she might have had on the subject was quickly wiped away at the first brush of his finger against her sex. "You're wet," he growled with audible pleasure into her mouth. He rubbed the callused pad of his finger over her folds and nibbled her bottom lip at the same time.

Penelope gasped and closed her eyes. He stroked over her, rubbing at a particularly sensitive spot, and then slipping his finger within her. Her hands tightened on his shoulders and she whimpered into his mouth as he thrust his thick finger in and out of her. It felt better than anything had in her entire life. She would explode from pleasure if he continued.

His breathing grew ragged and he groaned. "You're so tight, Penny. I want to be inside you," he rasped in a voice thick with desire.

Penelope made a series of unintelligible noises under the onslaught of the magic he was weaving around her pussy. He ground his palm against that sensitive place as he stroked into her.

"You feel so sweet," he murmured close to her ear. "I bet you taste delicious."

Those crude, forbidden words stabbed through her, making her feel wanton and wanted…that combined with his hand working her, caused pleasure to explode over her body and ripple out, overwhelming her. He covered her mouth with his, consuming the sounds of her climax.

The pleasure still tingled through her body when she whispered, "Aidan, please. I want you. I want more. I want you inside me."

"You're drunk with lust, Penny. I've already taken you too far. You don't know what you're saying."

"I do know," she insisted and laid a kiss on his lips.

"No. We can't. I won't ruin you. I'm not—" He brushed his lips over her forehead and she closed her eyes, enjoying the intimate gesture.

"You're not what?" she murmured.

He slipped his hand out of her skirts. A finger brushed her cheek, and the air stirred. Penelope stood, her face tipped up, lips parted, eyes closed as pleasurable, languid shock stole her ability to move.

A dove cooed in the rafters and fluttered its wings. She opened her eyes and he was gone.

* * * * *

The carriage lurched and slammed Gabriel back against his seat. He let out a sigh that blew a tendril of his long black hair away from his face. *Mon Dieu* but humans did not know how to travel comfortably. He closed his eyes as the first wisps of the hunger curled in the pit of his stomach, coalescing into something greater, something less controllable, far too quickly for his taste.

"My, I hope it's not too long before we arrive. I wonder how long a trip it is from Boston to New York. Feels like we've been traveling forever."

Gabriel focused his gaze on the young woman who sat in front of him. Her dress and black cloak were buttoned to her chin against the chill of the day. A fashionable, jaunty hat was firmly set upon her small head of upswept brown hair. "Only about 190 miles as the crow flies."

"Yes, but we are not crows."

Speak for yourself. He wished he'd been able to take animal form for this journey and avoid a lengthy trip by uncomfortable carriage. But he needed to save *sacyr* for now, for he would need much of it to travel between worlds in the coming days.

"I'm Regina," the woman said.

Gabriel reached out and clasped her hand, bringing it to his lips for a kiss. He raised his gaze and watched her brown eyes widen as he flipped her hand at the last moment and allowed his lips to linger on her skin of her wrist, sipping her essence.

"Gabriel," he answered so close to her skin his name brushed her. He could feel the blood pumping through her veins, could hear it surging through her heart. It would be nice to wait until he arrived in New York to feed, but he had a feeling the *sacyr* would not allow him that. Not now. Not when the equinox was so close.

Regina drew her hand away. A curious little smile curved her lips. "Where are you from, may I ask? I hear an accent but cannot place it," she said. Her cheeks were flushed and Gabriel knew his touch had affected her.

Gabriel waved a hand. "Originally, France, but I travel a lot."

"Ah, France! *Je parle un peu le français.*"

The woman prattled on, but Gabriel hardly heard her. He was far too busy controlling the hunger that was little by little growing stronger. Normally, he had excellent control, but the impending equinox threw him off. His body now demanded sustenance even though he'd fed well on the boat coming over from Europe.

Much was afoot. The One was coming. He could feel it in his bones, through his blood. They'd embraced every marked human they could find in order to find him. Time grew short, the equinox drew near, and the danger became great, brewing a supernatural war. The One would arrive soon. Even now the marked poured into New York City, not understanding why, merely called by the rising energies of the coming battle. Indeed, if they did not hear the call, events within their lives would force them to New York, to the Tenderloin District and, finally, to the Sugar Jar and Gabriel.

It was important he get back. Perhaps the One they sought had already arrived.

"Gabriel?" The woman reached out and touched his knee in a flirtatious way. Gabriel fought the growl that threatened to trickle through his lips. "I asked where you'd been born. I am merely trying to pass the time in an amusing way. Forgive me if you think I'm prying."

Gabriel narrowed his eyes at Regina's throat. He knew a warm vein pumped there, under the fold of her cloak. *Non,* the hunger was not being easy with him today. "You seem to want to know all about me, and so I shall tell you. I was born in the year of our lord 1610 in a small village in Bretagne. It is a region of France to the west of Paris."

"1610? But that's imposs—"

"Impossible that I should be 280 years old? I assure you it is not, *mademoiselle*. In fact there are others far older than I."

Regina's eyes widened in alarm and Gabriel almost pitied her…almost. "You are quite mad, sir!"

"You wanted to know about me and so you shall know. As I said, I was born in Bretagne to a poor family. Indeed they could not afford to eat. So, myself, a child of uncommonly good looks, they sold to an artist in Paris when I had but ten years in order to be a model. The artist, his name was Guillaume de Sant, was a lover of men, but not of children." He waved his hand. "He never amounted to anything as a painter. He was a man ahead of his time in that regard, but I digress. But what is wrong, my dear, Regina? You've grown pale. Are we not passing the time in an *amusing* way?"

Gabriel could hear Monia, his *mère de sang*, even now...*never play with your food*. But it was so much fun!

"Driver, halt!" Regina cried.

"*Non*. You will sit quietly and listen to my tale," Gabriel commanded, using a bit of glamour.

Regina lowered her eyes dutifully. "Do go on."

"Guillaume had a lover named Jacques who took a liking to me. Even though I wanted nothing to do with Jacques, Guillaume grew increasingly jealous. When I turned eighteen, Guillaume told me to leave his house. This was not a good time in France. There was much hunger and unrest. I did manage to find work and a place to live and then...I fell in love. I had eight years of happiness with her. When she died I was ruined with grief. I would have joined her in death, I think, had it not been for Madame Monia and her lover, Vaclav."

"Madame Monia?"

"*Oui*. She took me to her *auberge de plaisir*. Um...that is place where the Demi-Vampir can live and feed and be under the protection of the fully Embraced. Like a brothel, you know?"

"Vamp...*Vampir?*" Regina's eyes widened. "Like vampire? Like the creature in the folk tales and penny bloods?"

"*Oui*, that is correct, but you are calm," he commanded. Using glamour on humans was ridiculously easy. Gabriel had run into few able to resist.

"I am calm."

"*Exactement*. Anyway, we are nothing like the creatures depicted in fiction or folklore."

"But—"

"Shh...listen. Demi-Vampir are the unfortunates who are not strong enough to be full Vampir. They feed off sex, pleasure, lust whatever you want to call it. In any case, I was food for the Demi-Vampir for nearly seven years."

"You had sex with half vampiric creatures for nearly seven years?"

Gabriel raised a brow. "But you are quick, Regina. Yes. It was not an unpleasant time. You'd be surprised how much pleasure even a Demi-Vampir can bring you. Of course, it's nothing compared to the pleasure one of the fully Embraced can bring. Humans who lay with a fully Embraced Vampir nearly always become addicted. In any case, one day I fell very sick. Again, I nearly died, but my mistress had grown fond of me and so she Embraced me in order to save my life. I was strong enough to pass through the Demi and attain full Vampir-hood." Gabriel sketched a bow from his sitting position. "And here I am."

Regina merely frowned at him. Gabriel knew well it was all far too much for her human mind to grasp. He sighed. It entirely ruined his fun. "You are tired, Regina."

"I am?"

"*Oui*, very, very tired. You want to sleep now and you will remember none of this conversation upon awakening. *Repetez, s'il vous plait.*"

"I want to sleep now and will remember none of this conversation upon awakening."

"*Oui.*"

Her head dropped and her eyes closed. "Zzzzzzz."

Gabriel rolled his eyes. "Oh, wonderful, she snores." He moved over to sit beside her, his fangs already lengthening. He tipped Regina's head to the side, unbuttoned her cloak, and sank in. He'd sate the *sacyr* now and hope the One would be waiting for him back at the Sugar Jar.

About the author:

Anya Bast writes erotic fantasy and paranormal romance. Primarily, she writes happily-ever-afters with lots of steamy sex. After all, how can you have a happily-ever-after WITHOUT lots of sex?

Anya welcomes mail from readers. You can write to her c/o Ellora's Cave Publishing at 1056 Home Avenue, Akron OH 44310-3502.

Why an electronic book?

We live in the Information Age—an exciting time in the history of human civilization in which technology rules supreme and continues to progress in leaps and bounds every minute of every hour of every day. For a multitude of reasons, more and more avid literary fans are opting to purchase e-books instead of paperbacks. The question to those not yet initiated to the world of electronic reading is simply: *why?*

1. *Price.* An electronic title at Ellora's Cave Publishing and Cerridwen Press runs anywhere from 40-75% less than the cover price of the <u>exact same title</u> in paperback format. Why? Cold mathematics. It is less expensive to publish an e-book than it is to publish a paperback, so the savings are passed along to the consumer.

2. *Space.* Running out of room to house your paperback books? That is one worry you will never have with electronic novels. For a low one-time cost, you can purchase a handheld computer designed specifically for e-reading purposes. Many e-readers are larger than the average handheld, giving you plenty of screen room. Better yet, hundreds of titles can be stored within your new library—a single microchip. (Please note that Ellora's Cave and Cerridwen Press does not endorse any specific brands. You can check our website at www.ellorascave.com or

www.cerridwenpress.com for customer recommendations we make available to new consumers.)

3. *Mobility.* Because your new library now consists of only a microchip, your entire cache of books can be taken with you wherever you go.

4. *Personal preferences are accounted for.* Are the words you are currently reading too small? Too large? Too...**ANNOYING**? Paperback books cannot be modified according to personal preferences, but e-books can.

5. *Instant gratification.* Is it the middle of the night and all the bookstores are closed? Are you tired of waiting days—sometimes weeks—for online and offline bookstores to ship the novels you bought? Ellora's Cave Publishing sells instantaneous downloads 24 hours a day, 7 days a week, 365 days a year. Our e-book delivery system is 100% automated, meaning your order is filled as soon as you pay for it.

Those are a few of the top reasons why electronic novels are displacing paperbacks for many an avid reader. As always, Ellora's Cave and Cerridwen Press welcomes your questions and comments. We invite you to email us at service@ellorascave.com, service@cerridwenpress.com or write to us directly at: 1056 Home Ave. Akron OH 44310-3502.

Discover for yourself why readers can't get enough of the multiple award-winning publisher Ellora's Cave. Whether you prefer e-books or paperbacks, be sure to visit EC on the web at www.ellorascave.com for an erotic reading experience that will leave you breathless.

www.ellorascave.com

Printed in the United States
121369LV00001B/7/A